THE MILLINER AND THE DETECTIVE

"Good morning, Detective Turner."

"Well, well well, if it isn't our favorite milliner, Ms. Brenda Midnight." The way he emphasized the "Ms." I knew I was in trouble. "Funny," he said, "my partner and I were just talking about you. Like in how come Ms. Midnight's name always pops up whenever there's trouble in the neighborhood?"

"Trouble?"

"Don't give me that innocent crapola, Ms. Midnight. You didn't call to inquire as to my hat size, now did you? We've got ourselves a murder, and your ex-husband, Nado P. Sharpe, is right smack in the middle of it."

"It must be some kind of mistake," I said. Given their bad attitude, the last thing in the world I wanted to do was to tell the detectives how to do their job.

Then came the inevitable warning. "Remember, Ms. Midnight, don't you go getting any cockamamie ideas about interfering with our investigation. Stay out of this one. Go make some hats, leave the police work to us."

I had a hundred questions to ask and a thousand reasons to keep my mouth shut. But first and foremost, I had to find Nado.

Other Brenda Midnight Mysteries by
Barbara Jaye Wilson
from Avon Twilight

ACCESSORY TO MURDER
DEATH BRIMS OVER

BARBARA JAYE WILSON

DEATH FLIPS ITS LID

A BRENDA MIDNIGHT MYSTERY

AVON

TWILIGHT

This is a work of fiction. Names, characters, places, and incidents either are the product of the author's imagination or are used fictitiously. Any resemblance to actual events, locales, organizations, or persons, living or dead, is entirely coincidental and beyond the intent of either the author or the publisher.

AVON BOOKS, INC.
1350 Avenue of the Americas
New York, New York 10019

Copyright © 1998 by Barbara Jaye Wilson
Inside cover author photo by Gene Daly
Published by arrangement with the author
Visit our website at **http://www.AvonBooks.com/Twilight**
Library of Congress Catalog Card Number: 98-92460
ISBN: 0-380-78822-5

First Avon Twilight Printing: October 1998

AVON TWILIGHT TRADEMARK REG. U.S. PAT. OFF. AND IN OTHER COUNTRIES, MARCA REGISTRADA, HECHO EN U.S.A.

Printed in the U.S.A.

WCD 10 9 8 7 6 5 4 3 2 1

Dedicated to Gene Daly

ACKNOVLEDGMENTS

For being such a great place to live and work and walk X-Dot Potato, I thank my neighborhood, Greenwich Village. It stimulates and percolates. Layers of history ooze up from its cobblestones, yet there's always something brand-new around the next corner.

New York City's got just about everything anybody would ever want, plus a lot of stuff nobody would ever conceivably want—and it's got it all to dizzying, stultifying excess. Everything, that is, except space. Space is the one thing New York doesn't have nearly enough of, and never will.

All together, the five boroughs boast a population of over seven million people. On Manhattan alone there's a million and a half, piled up skyscraper high on a twenty-six-square-mile chunk of bedrock and paved-over landfill surrounded by questionable waters. Every last one of that million and a half desperately wants more space. Many of them will do just about anything to get it.

Like I often say, they're all looking for a place to hang their hat.

I'm a milliner. To hang my many hats, I've got 589.7 square feet down in Greenwich Village. Because of the relatively high ceilings in prewar construction, that adds up to slightly over a million cubic inches—1,019,001.6, to be precise. A little more than half of that is my apartment, a one-room condo I inherited. The rest—an elevator ride and a two-minute walk over to West Fourth Street—is my hat shop, Midnight Millinery.

One spring afternoon, I sat at my worktable in the shop. Before me was my sketchbook, opened to a blank page.

Pencil poised, I stared at that page. I was supposed to be doodling ideas for summer hats. The creative juices weren't exactly flowing, so mostly I worried about how to scrape up Midnight Millinery's rent.

The last time the rent was late—which was, by unfortunate coincidence, the last time the rent was due—the landlord, a no-nonsense kind of guy, had made a special limousine journey down to the Village to inform me that the next time I was late he'd toss me and my hat blocks out onto the cold, hard cobblestones. "Brenda Midnight," he'd said, taking a big draw on his well-chewed cigar stub, "need I remind you that your rent is due on the first of the month, *not* after my second threatening letter, *not* after my first threatening in-person visit?"

I think he rather enjoyed the threatening in-person visits. They gave him a chance to act tough. Intimidating tenants probably made him feel taller than five-foot-seven. He owned several properties in the neighborhood, most of them small apartment buildings with ground-floor storefronts, most of them poorly maintained, a fact I brought up each time he came around. Not that he paid any attention to my list of grievances.

Thanks to a big-selling beret, I'd had a successful spring season. The problem was cash flow. It's like this: As part of my business I wholesale to boutiques, many of which barely squeak by. They blatantly ignore the net thirty notice printed on the bottom of my invoice and don't pay me until after my third threatening letter or second threatening in-person visit.

I'd been in business long enough to know how to plan around the slow payers. But last month a felt broker called out of the blue and offered me a fantastic deal on top-quality luscious felt bodies and hoods in fashion-forward fall colors. I'd have been a fool not to jump at the opportunity, but with my credit rating—or lack thereof—the broker insisted I pay up front. That's why I came up a little short at rent time.

Of course I'd explained all this to the landlord. He'd sighed mightily, filling up the place with foul cigar smoke, and agreed to a two-week extension. "Miss Midnight," he'd said, "this is positively the last time I'm gonna be a nice guy."

That was last month.

Here I was, on the verge of being late again with the rent. This time it wasn't because of an irresistible deal; this time I had only myself to blame. My summer hat collection was late at a time when, due to the fizzling ozone layer, everybody wanted summer hats. If I could crank out a bunch and get them up in Midnight Millinery's window, my money problems would vanish.

It's just that I never was much good at cranking out anything. I do couture.

Disgusted with my lack of progress I slammed the sketchbook shut and plopped a square of straw cloth on my design head block. Sometimes it's better to work out designs in three dimensions. I blasted the straw with steam, fastened it with pushpins, stared at it, removed the pushpins, shifted it around, and stared some more.

Suddenly the day darkened. Thunder rumbled off in the distance. Jackhammer, a five-pound Yorkshire terrier, scrambled out of his bed of piled-up fabric scraps. I picked him up and stepped outside to check out the weather situation. The temperature had fallen dramatically. Plastic shopping bags swirled by in the wind. To the west, blackish green clouds filled the sky. A light rain began to fall. Jackhammer and I went back inside and watched as the rain turned into a torrential downpour. The thunder moved in close; flashes of lightning streaked through the sky.

The storm blew itself out in ten minutes. Broken twigs ripped from the trees lay on the cobblestones and glistened in the sun.

By then I was completely distracted from my work. Any creative juices that had managed to dribble out were now dammed up. My summer collection would have to wait yet another day. I told myself it wasn't so bad; I'd planned to close up early anyway to get ready for Johnny Verlane's bon voyage party.

Johnny was my ex-boyfriend. Several times we'd tried to make a go of it; several times, due to mutual pigheadedness, we'd failed. We've broken up over interior design; he has atrocious taste in rugs. We've broken up over music, books, art, and food. We've broken up over the shortest route to Balducci's. You name it. We break up at the drop of a hat, and I've got a lot of hats to drop. Lately, however, I'd been giving some thought to the idea that maybe, just maybe, there was an outside chance that if both of us swallowed enormous amounts of pride, we could possibly make it work.

I wanted to make an impression that would haunt him throughout his trip. I was thinking about what to wear to the party when I heard the most god-awful racket outside. I looked out the shop window. This time it was no storm, at least not in the normal sense.

A ratty old van jolted to a stop in front of the shop. It was the color of overcooked canned peas splotched here and there with dark gray primer. The driver's door jerked open. Out came a tallish skinny guy in wheat-colored jeans and a red-and-blue-striped knit shirt. He looked up and down the street. I couldn't see his license plate, but didn't need to. Obviously this was no New Yorker. I was positive he wasn't looking for Midnight Millinery, but to be on the safe side, I locked the door and flipped over my OPEN sign to CLOSED.

He loped over to my door, cupped his hands, and peered through the glass. Before I had a chance to duck down behind the counter, he caught sight of me and knocked.

I pointed to the closed sign and shook my head.

He smiled—a big toothy grin—and pounded on the door, hard enough to rattle the glass.

Jackhammer, still tense from the storm, turned into five

pounds of protective fury. He flung himself at the door, snarling and growling, his long red, blond, and black hair flying. Still, the guy kept pounding.

At first I was merely irritated, but when it became apparent he was not going to give up, I got scared. The fact that crime had plummeted to an all-time low didn't give me much solace. I was two seconds away from calling a couple of cops I knew at the Sixth Precinct when the guy stopped pounding, stood back a ways from the door, and shouted, "Brenda Sue, you let me in right now."

Brenda Sue?

Nobody in New York had ever called me Brenda Sue. It couldn't be. But if there was one thing I'd learned, it was that sometimes stuff that couldn't be, actually was. Unfortunately this was one of those times. I shushed Jackhammer and crept closer to the door to get a better look.

It had been a very long time. His hair was different now. He'd shaved the sides and somehow got the top part to stick straight up four inches like a flattop gone to seed. He still had twinkly green eyes and fourteen freckles splattered across his nose. I grabbed Jackhammer, unlocked the door, and inched it open. "Nado?"

He flashed another toothy grin. "You look so surprised, Brenda Sue. Didn't you get my postcard?"

"Postcard? No. I didn't get any postcard."

"Well, I sent one, but no matter. I'm here. I had one hellava time finding this place. The streets don't make much sense, know what I mean?"

It was true. Village streets twisted off Manhattan's main grid pattern and West Fourth was the twistiest of all.

He clomped past me into the shop. He still wore cowboy boots, a suburban cowboy. "I see you're making hats."

I nodded.

"Well, you always did like hats. What I wanta know is where you got the Midnight crap from."

"Long story," I said.

No way was I going to explain to Nado P. Sharpe, my

first ex-husband, about how after divorcing my second ex-husband, I'd named myself after my shop, which I'd named after the OPEN 'TIL MIDNIGHT sign painted in the window by the previous tenant, a deli fronting a numbers-running operation.

"If you want my opinion, Brenda Midnight sounds dopey," he said, "like you're some kind of spy."

I didn't want his opinion. I thought back, tried to remember what I'd ever seen in Nado. Perhaps nothing; we had been married less than a year. "Why are you here?" It came out sounding ruder than I'd intended.

If Nado was offended he didn't show it. He shrugged. "I had an urge to see you, Brenda Sue. That's all. I sent the postcard, hopped in the van, and here I am."

I suspected there was more to the story. "Come on, Nado. Truth."

He shook his head. "Damn, you can always tell, can't you? Okay, truth: Kathilynda and I had a huge blowup. I needed some time away from her. I've never been to the Big Apple, so I thought what the hell?"

Kathilynda. That name brought back a flood of rotten memories. Kathilynda Annamarie Cooper was Nado's second wife, a fact that had nothing to do with why I couldn't stand her.

Nado continued. "I needed a break from the business anyway."

"Is the business still hot dogs?" I asked.

Over the years, whenever things turned lousy, one thought always perked me up: It could be a whole lot worse. I could still be married to Nado, the man who, behind my back, invested what little money we had into a drive-in restaurant and created Sharpe's Hiway Haute Doggerie. Hot dogs, for chrissakes.

"Hot dogs it is," he said. "You, I suppose, are still a vegetarian?"

"That's right," I said.

"You're missing out, Brenda Sue. I make one hell of a

good hot dog. I'm thinking of franchising the concept, going nationwide."

I put my hands over my ears. "Stop, I don't want to hear it."

"Tell you what, Brenda Sue, I'll take you out to dinner and tell you all about it."

"Sorry, I've got plans. A party. A friend's party."

"You have a date for this party?"

"Yes. Well, no. I mean, not exactly. What I mean is, I'm meeting someone. The host." Nobody ever said I had to tell my first ex the precise truth.

"Where I come from," said Nado, "and if I may remind you, where you used to come from, a proper gentleman picks up his date and escorts her to and from the party."

"Excuse me," I said, "but where we come from . . ." I trailed off, lost in more memories.

Belup's Creek, otherwise known as back home, was named for its founders and subsequent developers, the Belup brothers, Samuel and Bruce. The creek itself was often referred to as Belly Up Creek, in honor of the supine position of the last fish seen anywhere in the vicinity. Technically, Nado hadn't been the boy next door, living as he had several blocks away, but in Belup's Creek, thanks to the Belup brothers' lack of originality, all the next doors looked pretty much alike, so he may as well have been.

Nado's voice brought me back to the present. "Come on, Brenda Sue, let me take you to the party. I'll show these New York fellas how to treat a lady."

I thought again of Johnny and the impression I wanted to make. Maybe it wouldn't be such a bad thing to show up on the arm of another man.

2

Nado stuck around the shop long enough to look at my display hats. "You know, Brenda Sue, if you ever need a real job you can always make lampshades." After yukking at his own joke, he said he had to go.

That was a relief. I'd been afraid he would ask to stay with me. I let the lampshade comment slide and walked him to the curb.

Hard to believe that Nado's rattletrap had made it the fifteen hundred or so miles from Belup's Creek to New York. From all angles the van was way out of whack; the most dramatic tilt was leftward. Nado tugged hard at the door; it didn't budge. "Some goddamned idiot sideswiped Kathilynda at the mall. Screwed up the door," he explained. He rested his left foot on the doorframe for leverage and pulled again. Still no good. Scowling, he backed up, cracked his knuckles, and narrowed his eyes. "All right, this calls for the big guns. Get a load of this, Brenda Sue." He spun around a couple of times, then, in a surprisingly elegant rapid one-two motion, kicked the door with the side of his boot and yanked the handle. The door creaked open—not all the way, but far enough for him to squeeze inside.

"Why don't you use one of the other doors?" I asked.

"It's a guy thing, Brenda Sue. You're not expected to

understand." There was that dopey tooth-baring grin again.

I couldn't remember why I'd ever married Nado, but I sure as hell remembered why I divorced him.

"Hop in," he said. "I'll give you a lift home."

"No thanks. I want to stick around here a bit longer to straighten up. Besides, home's within shooting distance." I pointed around the corner and across the street to my building. "If you want to go to that party, come by my apartment at ten."

"Ten? That's goddamned late for a weeknight."

"It's a New York thing, Nado."

With a shudder the van started, lurched down the street, around the corner, and Nado was gone in a stifling puff of black exhaust. Embarrassed, I looked up and down the street to see if anyone had seen me in the company of such a blatant polluter. Of course there was Mrs. Baxter. She spent all day every day leaning out her window, arms resting on a pillow-covered windowsill. She'd seen a lot worse. There was also a homeless man. I figured he'd seen a lot worse too.

Later, back at the apartment, I sifted through my closet for an appropriate party outfit—something memorable but not showy, sexy but not sleazy, and I began to have second thoughts about taking Nado to Johnny's party. My discomfort no doubt stemmed from guilt that my motivations were a tad less than pure. Plain and simple, I wanted to make Johnny jealous, a nefarious scheme doomed to backfire.

Johnny and I may have bungled our romance, but we remained good friends and I was proud of his rise to fame from his first part in a twenty-second aftershave commercial to the starring role in the *Tod Trueman, Urban Detective* TV series, a show that consistently rated in the top ten. Now, every female in the entire country over age six went gaga over his high cheekbones and the way his thick dark hair fell over his smoky gray eyes.

With the idea that when you're hot, you're hot, Johnny's

agent, the inimitable Lemon (Lemmy) B. Crenshaw, decided the time was ripe to take Johnny to Los Angeles in
pursuit of a movie deal. Hence the big send-off party.
Lemmy had invited virtually everybody he and Johnny
knew.

I'd slipped into my backless black bias-cut swath of silk,
and was in the process of tilting a zany, yet sophisticated,
bright red disk hat dramatically over my left eye when the
doorman buzzed and announced that Mr. Sharpe was on his
way up. I made one last tiny adjustment in the angle of the
hat, then answered the door.

"Lookin' good, Brenda Sue," said Nado.

I wished I could say the same for him. He'd obviously
made an effort to dress up. The results were, well . . . to be
kind, a little on the pastel side for New York. If the too-
short light blue creased slacks, white knit shirt, and blue
and white seersucker jacket weren't bad enough, he completed the ensemble with pointy white patent shoes and
yellow socks.

Jackhammer gave those shoes a sniff and, I swear, rolled
his eyes.

As Nado walked through the foyer he caught a glimpse
of himself in the mirror and frowned. "Sure do wish I'd
had time to get a haircut."

Nado's van was parked right in front of my building.

"You drove?"

"Sure, what else?"

"Walk, bus, cab. Driving's more trouble than it's worth.
You should have left the van at, um, you know, where
you're staying." I was reluctant to bring up the subject of
his accommodations, still afraid he'd ask to stay with me
and more afraid I'd say yes, even though I had no space,
no extra bed.

"That fleabag hotel," he said, "is not exactly your valet
parking kinda place."

"Oh." So he had a hotel room. Good.

"Overnight parking in this city costs as much as my room."

That statement said more about his hotel than the cost of parking in New York. While I couldn't offer him a place to stay, I could maybe do something to ease his parking problems. "I think I can get you a parking space. For free."

"Cool."

I'd known Lance Chapoppel almost as long as I'd known Nado. We'd met back in art school in a ceramics class. What started out as a fancy teapot handle got Lance heavily into extrusion technology. He ended up landing a lucrative contract with a macaroni conglomerate, where he made a small fortune on a pasta patent. He owned a huge co-op apartment in a nearby luxury building. The apartment had come with a parking space. As far as I knew, Lance didn't use the space.

I called Lance from a pay phone and explained the situation.

"Come on over," he said. "I'll meet you in front of the garage entrance."

"You just got lucky," I said to Nado.

Lance's apartment building was about as far west as you can go on Manhattan without falling into the Hudson River. It was familiarly known around the neighborhood as the Hudson Shadow because of the dark shadow it cast over the quaint Village streets. As we headed over there Nado asked, "How come if this Lance guy is so rich, he doesn't have a car?"

"He doesn't need one," I said.

Perplexed, Nado shook his head. It was a difficult concept for someone from Belup's Creek.

I directed Nado to drive to the side of the building. Lance was already waiting.

I stuck my head out the window. "Hey."

"Hey yourself." When Lance smiled, his whole face got into the act. He was compact, muscular, and had beautiful wavy honey-colored hair that fell in a tangle a couple of inches below his shoulders.

Lance climbed in the van. I made the introductions.

"I'm mighty grateful to you," said Nado.

"It's nothing," said Lance. He reached across me and handed Nado the remote control.

Nado pushed the button and the garage door lifted, revealing a steeply sloping driveway. He rode the brakes all the way down into the garage.

Lance's parking space was in the corner. "This is it," he said. "Not much to write home about."

"Looks great to me," said Nado. He got the van situated and turned it off.

To be polite, I asked Lance how his wife Susan was. She'd latched on to Lance as soon as it became apparent that he'd someday make piles of money.

Lance shrugged. "She's okay."

From the Hudson Shadow Nado and I walked north. "Jeezus, Brenda Sue, where are you taking me?" He was clearly ill at ease on the dark deserted streets.

"It's perfectly all right." I checked the addresses on a row of abandoned warehouses on the edge of the meatpacking district. "Dweena found the party space. She's a former bouncer, knows her way around."

A couple of minutes later we found the party. Even I had to admit, from the outside the building looked a little dicey. The inside, however, was another story. Clean, mean, and industrial, white walls with a smattering of dark red brick, clear glass brick, and cement block. Beneath it all, highgloss, rich brown, thick plank floors.

Dweena was the official greeter. "What do you think?" she asked. She was outfitted for the occasion in microskirted silver-sequined dress and waist-length platinum wig.

She held a rhinestone-studded cigarette holder loaded with a candy cigarette.

"Very Hollywood," I said.

Dweena shook her head. "I find it a perfect example of postindustrial, postmodern, scavengeristic decor."

"I meant you, not the place."

"In that case, I thank you." She surveyed Nado. Her eyes flickered from the top of his head to his pointy white shoes. "I don't believe we've met. Brenda, do tell Dweena who is your gentleman friend with the fabulously weird hairdo." She extended a rather large hand.

Nado turned bright red and patted his hair. Then he shook Dweena's hand.

"Dweena, Nado. Nado, Dweena," I said.

"Pleased," said Dweena.

"Double pleased," said Nado.

"Nado is my first ex-husband," I explained.

"Oh, your very first ex. That's so cute."

Other guests arrived. Dweena turned her attention to them.

I grabbed Nado's hand and led him into the party.

"Fabulously weird?" said Nado. "What does she mean by that?"

"I don't know," I said.

"Well, that Dweena is six feet of glorious female. She lets it all hang out."

"Not quite," I said. Before I could explain how Dweena used to be a stockbroker named Edward with a handlebar mustache, Nado caught sight of Johnny.

"Holy shit," he said. "That's Tod Trueman, you know, the guy on *Urban Detective*."

"Johnny Verlane," I said. "The guest of honor."

"No kidding. You mean your boyfriend Johnny is Tod Trueman?"

"Ex-boyfriend."

Johnny spotted me and waved. Nado was off like a flash. By the time I caught up, he'd already introduced himself.

As always, Johnny was gracious. "Pleased to meet one of Brenda's ex-husbands," he said, pumping Nado's hand.

Over Nado's shoulder, Johnny gave me a puzzled look. I figured he was as surprised as I that I'd been married to Nado. I made a face. I didn't like how he'd made it sound like I'd been married dozens of times. The actual count was two. Well, three, but one of them I don't count, never mention to anyone, and rarely admit even to myself.

Lemmy Crenshaw joined us. Since I'd last seen him he'd pierced his left eyebrow, a look that complemented his shaved head.

Nado did a double-take. He'd probably never seen a pierced eyebrow before, at least not on a guy with a shaved head dressed in a business suit. Nado warmed up considerably when I mentioned that Lemmy was Johnny's agent.

"Really? An agent?" said Nado.

"Best agent in all of New York," said Johnny.

"That so?" said Nado. "In that case, Mr. Crenshaw, let's talk turkey."

Actually he wanted to talk hot dogs, or, more precisely, a lot of bull. Nado launched into a ridiculous rap about celebrity-theme hot dog restaurants. He wanted Johnny involved. At the mention of a Tod Trueman hot dog—condiments of Tod's choice—Johnny chuckled, shook his head, and wandered off. Lemmy, however, put his arm around Nado's shoulders and led him over to a corner where they could talk. "Tell me more, my man, tell me more. Oh, and by the way, where'd you get that groovy haircut?"

I stayed pretty close to Nado and kept my eye on him to make sure he didn't embarrass me any more than he already had. He finished talking to Lemmy, drank two beers, then flirted with the tall redheaded guest starlet from Episode Three, the one Tod Trueman had rescued from the clutches of an evil drug kingpin by a dramatic jump off the Brooklyn

Bridge onto a garbage barge where she was being held prisoner.

The toasts began. Along with everyone else, I raised my glass and wished Johnny good luck. While doing so, an ugly thought swirled around my brain and I realized that a tiny part of me wanted Johnny to fail. What kind of lousy friend was I? I answered my own question. I was the kind of friend who was comfortable with the way things were. I didn't think our relationship—whatever it was—would survive a movie deal. I couldn't get that thought out of my head, so I decided instead to get myself out of the party. I told Nado I was ready to leave.

"Now?" he moaned. "The party's just getting started."

"You stay," I said. "I can get myself home perfectly well."

"You sure?"

"Yeah."

"That's great, Brenda Sue. See you around. Oh, and thanks for finding me that parking space. I really appreciate it."

"You're welcome." So much for Nado's gallantry, so much for his proper gentleman who picks up his date and escorts her to and from the party.

I didn't make a big deal about leaving. I edged toward the door, winked at Dweena, and walked out into the night. When I was half a block away, I was surprised to hear Johnny call my name. "Brenda, wait up." I stopped while he caught up with me. "I wanted to talk to you alone, without your ex."

"You can't leave your own party."

"Of course I can. Lemmy and I have to take off soon anyway."

The moon was full or close to it, the air was clear, a perfect night to walk around the Village. Johnny and I spoke of many things, carefully avoiding the subject of us, but as we lingered in front of my building, he took my hand. I started to pull it away, decided not to.

"So," said Johnny. "I've been meaning to talk to you about this just friends stuff." He pulled me close.

Before I could decide whether to hug him back, a cab squealed around the corner. Lemmy cranked down the window and shouted, "Where the hell've you two been? I've been searching all over the goddamned Village."

"We've been walking," said Johnny, "and talking."

"Walking and talking," parroted Lemmy. "That's just dandy. We've got a plane to catch, and you're walking and talking. Bunch of craparama. Get in the goddamned cab."

"I wanted—" said Johnny.

"Now," said Lemmy.

"All right, all right," said Johnny. He pecked me on the cheek. "When I get back, Brenda, you and I are going to have that talk."

Lemmy yanked Johnny into the cab and they sped off.

3

Inspiration finally hit. By late afternoon of the next day, less than twenty-four hours after Johnny flew off to LA, I had a prototype summer hat pushpinned onto my design head block. It was kind of like a sun visor, except not. Yes, it had a visor, a little mini-brim to shade the eyes, but it was the huge sculptural side-mounted butterfly bow that really defined the look.

With a little bit of attitude—no problem for my customers—and a sprig of veiling, it could do double duty as a cocktail hat. I envisioned the window display with scores of brightly colored hats suspended from fishing line. The color would attract attention; the black would sell.

I was jubilant, but then right in the middle of a joyous rendition of "Midnight Millinery Has a Summer Line," a sharp pang stopped me cold. Johnny hadn't called. I'd halfway expected to hear from him when he got to Los Angeles. I thought we'd continue the talk Lemmy'd interrupted. I'd also expected Nado to call or drop by. The fact that he hadn't was probably for the best. I didn't have time to show my ex around town.

A little after five o'clock I went next door to Pete's Café for a meeting of our neighborhood business association. As organizations go, ours was loosely structured. We didn't

17

have a name, or a regular meeting time. We got together whenever anyone felt the need.

The reason for today's gathering was Julia's Trick Shoppe. A refugee from the rampant cute-ification of Times Square, Julia's had recently moved into a long-vacant burned-out storefront, the site of a former shoe repair shop. When his rent quadrupled, the shoe repair man, who'd been in that location for almost half a century, firebombed the place and disappeared. At first, when Julia took over and gutted the burned-out dark hole, everybody cheered. Then her sign went up and everybody freaked. There'd never been a store of its kind in the neighborhood. It was chock-full of slightly risqué cheap trinkets, loads of plastic vomit, and T-shirts emblazoned with off-color sentiments spelled out in rhinestones.

To make matters worse, the owner, Julia Pond, had moved into the apartment next door to mine. I called it the Randolph apartment in honor of the arrogant lying son of a bitch who'd once lived there. Even after Randolph had moved his selfish self to the Upper East Side, the apartment continued to attract truly offensive human beings—like Julia.

I arrived before the group got to the business at hand. Everybody was yakking about some guy who wanted to start a small-scale pig farm in a Charles Street garden apartment.

I headed straight to the bar, where Pete had laid out a delectable array of sandwich ingredients. I made a cheese on rye, heaped on several slices of yellow tomato, a couple of arugula leaves, and asked for a red wine. Pete generously furnishes sandwich makings for the meetings; whoever's feeling particularly flush picks up our drink tab.

I found a seat in the corner, listened to the general murmur, and reflected on how our concerns had changed dramatically. We shopkeeps originally got together after a daring daylight robbery in a now-defunct frozen yogurt store. We organized to figure out how to protect ourselves and our businesses from the burgeoning crime problem. Crime had since nosedived. Now we had time to worry about pig farms and plastic vomit.

Anna's shrill voice cut through the others. She ran the organic bakery over on Horatio. "I heard he's gonna get that variance from the city zoning commission. Like it or not, looks like we're getting a shitload of pigs."

"I can see it now," said Barry, stroking his black beard. He published a neighborhood advertising circular. "Greenwich Village, neighborhood of bohemian poets, painters, and pig poop."

Everybody started talking at once.

"We'll be the butt of every joke."

"Better a pig farm than a methadone clinic."

"I like pigs as much as the next guy, but they got no place in Greenwich Village."

". . . domino effect. Next thing we know, somebody'll be wanting to bring in chickens. You want to smell something bad . . ."

". . . who cares about pigs? We got ourselves a homeless problem again."

"I warned you," said Anna. "Word's out that we're a soft touch over here in the West Village. It set a bad precedent when we let that bum Elliot hang out."

I never really thought of Elliot as a bum even though he lived on West Fourth Street. Literally. He did odd jobs in exchange for food and clothes and occasionally money. "Come to think of it," I said, "where is Elliot? I haven't seen him for a day or so."

"Good riddance," said Barry. "Anna's right. We should have got rid of him a long time ago."

I disagreed, but kept my mouth shut. I didn't want to start a fight.

"Well, Elliot might be gone," said the lady who ran the florist shop on the corner, "but some new bum already took his place."

"That's what I mean," said Anna. "It's out of control."

Actually, it was our meeting that was out of control.

Pete stood up. Since it was his restaurant, he was our unofficial moderator and sometime referee. People listened to Pete. He was big, real big, well over six and a half feet big, but not fat. He wore his two hundred and forty pounds well. His round cherub face was framed by dark brown ringlets of hair. "We all know there are certain subjects we're never gonna agree on. I suggest we move on to Julia's Trick Shoppe. Although I've got to tell you, I checked with my lawyer. He says there's not a thing we can do except try to reason with Julia Pond."

"She doesn't look like the reasoning type," said Barry.

"That store is unseemly," said the florist lady.

Once again, everybody chimed in.

"Julia's Trick Shoppe sounds like some kind of whorehouse."

"That cute spelling . . ."

"This is an historic district, for chrissakes . . ."

Lots of gripes, few constructive ideas. The meeting rapidly deteriorated. In the end, a few of the attendees formed a committee to look into the problem. The tone of the meeting left a rotten taste in my mouth.

Not long after I got home, Elizabeth, my across-the-hall neighbor, knocked on my door. She'd been in Montana for two weeks visiting her boyfriend, Dude Bob 43.

"What a mess," she said. "My plane got delayed. Bomb scare."

"Are you okay?"

"Oh sure. It turned out to be nothing, a bologna sandwich in a brown paper bag. Full of nitrates, maybe, but not the kind that blow up."

Jackhammer raced into the foyer, took a flying leap, and jumped into Elizabeth's outstretched arms. Aside from me, Elizabeth was his favorite human. She gave him a quick scratch on the head, waltzed into the apartment, and headed over to the chair by the window.

She was decked out in a heavy black leather jacket, a gauzy skirt, and brand-new bright red cowboy boots, no doubt a gift from Dude Bob. She'd coerced her long silver and black hair back into a single braid. Errant wisps fought that idea and stuck straight out, making a halo around her head.

"I'm getting hitched," she announced.

"As in married?"

"That's right. Me and the Dude."

I managed to choke out a congratulations with as much enthusiasm as I could muster in the middle of the night for something I was decidedly unenthusiastic about. It didn't fool Elizabeth.

"Oh, for goodness' sakes," she said. "Brenda Midnight, I can read you like a book. You're afraid I'll hit you up for a deluxe custom wedding veil, and you'll either have to say no and risk our friendship, or yes and break your 'I don't do weddings' rule. Well, you can just relax. I'm not gonna ask for a stupid veil. I mean, really, can you imagine *me* in a veil?"

As a matter of fact, I couldn't. Not because of her age either. More because Elizabeth had never done a single conventional thing in her seventy-some years. I was concerned because her betrothed, Dude Bob 43, a man she'd met online and whose real name I could never remember, had done three tours of Vietnam and was mighty goddamned proud of his service to the country. Elizabeth had protested our involvement in Vietnam. She and the Dude swore to let sleeping wars lie. However, it's been my experience that these kinds of things have a nasty way of creeping back to the surface.

"I know what I'm doing," she said. "It's not like it's the first time I'm getting married, you know."

"But it *is* the first time in a long time," I said.

"This time, I'm old enough that maybe it'll be the last time."

I had no answer to that. The thought of Elizabeth moving

made me sad. "I'll miss you," I said. "I like having you across the hall. Your cookies, your—"

Elizabeth cut me short. "What the hell's wrong with you? Got your hats screwed on backwards? Whaddya think, I'm a complete fool? I'm not going anywhere. Me? Elizabeth Franklin New York City Perry? A dozen Dude Bob 43s couldn't drag me out of this town. No way. The Dude will move in with me."

"Both of you, in that apartment?" Elizabeth's apartment was a mirror image of mine. Flopping it over didn't add one square inch of space.

She folded her hands on her lap and smiled complacently. "I got it all figured out while my plane circled LaGuardia. Built-ins are the answer. The ceilings are high. I'll go vertical. Rig up one of those library-type ladders."

"What about the furniture you've got now?"

Elizabeth's furniture was very cool, an oddball assortment of architect-designed biomorphic chairs, low kidney-bean-shaped tables, and quirky lamps she'd collected over the years.

"You can have it if you want."

I wanted it, of course, but there was a problem. To make room, I'd have to get rid of the furniture I had—massive dark depressing things I'd inherited from my friend Carla—not my taste at all. Much as I hated my furniture, I couldn't bear the thought of getting rid of it. It would be disrespectful of Carla. "Can I let you know later?"

"Don't take too long," said Elizabeth. "I need to get started on the built-ins right away. Now, tell me what I missed while I was in Montana."

I filled her in on Nado coming and Johnny going and gave her a blow-by-blow of the business association meeting.

"I knew Julia Pond would be trouble," she said, "from the moment she moved into the Randolph apartment."

*   *   *

After Elizabeth left, I thought about my furniture—how whenever I opened the bottom drawer of the dresser, my friend's perfume wafted ghostlike into the room. How could I consider dumping it? Deep down I knew it was about much more than furniture. It was about loyalty, respect, life, and death. Furniture was about moving out. This was about staying put and moving on.

4

That night I dreamed about furniture—
an overstuffed brown wing chair, its up-
holstery scratched, and springs poked through its
seat. It smelled of mildew and cigar butts, and was trying
with all its might to suffocate me. I fought back. I pierced
its flabby padding over and over with a giant ruby-studded
hatpin. Before there was a clear winner in the struggle between milliner and chair, a loud buzz woke me. The
doorman was ringing my apartment.

I got up and, in a daze, stumbled over to the intercom.
"Hello?"

The doorman's voice was high-pitched with excitement.
"Some guy's on his way up . . . I'm sorry . . . tried to stop
him . . . he ran past me . . . got on the elevator . . . looks like
some kinda lunatic . . . long hair all over the place." He
paused as if waiting for me to say something. When I
didn't, he asked, "Do you want I should call the cops?"

I heard a loud knock on my door. Jackhammer barked
and ran full speed into the foyer.

"I don't know," I said into the intercom. "Hang on a
second."

I threw on my robe on the way into the foyer. Jackhammer, ever the protector, frantically sniffed at the crack under
the door. I looked through the peephole. It was Lance Chapoppel. The doorman had not exaggerated; Lance looked

deranged. Highly animated, he flapped his arms and walked in a small tight circle.

"Lance?" I said tentatively.

He brought his face close to the peephole. "Please, Brenda, open up."

I let him in and quickly went back and picked up the intercom. "No cops," I told the doorman. "He's a friend."

"Some friends you got," said the doorman. "Not that it's any of my business, but—" I clicked off the intercom.

Lance stood in the middle of the room, looking as if he wanted to do something but couldn't remember what. He had always been the calm, cool one, studied and precise in his movements. I'd never seen him the least bit rattled. I quickly closed up the sofa bed, rearranged the pillows on top, and motioned for him to sit down.

He slumped onto the couch. "How could you do this to me?" he said. "I thought we were friends."

Me? What had I done? "Tell me what's wrong."

He drew several deep breaths. "You got any booze?"

"Red wine okay?"

"Whatever."

I retreated to the kitchen, got a bottle of wine, a glass, and a corkscrew, and rejoined Lance. He grabbed the bottle, plunged in the corkscrew with a violent twist, yanked out the cork, poured a glass, gulped it, and poured another. He turned to me and said, "You're not having any?"

I shook my head. I had a full day of work ahead of me.

He topped off the glass again, then spoke. "This is awful. This is terrible. They're gonna think I did it."

"Who's they? What's it?"

"The cops, that's who."

"Cops?"

"That's right, cops—as in the police, those guys that are gonna bust me for icing that rat bastard my soon-to-be ex-wife Susan was screwing around with." He buried his head in his hands.

Oh boy. So much for the low crime rate. "Tell me what happened."

He jerked to attention and sat up straight as a broomstick. "It sure as hell wasn't the first time my lovely wife Susan cheated on me. I guess I always knew she married me for my money. Guess what? There are men who have more money. Susan was always trying to better herself. This last time was one too many. I got fed up, threw her the hell out."

"I'm sorry."

Lance raved on. "So what's my sweet little gold digger to do? No home, no money, and believe me, there wasn't gonna be any alimony either. No way. I made real sure I had the goods on her before I told her I knew what she was up to. Tearfully she ran to her latest paramour. I'll be goddamned if the son of a bitch didn't set her up in one of his apartments, right in the same building. Supposedly she 'rented' "—Lance made quotation marks in the air—"one of his studio apartments. Yeah, right, rent. So they'd like me to think. Ha. Like I'm gonna believe any money changed hands."

Lance was talking fast and furious. "Slow down," I said. "You said the same building. Do you mean where you live?"

"That's exactly right. Get this: The son of a bitch is the president of the co-op board. I'm damn glad he's dead." Lance smiled, and for a moment looked like himself. "Can you believe it? Murdered. Whacked. Slain. Iced. Offed. Any way you want to say it—Royce Montmyer, adulterer, is dead. Ha. Wanna know who did the deed?"

I nodded.

"It was that ex-husband of yours, Nado."

It was late. I admit, until that point, my mind had been wandering. Lance now had my full attention. "Nado? Wait just a minute. Back up, start over. How does Nado figure into all this?"

Lance was bad enough before, but by now he was three sheets to the wind, totally incapable of coherently relating events in any semblance of order. I summoned up all my patience and asked a series of questions. Slowly, piece by piece, I managed to pull most of the relevant information out of him.

It seems Nado, my sneaky, lying, conniving first ex-husband, had taken advantage of Lance's willingness to let him use his parking space. Nado hadn't merely parked his van in Lance's spot, he'd been living in the van, a latent hippy decades too late. I knew the man was cheap—yet another reason why I divorced him—but this really took the cake.

Lance's details were sketchy. Someone apparently had seen Nado asleep in his van and complained to the building management. It is, after all, a luxury building, hardly a place for riffraff. As president of the co-op, Royce Montmyer, the very same ''rat bastard son of a bitch'' who was having the affair with Susan, took it upon himself to confront Nado. When he did, Nado shot Montmyer through his ''rotten evil heart.''

No wonder Lance was scared. It wouldn't take the police long to learn of Susan's relationship with Montmyer. Once they figured out that Lance also knew Nado, they'd probably conclude that Lance hired Nado to kill Montmyer. In Lance's shoes, I'd be shaking too.

However, I wasn't in Lance's shoes; I was in my own, and I knew damned well Nado didn't shoot Royce Montmyer. Nado had more faults than the state of California, but a killer he was not.

While Lance nodded off, I reflected on my entire life, the good, the bad, but mostly zeroing in on the Nado years, which were for the most part in between. Nothing I dredged up from those memories showed Nado to be the least bit violent.

As I sat and thought, my window filled with morning light. I heard New York kick into gear. The upstairs neighbor got up, padded into her bathroom. Water whooshed through pipes behind my wall. Off in the distance garbage trucks mashed through the streets, squealing as they digested yesterday's trash.

I looked over at Lance, then shook him. His eyelashes fluttered for a moment, then his eyes popped open. "There's one thing I don't understand," I said. "What makes you think Nado killed Montmyer?"

"Doesn't matter what I think," said Lance sorrowfully. "Cops think so too. You see, I was pulling an all-nighter, working out a new noodle concept. I heard the big commotion, yelling and sirens, and went outside to see what the deal was. Some people in the building were already there, rubbernecking. They told me the good news about Montmyer. So I was hanging out thinking how cool it was that he got killed, when I saw a couple of cops shove Nado into a squad car and peel out. People said Montmyer caught Nado living there. It didn't take me long to realize what that meant for me. So I split and came over here."

I had a thought. It was, after all, a small world. "Did you get a look at the cops who took Nado away?"

He shrugged. "I didn't pay much attention. Nice suits, I think. A white guy; a black guy. Cops all look alike to me."

I smiled. "I think we're in luck. I'll go down to the precinct. I promise you, I'll have this all straightened out before lunchtime."

"Thanks, Brenda. I knew I could count on you."

He toppled over onto the couch, curled up, and in seconds he was out. Jackhammer leaped up and wound into the crook of Lance's knees.

5

So as not to disturb Lance, I pulled my telephone into the kitchen. Then I dialed the precinct and punched in Turner's extension as directed by a recording. He picked up on the first ring. "Detective Turner here."

"Good morning, Detective Turner." His first name was Spencer. I'd never once used it.

"Well, well, well, if it isn't our favorite milliner, Ms. Brenda Midnight." The way he emphasized the "Ms." I knew I was in trouble. "Funny," he said, "my partner and I were just talking about you. Your ears must be burning."

"Really? Talking about me?" I said in a futile effort to keep the conversation light.

"Yes, really," he snapped. "Like in how come Ms. Midnight's name always pops up when there's trouble in the neighborhood?"

"Trouble?"

"Don't give me that innocent crapola, Ms. Midnight. You know goddamned well what I'm talking about. You didn't call to inquire as to my hat size, now, did you? We've got ourselves a murder, and your ex-husband, Nado P. Sharpe, is right smack in the middle of it."

"It must be some kind of mistake," I said.

"Why don't you come down to the precinct and we'll discuss it?" said Detective Turner. "In fact, I insist you pay us a little visit. Shall I send a squad car?''

''That won't be necessary.''

I zigzagged my way down Hudson Street in an attempt to avoid the chunks of dug-up concrete and blacktop and lurching earth-moving equipment. The construction project had dragged on for years. Contractors dug holes, filled them up, dug them up again. The plan, according to the city, was to install a new water main. Everybody in the neighborhood suspected the real truth was that they dug for the glory of digging. By now some of the holes qualified for landmark status.

The latest excavation left a gaping cavity in the street in front of the White Horse Tavern. I paused and looked down into the hole. It revealed the city's innards, a twisted, rusted network of pipes and conduits and god knows what else. Amazing that anything ever worked. I was fascinated, but also in a hurry. I'd have to contemplate the unfathomable some other time. I tore myself away from the hole and hightailed it the rest of the way down to the precinct.

I stood for a moment outside the cop house to gather my wits. How much could I say without tipping my hand? My main objective was to spring Nado. Then I'd try to find out how much they knew about Lance. That might get tricky. If Turner didn't mention Lance, I wouldn't bring up his name.

I took a deep breath, pushed open the heavy glass door, and entered the precinct. Here goes nothing, I thought. The officers hanging around the first floor recognized me from previous escapades. No one paid the slightest bit of attention as I headed up the stairs to the grim institutional cubicle Turner shared with his partner McKinley.

Turner and McKinley were Johnny's friends. Early in his Tod Trueman career, the two detectives had given him lessons in how to walk, talk, and drive like a cop. They thought the world of Johnny. However, on the subject of me, they blew hot and cold. Due to circumstances quite beyond my control, I'd gotten tangled up in one or two of their cases and was responsible for netting them a couple of rather impressive collars. For various reasons, I let them take full credit for rounding up the villains. You'd think they'd be grateful; instead they'd made it excruciatingly clear that they preferred that I leave the police work to them.

I knocked lightly on the doorframe of the cubicle.

"Do come in, Ms. Midnight. So good to see you." Turner's voice dripped with sarcasm. I'd usually find him tilted back in his chair with his feet up on his desk, showing off ultra-expensive, hand-stitched, buttery-leather European shoes. Not today. He paced back and forth from one end of the cubicle to the other. His light wool custom-tailored suit fit close to his body, which, for a man near retirement, he kept remarkably fit.

McKinley stood in the corner of the cubicle, arms crossed, and gave me a dirty look. His suit, a blend of linen and silk, hung on his tall, thin frame with casual elegance. He gestured me toward a broken-down office chair. "Have a seat," he said. "Stay awhile."

Like I had a choice.

McKinley was black; Turner white. Serious scowls contorted both of their faces.

I sat as directed. "Detectives." I stuck an experimental smile on my face. Neither smiled back. Neither commented on the gorgeous spring day. Neither offered me coffee. They got straight down to business and grilled me. It went on for over an hour, during which time Turner stopped pacing, sat down, and rhythmically banged his clenched fist on his desk. The paper in his in-box fluttered with each bang.

I didn't understand their extreme anger. About halfway through the interrogation, a ponytailed undercover cop dressed in cut-offs and a marijuana T-shirt stopped in the doorway. He listened in for a minute, then shook his head and snickered.

Every time I tried to ask a question, they shut me up. Every time I tried to qualify the yes or no answers they insisted on, they told me they didn't want to hear embellishments. After what seemed like the hundredth no, I'd had quite enough. "Look," I said, "I know nothing about Nado. Except for an occasional postcard, we don't keep in touch."

"Uh-huh," said McKinley. "You expect us to believe that out of the blue your ex, some hot dog stand bozo, drops by and you set him up with a parking place for his van, which he lives in, and even though you don't know anything, you're positive your dear Nado wouldn't hurt a flea."

"Yes," I said, "but I didn't—"

"Yes or no," said Turner, a command I chose to ignore.

"—except I didn't know Nado was living in his van. What's the matter with you two? Don't you believe me?"

McKinley opened his mouth to say something. Turner waved him off, sighed, and said, "Oddly enough, Ms. Midnight, we do believe you. And for your further edification I will tell you we do not believe Mr. Sharpe was involved in the murder of Royce Montmyer. In fact, we have evidence quite to the contrary. However, we'd feel a tad more comfortable about the entire sorry affair if Mr. Sharpe would tell us so himself."

Given their bad attitude, the last thing in the world I wanted to do was to tell the detectives how to do their job, but it seemed so obvious I blurted out. "Why don't you ask Nado?"

"Son of a bitch got away," said McKinley.

"He what?" I was shocked.

"Goddamned Nado P. Sharpe absconded with our vehicle," said Turner. "Do you realize how this makes us look?"

The words "stupid" and "incompetent" immediately came to mind. Now I knew why the cop with the ponytail had laughed. I'm sure he wasn't the only one.

I had a hundred questions to ask, and as many reasons to keep my mouth shut. Why had Nado run away? Where had he gone? The air was charged with hostility. Time and conversation stopped while Turner and McKinley glared at me. I twisted and turned in my seat, looked down at my shoes, up at the ceiling. Afraid the tension would give me the giggles, I occupied my mind by mentally rearranging my collection of antique hat blocks so that they lined up in chronological order, beginning with a twenties cloche shape. I'd just put a man's forties fedora form in its proper historical slot when Turner broke the spell with a ridiculous, inane, irrelevant question. "As long as you're here, Ms. Midnight, perhaps you can tell us why the hell McKinley and I weren't invited to Johnny Verlane's going-away party, the one with all the babes?"

I couldn't believe it. They seemed more angry about Johnny's party than about Nado taking off in their car. I knew why they hadn't been invited. I tried to smooth it over. "It's Lemmy Crenshaw. He put together the guest list. He's still a little uptight about you guys." I referred to a mix-up where the esteemed detectives incorrectly believed Lemmy had murdered a feather salesman. Now, long after I'd straightened that out, Lemmy still held a grudge.

"That really sucks," said McKinley.

"Lemmy Crenshaw is a short, bald, hotheaded buffoon," said Turner.

"Lemmy probably didn't show Johnny the guest list," I said. Turner and McKinley were never going to like Lemmy. I didn't want them mad at Johnny too.

McKinley continued his rant. "Really, really, really sucks."

The detectives finally got sick of telling me how much both situations sucked and told me to leave. They claimed they had a ton of paperwork to do. On my way out, McKinley said, "If Nado P. Sharpe comes moseying around your place again, you'll be sure to let us know, won't you?''

"Absolutely."

"I mean it, Ms. Midnight," said McKinley. "If your ex saw anything, we may not be the only ones looking for him."

"I understand."

Then, of course, came the inevitable warning. In preparation Turner cleared his throat, straightened his shoulders. "Remember, Ms. Midnight, don't you go getting any cockamamie ideas about interfering with our investigation. Stay out of this one. Go make some hats, leave the police work to us."

Unfortunately, my visit to the precinct gave me new questions and no answers. What the hell was wrong with Nado? It didn't make sense that he'd run from the cops if he'd seen Royce Montmyer get plugged. It also didn't make sense that he'd run from the cops even if he hadn't seen anything. But then, when did anything about Nado make sense? And now, because of his stupid behavior, he could be in danger.

I was glad that Turner and McKinley didn't think Nado was involved in the murder, but what did they mean by "evidence to the contrary"? Did that mean they already had a suspect? Lance? It was unlikely they knew about Montmyer and Susan Chapoppel yet, but as soon as they found out, Lance would certainly be a suspect.

One good thing in all this: If Nado really had witnessed the murder, his testimony could clear Lance.

I wanted to check on something before talking to Lance. I stopped by Elizabeth's. "Are you still on good terms with the precinct captain?" I asked.

She gave me a what-are-you-mixed-up-in-now kind of sigh and asked, "What are you mixed up in now?"

I told her.

"I've got an ex just like your Nado," she said. "One

gigantic pain in the kazooie. I sure as hell wouldn't have taken mine to a party, especially a party where I had the hots for the host. You must have been out of your mind.''

"I don't have the hots for Johnny.''

"Oh, excuse me,'' said Elizabeth, slapping the side of her head with her hand. "How could I ever forget? You and Johnny are just friends.''

"Anyway,'' I said, "I didn't think it would be a big deal. My mistake wasn't in taking Nado to the party; my mistake was introducing him to Lance so he could use that parking spot. Poor Lance. He's the one in the middle of this.''

"From what you told me about his wife, Lance would have been in the middle no matter what. Now, in answer to your question, the precinct captain and I are thick as thieves. His bulldog Elmo is scheduled to spend a couple of days with me soon. That dog's a sweetheart. Enormous appetite, though.''

"Do me a favor and call the captain, see if you can pull any information out of him. Find out if the cops know about Susan Chapoppel's affair with Montmyer.''

Elizabeth made the call. Once she got through to the captain she didn't say much, mostly listened, and made sympathetic little sounds. She hung up the phone and shook her head. "Sorry. I couldn't get a word in. I didn't find out anything about Susan Chapoppel. The captain knows you're my friend, and he knows Nado's your ex. All he could talk about was how Nado stole the cop car. Your detective friends are a couple of first-class clowns. The uniformed cop first on the scene discovered Nado in his van, possibly inebriated. Turner and McKinley wanted to get a statement from him and decided to bring him back to the precinct themselves. They didn't bother telling Nado that he wasn't under arrest.''

"They love to intimidate people,'' I said.

"Nado was probably scared to death. The detectives raced their vehicle the wrong way down Hudson Street, siren blaring, a West Village wake-up call. Jerks ran their

car into a hole—you know, from the perpetual digging—
and it got stuck. Turner and McKinley both got out of the
car to push. While they huffed and puffed, Nado sneaked
into the front seat. As soon as the car rolled out of the rut,
your ex put the pedal to the metal. They found the abandoned car in the East Village. No sign of Nado. The captain
says the worst thing that could happen to a cop is to lose
a service revolver; the second worst is to lose a police vehicle. It'll be a cold day in hell before Turner and McKinley
live this down.''

Lance and Jackhammer were exactly as I'd left them. I
woke Jackhammer first, then roused Lance. He groaned and
rubbed his forehead with his fingertips. I imagined he felt
the effects of too much wine, too late, too fast.

He pushed his hair out of his eyes. "So?"

I tried to put a positive spin on things. No reason to get
Lance more upset than he already was. "We got lucky," I
said. "Those detectives you saw, the ones in charge, I'm
personally acquainted with them. They came right out and
told me they don't suspect Nado. That means they can't
possibly think you hired him."

"They probably think I blew the bastard away myself,"
said Lance. "No alibi, fabulous motive. Do they know
about Susan and Montmyer?"

"I don't know. I couldn't ask."

"When they find out . . ." Lance pulled his finger across
his throat. "I swear to god, Brenda, this really pisses me
off. If you hadn't brought your goddamned ex around, and
if he hadn't—"

"I sure as hell don't blame you for being mad, but it
could work out for the best. Nado might have seen who
did it. He can clear you."

Lance perked up. "That's wonderful. Why didn't you
tell me before?"

"There's one problem. Nado disappeared." I gave Lance

the rest of the details. When I finished, he wasn't any too happy. "I'm sorry," I said.

"I'm afraid sorry just doesn't cut it, Brenda. However, there is something you could do."

"Anything," I said.

"You find out who killed Royce Montmyer."

"Me? I'm a milliner, remember?"

"Oh, come on, Brenda. You think I haven't heard about your exploits? You nab killers every bit as well as you block hats."

Actually I'd never considered myself much of a blocker.

6

Lance paused on his way out. He looked very tired. "You know where to find me— that is, unless I get arrested."

With Jackhammer stretched out on my stomach, I lay back on the couch and thought about all the stuff I had to do. First and foremost, I had to find Nado and make sure he was safe. I owed him that much for old times' sake. Also, finding Nado would help me get back on Turner and McKinley's good side. If I got really lucky, and Nado had seen something in the garage, finding him might also get Lance out of trouble.

Lance was my second priority. He was a good friend. When I moved to New York, Lance had already been here a year. He took me under his wing and showed me the good galleries, the art bars, and helped me get my first day job. I'd help him out anyway, even if I hadn't been responsible for complicating his predicament.

Since finding Nado might kill two birds with one stone, it was the logical place to begin. I had an idea and called my friend Chuck Riley to see if he would help. He lived in the East Village, close to where Nado ditched Turner and McKinley's vehicle.

Chuck had caller ID. He knew it was me before I picked up. "Brenda," he said. "Glad you called. I've been meaning to call you to apologize for flaking out on

Johnny's bon voyage party. I was gonna go, but I got into this intense cyberblab with a team of wacky physicists.''

''That's okay.'' Nobody expected Chuck to show up at the party. Only three things were guaranteed to pry him away from his roomful of computers: Elizabeth, whom he adored; the band Urban Dog Talk; or food. Elizabeth had been in Montana getting proposed to, Urban Dog Talk had temporarily stopped gigging to regroup, and Chuck's favorite pizza joint now delivered.

''What did I miss?'' he asked. ''Any miniskirted starlets show up to bid Johnny adieu?''

''A few, but the reason I called was to ask—''

''Wait. Don't tell me. You decided to go in with me on my smell-o-veil idea. I'll infuse the net with any smell you want, be it rose petals at dusk or subway platform at dawn.''

''Chuck, the world is not ready for smell-o-veils.''

''There's historical precedent,'' he said. ''Back in the fifties—''

''Chuck, no smell-o-veils, okay? Now, listen up. I need your help.''

I made a long story short.

He interrupted once to tell me I was a jerk to take Nado to Johnny's party. ''Especially with you having the hots for Johnny and all.''

Why did all my friends insist on the same thing? I ran through the tired old bit of how Johnny and I were just friends, Chuck made the expected bitingly sarcastic comment, then I continued with the story of Royce Montmyer's murder and how Nado had run away.

''Chalk up another screw-up for Turner and McKinley,'' said Chuck.

''I've got to find Nado. He might be in danger.''

''What do you need me to do?''

''If I can get a photo of Nado faxed to you, can you make up some missing person posters?''

''Piece of cake. I'll help you plaster them up too. Urban

Dog Talk's got sophisticated postering equipment. I'll borrow their big bucket, professional paste, and high-quality brush.''

''You're a pal, Chuck.''

''You know, Brenda, there's one good thing about all of this. I'm glad Lance is finally dumping that no-good wife of his.''

''You know Susan Chapoppel?''

''I met her at a party a couple of years ago. Lance was out of town at a noodle convention. She snubbed me, wouldn't give me the time of day. As a social experiment, a friend told her I held the patent on a new Internet browser that'd blow away the competition, and that my company was planning an initial public offering. He convinced her the future was in new tech, not extruded noodles. She did a complete turnaround. She slithered over and tried to put the move on me.''

That sounded like Susan. ''So what happened?''

''Gentleman that I am, I told her to get lost.''

I dreaded what I had to do next. It took almost an hour to get up the nerve to do it. Then I procrastinated an additional half hour in case the world was going to end anytime soon. When it didn't, I took a deep breath, picked up the phone, and called Kathilynda Annamarie Cooper Sharpe.

My problems with Nado's current wife went way back, long before either of us married Nado, long before either of us even noticed Nado. Back then, pretty much none of the girls noticed Nado, or for that matter any of the other guys in our high school, not when Vinnie T came on the scene.

Tall, dark, handsome, leather-jacketed Vincent Torrence had an aura of danger surrounding him that made our teenage hearts sing. One day between classes Kathilynda and I stood before our adjoining lockers eyeing each other's split ends. Vinnie T swaggered up, leaned close, looked at me, then at her, then at me again, then he asked me to meet him at the drive-in on Friday night. Speechless, I nodded in agreement. Kathilynda shot me a look I remember to this day.

The date never happened. At the last minute, Vinnie T called and said he had laryngitis. He sounded awful, hoarse and feverish. The next day a friend called and asked why I'd stood up Vinnie T. "I didn't," I said. "He was sick."

"Not so," said the friend. "He waited for you at the drive-in. He got pissed off when you didn't show and ended up taking Kathilynda Cooper home."

Even Turner and McKinley could have figured out what had happened. Vinnie T hadn't called me. It had been Kathilynda, disguising her voice.

"Sharpe's Hiway Haute Doggerie, home of Belup's Creek's gourmet hot dogs. May I take your order?"

I recognized that nasal twang. "Kathilynda?"

"Who is this?"

I told her, cut through the small talk, and got to the point.

"Nado did what?" she screeched.

I repeated, "Nado stole a cop car."

"What the hell for? You caused this, didn't you, Brenda Sue?"

I started over from the beginning, downplaying the fact that Nado might be in danger. She stopped me before I finished.

"You mean Nado wasn't shacked up with you?"

"Of course not."

"Did he tell you we had a fight?"

"He might have mentioned it."

"Well, we had one, and it was a doozy. Then he hauled ass out of here and said he was on his way to New York to see you, and naturally I thought ... I thought you two were, you know. I mean you two used to be married."

"Nothing happened, Kathilynda."

"That's a relief. Where is Nado? I want to talk to him. I bet he's sorry he ever left Belup's Creek."

Reluctantly, I went on with the story. "So, I'm not sure where he is now, but I plan to find him."

Kathilynda reacted pretty much as I expected. Enraged, she cursed Nado for being stupid, New York City for swallowing up her husband, and me simply for being me. She wound down her tirade with, "I never did like you much, Brenda Sue."

In the worst way I wanted to tell her the feeling was mutual. I wanted to finally confront her about the Vinnie T episode back in high school. I fought that urge. I needed her cooperation to find Nado and I needed to find Nado. I bit my tongue and told her not to worry. "I've got the situation under control. I need to ask one little favor of you."

After a brief outburst, she promised to fax a photo of Nado.

"Please send it directly to my friend Chuck." I gave her the number.

"You better find my Nado," she said. Her voice caught and she started to sob.

In a way, I felt sorry for her. I understood her anger. I'd be mad too, and jealous, and scared. For one split second I considered growing up. I could let bygones be bygones. Because of what she did next, I'm damned glad I didn't.

With a quick sniffle she recovered her composure. "Oh, by the way," she said sweetly, "your name came up the other day."

"Really?"

"Uh-huh. Vinnie T came by the restaurant and we got to talking. You remember Vinnie T, don't you?"

A flash of anger quickly dissipated. I felt tingly all over. I reacted exactly like a fourteen-year-old. "What did he say? What did you say?"

"Well, I said that Nado was on his way to see you, that after several unsuccessful marriages you lived all by your lonesome in a pathetic New York slum, and that you were really, really, really fighting the drug addiction, but that you're still forced to turn an occasional trick. Vinnie T? He didn't say much after that.''

7

Kathilynda burned me up. Seeking solace, I grabbed Jackhammer, stormed out of Midnight Millinery, and went over to Elizabeth's to vent. She offered cookies from a fresh batch.

I bit down with great care in case this cookie experiment was one of her few misfires.

"What do you think?" she asked.

"Not bad. What's in it, banana?"

"Yes. Exquisitely paired with sweet onion."

"Interesting."

I gave Elizabeth the lowdown on Kathilynda.

"She sounds like a piece of work, all right."

"Now Vinnie T thinks I'm a drug-addicted hooker."

"I wouldn't worry about that. I don't know your Vinnie T, but I doubt he'd fall for that bunch of malarkey. In fact, I bet Kathilynda didn't tell him any such thing. She wanted to push your buttons."

"In that case, her ploy worked. I'm mad as a hatter."

Elizabeth laughed. "What we're really talking about here is closure. Your past is not resolved."

"You sound like a pop psychiatrist," I said. "I don't need to resolve anything. I grew up and got over it."

"Then why are you so upset? We've all got our Vinnie Ts buried in the past. Sometimes they get dredged up again. Mine had a convertible. Did yours?"

44

I smiled at the memory. "Candy-apple red with a custom leather interior, baby moon hubcaps."

Elizabeth leaned back and closed her eyes. A smile played across her face.

"Vinnie T wore a black leather jacket," I added, "even in summer."

"Ah yes, the obligatory black leather jacket. Timeless." Elizabeth sighed deeply, then snapped out of her reverie. "Enough about the unrequited. What's your next move?"

"I figure looking for Nado in New York would be like looking for a hayseed in a haystack, so I came up with a better idea. If Kathilynda comes through with a photo of Nado, Chuck promised to make a missing person poster. We'll slap them up all over town. Put the whole city on alert."

"Good plan. How's your friend Lance doing with all this?"

"Not good. He wants me to find out who killed Royce Montmyer."

"And?"

"Well . . . I guess I sort of said I'd look into it."

"Shame on Lance Chapoppel for encouraging you, and shame on you too, Brenda Midnight, for agreeing. What do you think you are anyway, some kind of honorary detective? Maybe you got lucky a couple of times. That doesn't mean you're qualified to chase after every killer who comes down the pike."

"I've got to help Lance. Because of Nado, I feel responsible."

"Don't give me that crap. Know what I think? You're beginning to like this detective work. You know damned well what Turner and McKinley will say."

"Rest assured. They've already said it."

On my way out Elizabeth asked if I'd made a decision about her furniture.

"Soon," I promised.

*   *   *

From Elizabeth's apartment door to mine it's a straight shot. As Jackhammer and I traversed the six feet of renovated hallway, he got attacked. Being six inches tall, he didn't know what hit him. From my higher vantage point, I saw the twenty-pound orange striped cat tear around the corner, but not in time to stop it from swatting Jackhammer. It then zoomed back around the corner.

Jackhammer squealed bloody murder. I scooped him up. When he shook his head, blood spurted out.

Elizabeth dashed into the hallway. "What happened? Is our little guy all right?"

"I think so," I said. "A huge cat came ripping around the corner and swatted him." I probed for damage. "I'm pretty sure the blood is all from his nose."

"Goddamned bushwacker cat. A mangy yellow thing, right?"

"Yes."

"Guess whose?" Elizabeth jutted her chin toward the Randolph apartment, now occupied by none other than Julia Pond, proprietress of Julia's Trick Shoppe, blight of the West Village.

"I should have guessed."

Jackhammer stopped squealing and licked my cheek. "He's all right," I said. "A little humiliated is all."

Julia's apartment door burst open, and Julia herself stepped into the hallway. She had on a shapeless flower-printed muumuu-type dress, her bleached blond, black-rooted, chopped-off, fried hair partially tucked under a stretch knit turban. She ignored Elizabeth, Jackhammer, and me. "Oh, Irving," she called. "Playtime's over. Time to come home to Mama Julia."

The orange cat slunk back around the corner and ducked into Julia's apartment.

In the interest of harmony and community I've been known to let a lot roll off my back, but not in this case. Jackhammer had been hurt. That didn't roll well at all. It got stuck halfway down. "Your cat attacked my dog," I said.

Julia regarded me with scorn.

"You shouldn't let your cat roam the hallway unattended," said Elizabeth.

Julia scowled at Elizabeth. "Irving does not roam." Her voice boomed. "Irving patrols for rodents."

"This building doesn't have rodents," I said.

"We've got a rule against unleashed animals in the common areas," said Elizabeth.

Julia put her hands on her hips. "Oh, you do, do you? I choose not to obey that rule."

I pointed to blood drops on the ceramic tile floor. "Your cat bloodied Jackhammer's nose."

Julia snorted. "And that, I suppose, is Jackhammer?"

I nodded.

"That explains it, then. My Irving thinks the little pipsqueak is a rodent."

With that she stepped inside her apartment and slammed the door.

"That lady's cruisin' for a bruisin'," said Elizabeth.

I stood Jackhammer on the kitchen counter and gently wiped off his little black nose. The bleeding had stopped. I inspected him for further damage. It appeared he was in one piece, though shaken. He perked up when I offered him a steamed green bean, which he swallowed whole. Then he curled up on the couch and went to sleep.

I decided to do the same. It had already been a very long day and if Chuck and I went out hanging posters, it would be a long night. Before napping, I checked my answering machine.

There was a long-winded, incomprehensible message from Johnny. Cars honked in the background. He must have called from a car phone while tooling down some eight-thousand-laned freeway. I hoped to hell he wasn't behind the wheel. Johnny was a lousy driver. I played his message back several times. If he said anything pertinent to our nonrelationship, it got lost in the muddle.

Next, a garbled message from Chuck. No traffic noise, but the sound kind of whooshed in and out. Maybe my machine was screwed up. After a few replays, I figured out what he had to say. Kathilynda had faxed the photo of Nado. The last part of his message was all too clear. "Don't tell me you were actually married to this Nado guy. He looks like a dweeb."

My nap was a complete washout. I worried about Nado. I worried about Lance. I worried about what Elizabeth had said about me going after Royce Montmyer's killer. She needn't have worried. I hadn't done anything yet. I didn't know how to proceed.

What did I know about Royce Montmyer? He'd been shot dead. He'd been having an affair with Susan Chapoppel. That meant he had bad taste. Did it also mean he had an angry wife who perhaps preferred widowhood to a cheating husband?

I also knew Montmyer was president of his co-op board. Had he misused his power, greased his palm with kickbacks?

He owned at least two apartments in his building, his and the one Susan had moved into after Lance threw her out. Did he own other apartments? Was he a landlord? Landlords are not exactly universally loved. Could he have been killed by an irate tenant?

Later that night I took a cab over to Chuck's boarded-up East Village storefront. His place looked like the inside of a television set. A six-foot wall of computer magazines divided it into two rooms, both chock-full of antique and state-of-the-art electronic equipment. He had at least four computers running at all times. Wires and cables crisscrossed the floor, ran up the walls, and hung from the ceiling. Chuck was an electronics genius. Every so often he took a consulting job, made a pile of money, then goofed off until he spent it all.

I was shocked when I saw him. Instead of his usual ripped jeans, he had on a pair of baggy red and orange plaid trousers. If I wasn't mistaken, his T-shirt had fewer holes, and a new earring cut from a chunk of circuit board dangled from his left lobe.

"Formal affair?" I asked.

"Very funny."

He led me over to his graphics computer. An image of Nado stared at me from Chuck's gigantic monitor. "Fax was lousy," said Chuck, "so I whipped it into my trusty photo retouch program and sharpened it up."

"It looks great," I said. "Exactly like Nado."

Chuck laughed. "How long ago were you married to him?"

"Long enough that I can't believe it either."

Chuck got busy on the computer. He pointed and clicked and moved elements into place. "How much reward?"

I hadn't thought about that. Lance would probably pay. "I don't know. Five hundred?"

"What if we just say 'generous reward'?" He typed the words, moved them into place, enlarged the type. "You want to say something like 'last seen in East Village'?"

"I guess we better."

"Okay. Midnight Millinery's phone number or your home?"

"I was kinda hoping neither. You know, in case Nado saw something and whoever did it saw Nado and—"

"Don't sweat it, Brenda. How about if I set up a dummy number and route any calls over to Midnight Millinery?"

"You can do that?"

"Piece of cake. Just remember to change your message to something anonymous."

While Chuck's laser printer spit out the posters, and Chuck mixed paste, I consulted a city map and tried to plot out a strategy for postering. I'd just concluded it was impossible to get posters distributed throughout Manhattan when Chuck's door buzzer went off.

"Dweena's right on time," he said.

"Dweena?"

"I asked her to help out. We need wheels if we're gonna get this job done tonight."

I had a very bad feeling. I opened the door. Dweena stood in the hallway. She had on a skintight black catsuit, high black boots, a long black wig, and black sunglasses. I looked beyond her through the glass front door and saw a shiny black sedan parked at the curbside. "Diplomat?" I asked.

"As you know," said Dweena, "I specialize."

Once, when she was between careers, Dweena had apprenticed as a car thief. She'd since moved on to better things; to keep in practice she occasionally boosts a car for a joyride or a short errand. To promote justice, she targets diplomats' vehicles. They park wherever they want and claim diplomatic immunity. The mayor is up in arms about the flagrant abuse. Dweena evens the playing field.

Slapping up posters wasn't exactly legal, but I was willing to risk the consequences to find Nado. Slapping up posters in a stolen diplomat's car was a whole hell of a lot more seriously illegal. I was scared.

When it was all over, I had to admit, Chuck was right. It was efficient. In two hours we were done. Dweena dropped Chuck off, parked the diplomat's car on Avenue C—creative relocation, she called it—then she and I cabbed it back to the West Village.

"See?" she said. "There was nothing to be so nervous about."

I stopped by the shop on my way home and changed the answering machine tape so that the greeting said simply, "Leave a message." That was that. Now all I had to do was wait for the calls to pour in.

*   *   *

That night I dreamed about another chair. This time it was a friendly chair, one of Elizabeth's. It oozed under my door and danced and pirouetted around the apartment. For an encore it transformed into a hat, took a bow, then oozed back out.

8

Early the next morning I hurried over to Midnight Millinery, anxious to listen to all the calls that had come in about Nado. I was greatly disappointed. So far, the posters had netted only one call, and it was a prank. "That guy on the poster?" said the caller. "He's the one got me pregnant. Hahahaha."

I tried to cheer myself. The posters hadn't been up long enough to get real results. Still, I had to face the fact that the poster idea might be a dud. Finding Nado might not be so easy.

Then there was Lance. If I was going to help him, I couldn't just sit back and wait for the poster to get results. For one thing, Nado might not know anything anyway, in which case finding him wouldn't do Lance any good. The more I thought about it, the more I realized I had to do some poking around into Royce Montmyer's life to find out who might want him dead. Damn. Despite what Elizabeth and Turner and McKinley thought, I really hated this kind of stuff.

I called Lance. He was grumpy at first, but seemed a bit happier after I told him about the posters. I didn't bother him with details like the first call being a failure.

"Sounds good, Brenda."

"Now," I said, "to proceed with part two of my investigation I need to ask you some pertinent questions about the deceased.'' I sounded ridiculous, a bit like vintage Tod Trueman before Turner and McKinley got hold of Johnny and taught him how to act like a cop.

Lance laughed. I must have sounded ridiculous to him too. ''Sure, Brenda. Go ahead.''

''All right. Was Royce Montmyer married?''

''Yes, he had a wife, Maris Montmyer.''

''Great. A jealous spouse who's not you.''

''I don't know, Brenda. Maris Montmyer doesn't seem the jealous type.''

''What do you mean?''

''Too self-involved. I think the two of them had an agreement to go their separate ways.''

''Did he have any other . . . you know . . . besides Susan?''

''Not that I know of, though I wouldn't be surprised.''

''What about business associates? What did Montmyer do for a living?''

''I got the impression he worked for himself.''

''You mentioned he owned Susan's apartment. Any others in the building?''

''Yeah. I think so.''

''Did the cops talk to you yet?''

''No, but I'm sure they're watching me. I feel eyes, Brenda. Know what I mean?''

I didn't, but I said I did, and hung up.

One way to find out about Royce Montmyer, his loves, his business deals, his life, and his death, would be to snoop around the Hudson Shadow and ask a bunch of questions of anyone willing to talk. That way, however, required that I spend time away from Midnight Millinery. If I could get hold of the minutes of the Hudson Shadow's board, I could streamline the process, and do it from the comfort of my own store.

If anybody could help me procure the minutes, it was

Irene Finneluk. By night, Irene performed on the amateur strip circuit, specializing in the shimmy. By day, she was a powerful real estate broker, specializing in Upper West Side luxury properties. I'd first met Irene as a customer when she bought a gigantic-brimmed straw hat to use in her act. Later, we became friends and coconspirators. I hadn't seen her since we'd set up a sting to outscam a big-time scammer.

"Brenda," she said. "You poor thing. I was just this minute thinking about you. You must be spitting mad, or depressed, or something. I know I would be."

"Me? What would I be mad, or depressed, or something about?"

"Oh, of course," she said. "I should have known. You were in on it the whole time, right?"

If I was in on something, I didn't know it. "In on what?"

"The publicity stunt. Smooth maneuver for Lemmy Crenshaw, bless his little agent heart. Wonderful timing, having the news break with the season finale of *Tod Trueman*. A brilliant touch."

Damn. Johnny would be really mad at me. I'd been out plastering up posters and forgot all about the *TTUD* season finale, a two-hour special. Johnny said it was the best episode yet. He must have been calling to remind me to watch when he'd left that garbled message on my machine.

Irene went on. "They were very convincing. I guess that's because they're good actors. Actors act; that's what they do. Did you get a load of that rock? Even though it was all an act, I bet you still shit a brick when you saw the size of that sparkler."

"Rock? Sparkler?"

Dead silence. Finally Irene said, "You really don't know, do you?"

"Don't know what?"

She sighed. "I hate to be the one to tell you, but right after the *Tod Trueman* finale, after Johnny had rescued that beautiful heiress with the long wavy blond hair in the turquoise hot pants from the clutches of the evil drug kingpin, after the fadeout with the passionate kiss, the lead-in to the news showed the real-life Johnny Verlane with the real-life blond. She was showing off a real-life new engagement ring and blathering about how they'd met on the set months ago and had managed to keep their romance secret until now.''

Oh. Before my heart came to a complete stop, I managed to squeak out, ''That? Sure. I knew about that.''

Johnny? Engaged? But I thought . . . when he said . . . I closed my eyes. Images of Johnny ran through my head.

''Well, thank goodness you already knew,'' said Irene. ''Otherwise it would have been quite a shock. So anyway, it's good to hear from you.''

It took a moment to pull myself together enough to tell Irene why I'd called. When I finally did, I chose my words very carefully. ''Hypothetical,'' I said. ''Say I've got this friend who needs to investigate the president of a certain Manhattan co-op board. My friend would like to take a look at the minutes from the board meetings. Would that kind of information be available?''

''Hypothetically speaking, anything's available if you know whom to call, how to ask, and how much to offer.''

''I thought so. How would you suggest I advise my friend?''

''First, Brenda, cut the friend crap.''

''I was that transparent?''

''Yeah. Like a Madison Avenue boutique window. Now tell me what the hell you're doing poking around the Royce Montmyer murder. And don't tell me it's not *that* murder, because I know better. It's kinda funny. Anywhere else in the world, an on-site murder would put a crimp in sales, at least temporarily. In your wacky West Village, such cachet could actually drive prices up.''

Briefly, I explained my involvement.

''Your ex sounds like a real winner,'' she said.

"It was a long time ago," I said. "So, do you think the minutes would help me?"

"Maybe. Although minutes are notoriously sterile. You'll have to read between the lines."

"Does that mean you'll get them?"

"Consider it done. It so happens I know the vice president of the management company that runs the Hudson Shadow. He's an avid fan of my strip act. If I promise to toss him a pastie, he'll fax me the board minutes, no questions asked. Theoretically, I could have them this afternoon."

"Thanks, Irene."

"Promise me you'll be careful. You've been lucky a time or two, but—"

"I know what you're going to say. Don't worry, I know my limitations."

"Good. I'm glad Johnny's engagement was a publicity stunt, but I warn you, Brenda, that Johnny Verlane is hot stuff. If you don't snap him up, I will."

I forced a sound out of my throat that I hoped sounded like a chuckle. It wasn't.

Johnny often escorted the guest starlets who appeared on the Tod Trueman show around town. Lemmy said it was to keep the rumor mill well fed, the gossip columnists gossiping, and the public confused. Now I was the public and I didn't like being confused. This engagement bit was a whole new ball of wax. It could be the real thing. I had to come to grips with that.

And I had to come to grips with something else too. No matter what I told my friends about Johnny and I being just friends, deep down I kind of thought it might be nice if it were otherwise. And I thought Johnny kind of felt the same. I thought that's what he wanted to talk about before he left for Los Angeles. Just because he'd said he wanted to talk to me didn't mean what he wanted to talk about was what I thought he wanted to talk about. Here I'd been worried about how to turn him down—thinking maybe this time I wouldn't, maybe this time I'd say yes—but if Johnny wasn't asking, I had no decision to make.

The mailman came by Midnight Millinery and dropped off my mail. I sifted through, pitched the catalogues and a couple of You Have Won–type solicitations. The only legit mail was a Con Ed bill and two postcards from Nado. One showed an old photograph of the Belup's Creek creek majestically snaking through what would later become a subdivision. On the back of that postcard Nado had written: "Headed toward the Big Apple. See ya soon." So, he really had sent a card. I'd assumed he'd lied about that. The post office had been speedier with the second card, postmarked the day before. When the system works, it works well. That card had a shot of the Empire State Building lit up with red lights. "Having a wonderful time. Don't worry."

Yeah, right. Like I wasn't going to worry. Damn him.

While waiting for calls to come in about Nado and for Irene's fax to arrive, I squeezed in some real millinery work. I needed hats soon. The faster I got my summer hats up in the window, the longer my selling season, the more hats I would sell, the more money I would make, and the more likely I'd be on time with Midnight Millinery's rent.

I had a basic shape. The next step in creating my summer line was to decide on color and fabric. Was chartreuse over? Would hot pink make a comeback? I saw taxicab yellow on the horizon. My gaze wandered to Nado's Empire State Building postcard. The light fell over the building, bathing its upper floors in red. It wasn't the red that attracted—personally, I was sick to death of red—what I liked was the translucent glow.

I got out my box of fabric scraps, found some silk organdy, and experimented. The organdy was a pain to work with. The very feature I liked—the translucence—was the problem. The seams showed through. The edges had to be

finished, which translated into exactly double the work.
Worth the effort? I was considering that question when the
phone rang.

That Chuck sure had a way with wires. Thanks to him,
the telephone circuitry figured out that the incoming call
was a fax, the machine kicked into gear, and thirty feet of
paper spooled out. I cut the pages apart and sat down at
the vanity to read.

I wanted to be like a fly on the wall, but it wasn't like that.
Irene was right. Board minutes were sterile. Motion to get
new uniforms for the doormen, seconded. Vote: All six
board members in favor. Hand it over to such and such,
who knows about this and that. Landscaper needs to be
reminded of the proper way to dispose of cuttings. So and
so will write a letter. Resident complaint regarding dead
water bug in hallway for over a week. Check to see if the
new super changed the sweeping schedule. Repaint. Repair
roof.

Kickbacks? I'd have to check further. Garage security.
That gave me chills. A proposal to install a video security
system had been voted down. Royce Montmyer had been
one of the nays. I'd bet there'd been a few seconds at the
end of his life, as he watched the warm pool of his own
blood spread out on the cement floor of the garage, when
Royce Montmyer wished he'd voted yea.

By the time I'd slogged through two years' worth of
monthly meetings, a pattern emerged, something I hadn't
thought of before. Co-op boards have the power to reject
potential buyers and they don't have to say why. The Hudson Shadow's board didn't seem to be overly fussy; they
gave a quick go-ahead to most applicants. However, in a
couple of instances a buyer had been turned down, and the
next buyer was also turned down, then the next. One apartment had six different buyers rejected in as many months.
The seventh applicant, Royce Montmyer himself, was ap-

proved. I had a suspicion he didn't pay anywhere near the original asking price.

Every buyer who'd been turned down, every seller who'd had a buyer turned down, and every broker who'd lost a deal, all had reason to hate Royce Montmyer. Had one of them hated enough to kill?

Once again, I learned the hard way that real life had absolutely nothing in common with a *Tod Trueman* episode. In a *Tod*, Johnny would have received the fax at poolside, glanced at it while clinking crystal champagne flutes with a beautiful guest starlet, and bingo, right before the commercial break, he'd figure out who the bad guy was, how to trap him, and, if that wasn't enough, how to get the girl. That, I didn't want to think about.

I, stuck in real life, hadn't the foggiest idea where to begin.

9

I called Lance and started to tell him what I'd found out.

"Excuse me, Brenda, but I don't want to hear about the board right now. The doorman told me they called a special emergency meeting to talk about me. They want to throw me out on the grounds that I created a hazardous condition in the parking garage that led to the death of Royce Montmyer."

I'd considered Nado to be a lot of things, but never a hazardous condition. "Can the board do that? I mean, you own the apartment."

"They can make a lot of trouble. I did violate the bylaws. It will probably come down to who's got the biggest, baddest lawyer."

An image of three-hundred-pound lawyers converging on the Hudson Shadow popped into my head. I squelched it; this was no joke.

Lance continued. "My patent attorney referred me to a real estate attorney, who said it would help if I could get Nado to swear he'd never met me, that I had no knowledge of him parking or living in my space. It's important that you find Nado soon."

"The response to the missing person poster has been amazing. I've got a bunch of leads to follow up." Big exaggeration. I hated this. I promised myself to never again get in a position where I had to lie to a friend.

"Good," said Lance. "Keep me informed of your progress."

"Of course."

"You be careful, now, Brenda. I'd never forgive myself if something happened to you."

I thought Lance knew me better than that. I would never endanger myself. I don't fly, eat meat, or carry large amounts of cash to the garment center. I most certainly don't put myself in the way of killers.

I got back to work. I cut out three hats at once, then sewed assembly-line style. Henry Ford would be proud. My mind wandered from Nado's disappearance to Royce Montmyer. I considered possible killers and possible motives. Who done it? The wife Royce Montmyer had cheated on, or somebody who got screwed by his real estate shenanigans? The popular notion was that nine times out of ten the spouse did it, so that seemed a good place to start.

I congratulated myself on a rapid and good decision. Soon I uncongratulated myself. The decision to start with Maris Montmyer was a long way from actually starting. How best to proceed? Break into her apartment to look for incriminating evidence? Not this milliner. Interrogate her friends? Not likely.

What happened next was even less likely. In retrospect, what happened next was so unlikely as to throw it into the realm of stuff that always happens to Johnny in a *Tod Trueman* episode. However, it was real, and it happened to me.

There I was, sewing French seams around a curve in translucent silk organdy. The bells on the door jangled and an elegant woman glided in. She trailed many layers of yellow chiffon behind her. She had on gold-framed designer sunglasses and gold toe-baring sandals. She was attractive, late fifties or early sixties, with a deep preseason tan, and the kind of hair that could either be gray or blond, depending on context and attitude.

Jackhammer trotted over and sniffed at her platinum-painted toenails.

She reached down and scratched him between his ears. "Nice little doggie."

"Let me know if I can be of help," I said.

She looked at all the hats on display. I noticed that she was attracted to a completed bowed visor, although she didn't try it on.

She wandered over and watched me work. "Do you do custom work?"

"I sure do. That is, everything but weddings. I don't do weddings."

She laughed. "This is certainly no wedding. I need widow headgear. You know, a hat with a heavy black veil."

No one had ever asked me for mourning millinery. At a loss for words, I turned to cliché. "I'm terribly sorry for your loss."

"Don't be. My husband, the arrogant, philandering son of a bitch, got himself murdered, shot through his cold hard heart. You must have heard about it. It happened right here in the neighborhood."

No. It couldn't be. I pulled a number five millinery needle from my pincushion and jabbed it in my palm to see if I was dreaming. It hurt; I seemed to be awake.

She doffed her sunglasses with a flourish and smiled. "I'm Maris Montmyer, grieving widow of Royce Montmyer."

I gave the needle another jab, to be sure. Ouch. In mild pain, severe shock, and fresh out of suitable clichés, all I could come out with was, "Pleased to meet you."

"Likewise," she said.

I knew next to nothing about funeral etiquette. "So," I said, "about the funeral. Does your religion specify any—"

"Oh hell no. I can wear what I goddamned please. My only requirement is a heavy veil. I don't want anybody to see in."

"Right. Heavy veil. I can understand. You need privacy in your moment of sorrow."

"Screw sorrow. I already told you, I'm glad he's dead. What I'd really like to do is tie his low-down cheating carcass to the bumper of a cab, give the driver a C-note, and tell him to drive around 'til the money runs out, then dump whatever's left of Royce in the Hudson. However, I'm afraid the law frowns on such actions."

Strange behavior, I thought. Had she acted like this when the cops questioned her? Maybe it was some kind of reverse psychology. If she'd killed her husband, she'd be expected to hide her contempt for him; by not doing so, she confused the issue. Or perhaps she had an ironclad alibi and no reason to hold anything back. If only I could think of a way to ask. "Will it be an afternoon funeral?" I asked, as if that would make any difference in the design of the hat.

Maris Montmyer eased herself gracefully onto the vanity stool. She leaned forward and examined her face in the mirror. Finally she answered my question. "Late afternoon. Royce's will left no specific instructions regarding funerals and whatnot. I wasn't even going to have one; then, behind my back, Royce's goddamned inconsiderate sleaze of a brother went right ahead and scheduled a memorial service. Can you believe the gall? He didn't consult me about the date until he'd already invited everyone." She spun around on the stool so she faced me. "So, guess what day the asshole picked?" She paused, as if she expected a response.

I shrugged my shoulders.

"Two lousy days after my face-lift, that's when. I'll be a purple pulpy mess. My brother-in-law says to me, 'What's the big deal, Maris? Reschedule your lift.' Arrogance runs in that family just as sure as rotten teeth and flat feet. Everybody knows you don't reschedule with Dr.

Ruggetay.'' She looked at me like I was supposed to know of whom she spoke.

I gave her a blank look.

"You haven't heard of Dr. Ruggetay?"

"No, I don't think so."

"Oh, my dear, you have so much to learn. The man's a genius, a true artist with the scalpel. He does absolutely everybody who's anybody. He's booked up at least three years in advance. Reschedule? Heavens. That is quite out of the question. Yet I must go to the stupid memorial service. A dilemma."

"Now I understand your need for a heavy veil."

"You got it. A proper old-fashioned widow's veil might do the trick. Do you think you could whip me up a little something to hide the ravages of surgery?"

"I'd be happy to," I said.

Wadded up near the bottom of my box of trimming I found a piece of super-dense veiling. I gave it a shot of steam, draped a layer artfully over the widow Montmyer's face, and fastened it in place with a hairpin.

She twisted her head this way and that, looked hard into the mirror.

"Can you see out?" I asked.

"Fabulous, yet no one can see in. If hats with veils were to come back into style, we wouldn't need men like Dr. Ruggetay."

I gathered up several hats for her to try on with the veil.

She picked a denim pillbox style. "Can you make it up in black velvet with satin trim?"

"Yes. How soon will you need it?"

"Sooner than soon. Tomorrow; I need it with me when I purchase a mourning ensemble. If need be, I'll pay a rush fee. I can send a messenger by to pick it up, say, tomorrow morning."

That wouldn't do. I wanted to see her again after I'd had

time to think. "Tell you what. Since you're in the neighborhood, why don't I drop by in the morning with the finished hat? We should do a final fitting to assure that the veil drapes nicely."

I couldn't believe my good luck. I dropped what I'd been doing and stayed at the shop until I finished Maris Montmyer's widow hat. Then I took it over to Elizabeth's to show her.

"Maris Montmyer told me she could see out, but I'm worried," I said. "This is an unusually dense veil. What if she trips and falls and breaks her neck and sues me?"

"For what? Millinery malpractice? For goodness' sakes, Brenda, you're too paranoid. No offense, but why would anyone want to sue you? You don't have a pot to piss in. If you're so concerned, why not put the hat on and see how well you can see out?"

"Bad luck," I said. "You know how the groom isn't supposed to see the wedding dress before the ceremony? It's like that. Except different."

"You, Brenda Midnight, are superstitious?"

"Not usually, but this is special. You probably have to be a milliner to understand. There's an old saying, goes something like, 'She who dons the widow's veil' . . . I forget the rest, but it's bad news."

"Hogwash. Give me the damned thing. I'll put it on. I'm not superstitious. And even if I were, so what? What would happen? One of my exes is gonna croak? Ha. Most of them have already got one foot in the grave." She grabbed the hat from me.

"No, Elizabeth. Don't. I just remembered the rest."

She jammed it on her head.

"It's 'shall ne'er marry'—"

Elizabeth yanked the hat off. "What have I done?"

"It's okay. It's a silly superstition."

"I killed Dude Bob, didn't I?"

"No, no," I said. "Nothing like that. It means that some

little bitty thing might go wrong, like maybe when Dude Bob comes to town, his plane will be late, something like that.''

''You're sure, now?''

''Positive.''

''You really had me going there for a minute,'' said Elizabeth. ''I guess I'm more superstitious than I thought.''

''Sorry.'' I wished I'd kept my big mouth shut.

''Now that we've got that squared away,'' said Elizabeth, ''give me the poop on the widow, Maris Montmyer.''

''She's attractive.''

''I don't care what she looks like. What I want to know is did she bump off her husband? As any cop'll tell you, it's always the spouse.''

''Believe me, I thought about that. She's so blatantly not grieving, it could be an act to throw me off, but why would she want to throw me off? She doesn't know I'm on. She has no idea I'm involved.''

''I wouldn't be so sure about that,'' said Elizabeth. ''What if she does know? She could have found out that Nado is your ex, or that Lance is your friend.''

''How?''

''Lance could have mentioned it to a neighbor, who mentioned it to someone else. You get the picture. Maris Montmyer wants to know exactly how much you know. That would certainly explain the bizarre coincidence of her happening to show up at Midnight Millinery and revealing intimate details that are none of your business. You've gotta admit, that's real Tod Truemanish. Speaking of Tod, have you heard from Johnny?''

''No.''

Later that night I went back to Midnight Millinery to check the answering machine. No new calls about Nado, not even a prank. Obviously, I needed a fresh tactic. Since Nado dumped Turner and McKinley's car in the East Village, I figured it wouldn't hurt to go check out that neighborhood in person.

I called Chuck. He knew the East Village like the back of his hand. "Want to take a walk around your neighborhood tomorrow?" I asked.

Chuck didn't want to talk about walks. He was mad. "I talked to Elizabeth today," he said. "Did you know she was gonna marry Dude Bob?"

"She mentioned it. Yes."

"Why the hell didn't you tell me?"

There were a lot of reasons, the main one being that Chuck was kind of sweet on Elizabeth. Not that he'd ever come right out and admit it. "I thought she should tell you herself. Wouldn't you rather hear it from her?"

"I'd rather not hear it at all, goddammit. I don't know what Elizabeth sees in that creep."

"No accounting for taste," I said.

"You should know all about that," he said. "Speaking of Nado, any response from the poster yet?"

"No. Lance is getting antsy. That's why I want to take a look around the East Village. You up for it? Late tomorrow morning?"

"Yeah, what the hell."

10

The Hudson Shadow loomed up ahead. In real estate lingo, the building was a luxury residence. To me it looked like a twenty-five-story eyesore, a big hulking blue brick box. In the late sixties a fire leveled an abandoned dockworkers' flophouse on the site. A developer snapped up the parcel of land and announced plans for an apartment building "unlike anything the West Village has ever seen."

Well, West Villagers had pretty much already seen it all, and they didn't want to see this particular building on this particular site. Different factions opposed the building for different reasons; but everyone united in concern about the shadow it would cast. Trees and flowers would die. Muggers would lurk.

Elizabeth remembered a sleep-in protest at the construction site. She and about twenty others had greeted the early morning bulldozers with songs of peace and love. They tossed flower petals on the ground. The heavy machinery crunched on; the protesters went home; the building went up in record time. In the eighties, it went co-op.

I'd never given the Hudson Shadow much thought one way or the other. It was just the big building where Lance lived, and more recently where Nado had parked, and Royce Montmyer had died. I looked up at it and saw that the building was plug-ugly. I marveled at the blueness of the brick; perhaps meant to replace the sky views it blocked.

I walked down two steps, between two potted palms, through heavy glass revolving doors, and into the lobby of the Hudson Shadow. It had been hideously redecorated since I'd last visited. Every conceivable surface had been covered with mirrors, every edge trimmed in highly polished chrome. Everywhere I looked were images of me and my Midnight Millinery hatbox. I could almost see my face in the super-shiny terrazzo floor.

I stopped before an intimidating mirrored pulpit-like desk and told the doorman my name. He waved me toward a bank of mirrored elevators. "Mrs. Montmyer is expecting you."

The walls and ceiling of the elevator were mirrored. My image reflected infinitely in five directions. At first I didn't know whether the effect was transcendental or nauseating, but by the time the elevator reached the twenty-second floor I had a definite opinion. With a double-bong sound the doors opened, and I staggered off. It took a moment to get my bearings, then I found the Montmyer apartment at the end of a long hallway. I used a brass knocker in the center of the door.

From inside I heard Maris. "Be with you in a minute."

It was more like three minutes before Maris Montmyer opened the door. She had on beige linen trousers, a white silk blouse, and a patronizing smile.

I smiled back. "Good morning."

The mirrored theme of the lobby and elevator spilled over into the Montmyer apartment. Mirrors everywhere. I surmised that Royce, or possibly Maris herself, had been the designer on the lobby project. That alone, in my opinion, was motive for murder.

Everything in the apartment that wasn't mirrored blazed white. Overstuffed, oversized couches and chairs were covered with white on white brocade. Crystal-based lamps sat on white marble tables. Beneath it all, a deep-pile white rug.

Maris directed me into a sunken living room. "Have a seat," she said, indicating the couch with a flick of her wrist.

I put the hatbox on a mirror-topped coffee table, sank into the plush pillows. "Lovely apartment," I said, forcing sincerity into my voice.

Maris sat on a chair next to the couch. She tilted her chin toward the hatbox. "Thank you. So kind of you to bring my mourning hat in person."

"My pleasure," I said.

"Well, I appreciate it. I have so much to do before my face-lift. Royce's timing couldn't have been worse. Oh well, I suppose I can't complain. At least he's dead."

That was it—my opening, a chance to ask about her brazen attitude. All I had to do was open my mouth. I chickened out. "Shall we try it on now?"

"Might as well get it over with," she said.

I took the hat out of the box and placed it ever so gently on her head. I spent a few extra moments fussing with the veil. Then, with my hands spread wide under her face, I presented herself to herself. "Voilà."

Maris Montmyer had no problem locating a mirror. She studied herself from all angles from the comfort of her chair. After what seemed like a long time, she came out with a "Hmmm." A minute passed, another "Hmmm." Then she said, "I'd like it tilted forward a bit. Can you do that for me?"

I did so.

"And a little to the side, perhaps?"

I did that also.

The adjustments gave the hat a jaunty look, hardly proper for a memorial service. She might as well show up in a veiled beanie with a propeller on top.

"That's it," she said. "Perfect. I must say, I'm thrilled with the way this turned out."

"Thank you." I took the hat off her head and nestled it back in the hatbox, all the time trying to get up the nerve to ask her. I'd never have a better chance. I took a deep breath. "Mind if I ask you something?"

"I suppose not."

"You don't hold back much, do you? I mean—"

"If you mean my contempt for my dead husband, you're quite right. I hated the bastard and I don't care who knows."

"Aren't you afraid the police will think you, well, you know . . ."

"Whacked him myself?"

"Right."

"How very touching. Thanks for your concern. Under normal circumstances, you'd be right. The thing is, I have a wonderful alibi for the evening in question."

"I see." Did I dare ask more? Perhaps I'd already gone too far.

Maris, however, seemed eager to elaborate. "You see, my dear, I was in jail. Rounded up—by mistake, of course—with a bunch of streetwalkers. Apparently someone thought they'd seen one of the prostitutes with a bomb. I was out getting a breath of fresh air in the newly trendy meat district to the north of here. The next thing I knew, wham-bang I'm searched and in the wagon. At the time someone was blowing away my dearly departed, a handsome young police officer was inking my fingertips at our friendly neighborhood precinct. Now, I hope you'll accept a check."

"Of course," I said.

Maris Montmyer's alibi stank to high heaven. It stank more than the meat market. It was too convenient to convince me. She could have hired a hit man to kill her husband, then called in the bomb scare and made sure she got herself busted in the hooker sweep. I'd have to look into this.

I checked my watch. Too late to go to Midnight Milli-

nery and get any appreciable amount of work done, too
early to go to Chuck's. Since I was already in the building,
I decided to drop by Lance's to see if he had an extra
garage-door controller. I needed access to the scene of the
crime.

I went back to the lobby and had the doorman buzz
Lance's apartment. "Busy today, aren't we?" the doorman
said. Then, for the second time that day, he watched me
cross the lobby to the elevators.

The door to Lance's apartment was ajar. I called to him.
"Lance?"

"Come on into the kitchen," he said. "I'm in the middle
of an experiment."

Lance's apartment was full of noodles—books on noodles, gigantic schematics of noodles, three-dimensional
models of noodles, prototype noodles, production noodles,
and, in the kitchen, a stainless steel pot of noodles boiled
on the stove. Lance plucked a few out of the water, tasted
one, tossed the rest into a cup, and wrote down the elapsed
cooking time in tenths of a second.

"Anything new on Nado?" he asked. He seemed in a
pretty good mood, considering.

"So far none of the leads from the poster have panned
out. However, I have good news." I told him how Maris
Montmyer had dropped from the sky onto Midnight Millinery. "I wouldn't exactly call that alibi of hers ironclad.
I'm going to check it out. Also, I think I should take a look
at the garage. Do you have an extra remote control?"

He did. "You might as well take this too," he said, re-
ferring to a key. "This is for the door that leads from the
garage to the basement. I've no use for it." Then he called
down to the doorman. "My friend Brenda Midnight is helping me out with a project. Make sure she has full access to
the building. She'll be coming and going at all hours."

A timer went off. Lance plucked more noodles out of
the water, ate one, cupped the rest.

"I thought they were done when they stuck to the wall," I said.

Lance laughed. "That's an oversimplification. The composition of the wall is a factor, also the shape of the noodle, the relative humidity, and the thrust with which they're hurled."

"In other words, like everything else in life, it depends."

"Right. You know, Brenda, I really love my work. Extrusion is so like life. You stick something in one end and sometimes, no matter how well you've planned, what comes out the other end is a big fat surprise."

I left Lance to his noodles. On my way out of the building I nodded to the doorman. He smiled and nodded back. Once outside, I walked around to the side of the building. I didn't have to be at Chuck's for a while yet, so I decided to take a quick look around the parking garage.

I pointed the controller at the garage door and pushed the button. A motor whirred, gears engaged, the door lifted, and I walked down the steep incline into the garage. About a minute later, the door clanked closed behind me.

Before, when Lance had shown Nado his parking space, I'd been too busy talking to pay much attention to the garage. Now, all alone, I marveled at the vast space. The ceilings were high, the expanse interrupted only by plain cement supporting columns. It smelled of gas and oil and grease and metal.

I walked all around. About half the parking spaces were filled with some kind of vehicle—car, van, motorcycle— all new, expensive, shiny, and for the most part undented. Tucked away in a corner behind a column, I spotted Nado's van—old, cheap, rusted out, creased, and leaking oil.

I hadn't expected to find it in the garage at all. The fact that it was there was terrific news. Turner and McKinley weren't playing games. They really didn't suspect Nado. If he were a suspect, the cops would've confiscated his van.

Lance couldn't move the van; Nado had the keys. And

of course Nado wouldn't come back for it, not if he thought the cops were after him. So, where else would it be?

All the doors were locked except for the dented driver's-side door, which was too messed up to lock. I remembered how Nado had kicked it open, duplicated his actions, and climbed inside. I hoped to find something to indicate where he'd gone, like maybe an address of somebody else he knew in New York. The results of my search were disappointing. I found dirty clothes, a bunch of flyers for Sharpe's Hiway Haute Doggerie, and a map of Manhattan with the location of Midnight Millinery circled.

I'd just kicked the door back open from the inside when I heard a grinding noise. The gears to the big outside garage door started up. I sure didn't want to have to explain to anybody why I was there. I ducked down in the seat and pulled the door most of the way closed.

I peeked through the crack of the door and watched as two late-model sedans rolled into the garage single file and pulled up next to each other. The drivers got out and walked around to the back of the cars. It looked as if both men put in a lot of time at the gym. They wore almost identical shiny suits, no ties, and had crisp white shirts open far enough to display gold medallions on their hairy muscular chests. They were straight out of central casting. Fear stifled my laughter.

The guy with the larger medallion took a carton out of his trunk and put it in the other guy's trunk. The guy with the smaller medallion took a smaller carton out of his trunk and put it in the other guy's trunk. Both got back in their respective cars and rolled out to the street. The whole exchange had taken under a minute. The garage door had remained open. Seconds later it shut. I was scared. Had Royce Montmyer witnessed a similar exchange, revealed himself, and been killed?

I got the hell out of there. I used the key to the inner door, ran through the basement, passed under pipes and cables, ran by the boiler room, gas meter room, laundry room, compactor room, recycling room, and telephone room. I ran all the way to the elevator and took it one floor up to the lobby. The doorman nodded again as I ran out the front door.

11

"Drugs?" said Chuck. "I'm like under-whelmed." He turned back to his computer.

"I'm not talking about some street dealer passing a baggie of oregano to a tourist," I explained. "This was major-quantity stuff, two cardboard cartons." I stretched my arms to show how big. "Probably jam-packed with contraband."

Chuck tapped furiously on his keyboard. He looked more bedraggled than usual, his face paler and greener, carrot-colored fuzzball of hair mashed down on one side, stuck out on the other. He had let me in with barely a nod, thrust a bag of generic barbecued potato chips at me, told me to help myself, and then plopped down in front of his computer. The whole time I talked, detailing the scene in the garage, he cursed at the words scrolling by on his computer screen, pretty much ignoring me.

I didn't give up. "What if Royce Montmyer stumbled onto a drug deal in progress? The drug dealers killed him so he couldn't rat on them. Or here's another possibility. He could have been part of the deal and it went bad."

Still no response from Chuck.

"I should talk to Turner and McKinley. I bet they'll listen. Then again, maybe that's not such a great idea. I wouldn't want them to know I was snooping, would I? Maybe I will anyway. So what if they get mad? It's my civic duty. What do you think? Chuck? Are you listening? Chuck? Do you hear me? Earth to Chuck, come in.'' I might as well have been talking to myself. ''Chuck?''

He rolled his chair away from the computer, looked at me with tired red-rimmed eyes, and said, ''We got trouble.''

Chuck popped the top off a can of beer. ''Want one?''

''No thanks.'' I said. I sank into his red beanbag chair and waited for him to explain.

I'd never seen Chuck this serious. He took a gulp of beer and wiped his mouth with the back of his hand. ''After Elizabeth told me she planned to marry Dude Bob 43, I did some checking on the Internet. I popped the Dude's real name into my search engine to see what it came up with.''

I tried to remember Dude Bob's real name. I always thought of him by his screen name.

''My first inquiry drew a blank, so I tried other search engines. Nothing. Then I went directly to a bunch of Vietnam sites. He should have turned up on any one of a dozen lists, but he didn't. Dude Bob 43 is a fake. He never did any tours of Vietnam, never received the medals, never was in any branch of the U.S. military. I don't know what he did during that era, but he sure as hell didn't do all the stuff he always brags about. I posted at every site I visited and asked if anyone remembered him. Nobody does. Bottom line: Dude Bob 43 lied to Elizabeth. He's a sleaze. I should have checked up on him a long time ago. I'll show you where I've been.''

He ran his computer through its paces. He typed, pointed, and clicked his mouse. The words ''not found'' came up on the screen again and again. I didn't understand where we were, but I had complete confidence in Chuck's abilities to maneuver in the cyber world.

''This is just a summary, of course, but I think you get the idea. I'm damned good at this. If he were here, I'd have found him.''

"Have you told Elizabeth?"

"Not yet. It'll break her heart. I want to try a few more places before I give up. Meanwhile, I promised Elizabeth I'd meet her tonight at Angie's for dinner. She wants me to go over the plans for her built-in furniture. So I've gotta pretend like everything's hunky-dory, like I'm thrilled to help her build furniture to make room so a big fake can move in and marry her."

"Want me to come along?"

"It wouldn't hurt. You could change the subject or kick me if I start to say something bad about Dude Bob."

"I'll be there," I said.

"Thanks, Brenda. I feel rotten. I had a hunch Dude Bob 43 was no damned good from the minute Elizabeth started to flirt with him online. I should have pulled the modem on their romance. Nipped it in the bud."

"Don't blame yourself," I said. "Elizabeth is one mighty strong-willed woman. Once she made up her mind, there was nothing you could have done to stop her."

I ran through the drug dealer story again. This time Chuck paid attention. He agreed that it might be significant—and dangerous. "Stay out of that garage, Brenda."

Next, I told him about Maris Montmyer. He got a kick out of that story at first, but after he thought about it for a minute, he came to the same conclusion as Elizabeth. "She didn't drop by Midnight Millinery out of the blue. Maris Montmyer knows who you are and what you're doing." When I told him I'd delivered a hat to Maris at her apartment, he blew up. "Promise me you won't do anything stupid like that again all by yourself."

"All right. Next time I do something stupid, I'll invite you to come along. Now, let's go for that walk."

The way Chuck sighed and pushed himself out of his chair, I'd have thought he was a hundred years old. "Sure," he said. "A stomp around the neighborhood might make me feel better."

*   *   *

We headed north on Avenue A. The streets seemed unu- sually tranquil.

"Is it true," I asked, "that the East Village has lost its edge?"

"Do you mean because of our Kmart? Or our multitude of brand-new straight-out-of-the-mall clothing emporia, or the spread of national franchise foodstops, or the fact that we're so goddamned trendy that a one-bedroom in this building right here will set you back more than—"

"Look out!" I shouted.

It was big, it was orange, it was on a dolly, and it was rolling real fast down a ramp that led out of the building, straight at us. I shoved Chuck so hard we both tumbled to the pavement. The orange object hurtled across the side- walk, inches from where we'd landed, and crashed into a dark green BMW parked by a fire hydrant.

"Holy shit," said Chuck. "Both those suckers are to- taled."

Two men ran huffing and puffing out of the building.

"Son of a bitch," said one.

"Boy, are we in trouble," said the other.

"Whaddya mean, 'we'? You're the idiot who pushed when I said pull."

A woman in a pin-striped power suit stormed out of the building, surveyed the situation. "What have you done? This is a total disaster. I'm holding both of you responsi- ble."

A man charged out of the sushi restaurant next door. He also wore a pin-striped power suit. "What have you done to my car?" His head spun wildly. He looked from the woman, to the two men, to Chuck and me. When no one answered, he pointed to the orange object. "What is that orange monstrosity? Will somebody at least tell me that?"

"That monstrosity," said the woman, "*was* my custom- built, four-thousand-dollar, fifty-cubic-foot refrigerator. It is vermilion, not orange. Now it is ruined."

"A refrigerator? You telling me a freaking refrigerator smashed up my Beemer? It's destroyed."

"Your Beemer," said the woman, "happens to be illegally parked."

"This could get real nasty," said Chuck.

"Let's hit the road."

"So you see, Brenda," Chuck said when we were a block away, "the East Village didn't lose its edge. We're still razor sharp, but we have a new set of worries. No more crackheads and junkies and muggers. Now our fancy cars get menaced by four-thousand-dollar custom-built designer orange refrigerators."

I corrected him. "Vermilion."

Chuck and I walked around some more. I stopped at several delis, personally dropped off Nado posters, and asked the proprietors to put them in the window. "It's important," I emphasized.

We passed by a community garden. "That's where that building collapsed last year," said Chuck.

The buildings to either side of the garden showed ghostlike impressions of the building that used to be. I was admiring the garden when I spotted a familiar face. Elliot. The homeless man from West Fourth Street. He was weeding a flower patch. What was he doing here?

I didn't know what to say. My previous conversations with Elliot had consisted of little more than a nod, a hello, and a how are you. Pete always handled the nitty-gritty of negotiations for sweeping up the sidewalk and repair work. I was thinking how I should call Pete and ask him to come over and talk to Elliot when Elliot saw me and waved.

I told Chuck to wait for me and went over to the flower patch. "Hi, Elliot. Pete and I have been wondering where you've been. We've been worried. Are you all right?"

"Never better," he said. "I'm on vacation."

"What do you mean?" I'd spoken too quickly, but if he was offended, he didn't show it.

"Somebody gave me a hundred-dollar bill, told me to get lost for a while."

"Really? Who?" That seemed highly unlikely.

Elliot shrugged. "I dunno. Just some guy."

"Well, we miss you. Are you thinking about coming back to West Fourth Street?"

"Yeah, maybe."

"Good. Until then, you take care, Elliot."

Elliot returned to his flowers. I walked over to where Chuck was waiting.

"So what was that all about?" asked Chuck.

"Elliot's talking nonsense," I said.

Chuck walked me by the intersection where Nado had ditched Turner and McKinley's car.

"I think I know why Nado picked this spot," said Chuck. "From Hudson he must have picked up Bleecker, and shot across town. Then he turned and ended up here on East Fourth. When he went past the playground he could see straight through to Fifth where all the cop cars park around the Ninth. He freaked, stopped here on First, and lit out on foot."

"Where the hell is he now?"

"Good question," Chuck confirmed with a nod.

White puffy clouds floated in a bright blue sky. The temperature was in the seventies, the humidity low. I breathed deeply. I felt guilty taking the time to walk all the way home when I had so much to do, but I did it anyway. I stopped once to marvel at the Kmart on Astor Place, and again to snicker at a guy in avant-garde cowboy garb who stood in front of a country-western theme restaurant, spinning a rope.

12

I got back to the apartment late, way past time for Jackhammer's midday walk. He was one grumpy little Yorkie. He pretended to be asleep, but under his reddish blond forelock I detected a half-open eye that followed my every move. I went into the kitchen and made a big show of banging cabinet doors. He roused himself, trotted in, planted himself at my feet, and stared up at me with soulful dark eyes.

"Now that I have your attention," I said, "let me explain."

While I threw together a broccoli, arugula, and carrot salad, I gave him a rundown of my day so far. Unlike Chuck, Jackhammer was riveted by what I had to say. He stayed at rapt attention until I gave him a broccoli floret, which he carried off to his bed.

My answering machine blinked, signaling one message. I recognized Kathilynda's twang. She had a lot of nerve to call after what she claimed to have told Vinnie T. Maybe she had called to apologize. I couldn't tell what she said. The message came out a garbled mess, like it had chewing gum in the works. I fiddled with the machine, popped out the tape, poked around inside. It looked normal to me. I put the tape back in, rewound, and listened again. No good. I needed a new machine. That came through loud and clear.

* * *

I took Jackhammer and headed over to Midnight Millinery. On the way I stopped in at Pete's Café and told Pete that I'd seen Elliot. "I'm afraid Elliot's got static in the attic," I said. "Can you imagine, he claims somebody gave him a hundred-dollar bill and sent him on vacation."

Pete, who knew Elliot far better than I, frowned and shook his head. "I tend to take Elliot at his word."

"It's absurd to think somebody gave him that kind of money."

"Maybe not," said Pete. "It's one sure way to get the homeless out of our neighborhood. Know what I mean?"

I realized what Pete hinted at. "You think someone from the business association paid him?"

"Could be. I'm gonna ask around."

The sign mounted on the door of Midnight Millinery promised in extra-bold seventy-two-point sans serif type: HOURS—NOONISH 'TIL LATE OR BY APPOINTMENT. It was a joke, and served mostly to taunt me. I didn't open up until four o'clock that afternoon, which gave me very little time to work before I had to meet Chuck and Elizabeth for dinner. Before I could get to work I had to listen to a whole slew of messages about Nado on my one and only fully functioning answering machine.

Quantitywise, things had picked up. Five messages had come in. Qualitywise, however, they left a lot to be desired. The first caller said Nado owed him two hundred thousand dollars, the next said Nado reminded her of her long-lost brother who'd ax-murdered her lover, one person said his hair was way cool, someone else asked, "Why would you even want to find such a geek?" The last caller burped and hung up. At least no one today claimed to be pregnant by Nado.

I wanted to call Dweena, but I waited until five. She was not an early riser. She picked up right away, and sounded perky. "Did those posters reel in your ex?"

"Caught some crank calls. I threw 'em back in. Meanwhile, I'm looking into another aspect of the case. The same night Royce Montmyer was murdered, a bunch of hookers in your neighborhood got rounded up because somebody reported that one of them had a bomb.''

''I remember. We don't have too many hooker raids over here. Live and let live in the wild, wild far West Village. Every so often somebody gets a bee up their behind and complains, and the cops are forced to do their thing. Saying there's a bomb would certainly assure swift action.''

''Maris Montmyer was arrested with the hookers.''

''The wife of the guy who got whacked? A married lady? Oh my. Dweena simply does not know what this world is coming to.''

''She told me she was in the wrong place at the wrong time. I think she engineered the raid to give herself an alibi.''

''Interesting theory. I'll put my ear to the ground. I'll let you know if I pick up any rumblings.''

''Thanks, Dweena.''

Murder had sure thrown a wrench into my summer line. The hats I'd started the day before were in various stages of construction. By the time I reorganized and got back on track, I had to leave to meet Chuck and Elizabeth. I closed the shop, popped Jackhammer in a canvas tote bag, and told him to keep his head down. Tommy, Angie's bartender and probable owner, allowed him in the restaurant on one condition: I had to pretend to sneak him in. That way, if an undercover health inspector happened to be lurking on the premises, Tommy would be in the clear.

Pastel-clad bridge-and-tunnelers were crowded three deep in the bar. They'd no doubt read that article in *New York* magazine that proclaimed Angie's to be the perfect neighborhood bar. Of course, the very fact that so many non-Villagers were there made it no longer a neighborhood bar, and no longer perfect—a concept Chuck and Elizabeth were in the middle of discussing when I joined them in a booth in the back room.

"Some scene in the front room," said Chuck. He pounded on the bottom of a ketchup bottle until the red stuff exploded out and flooded a platter heaped high with french fries. "It's like a down-to-earth nonquantum version of Heisenberg's Uncertainty Principle." He seemed to be in a much better mood than this afternoon.

"What the hell are you talking about?" asked Elizabeth.

"To paraphrase," said Chuck, "subatomically speaking, the very act of measuring screws up what's being measured, so you never get the right answer."

"I know all about Heisenberg," she said. "What's he got to do with Angie's?"

"It's abstract," said Chuck.

"Mr. Heisenberg was right," I said. "You never really know how much or what or where or who."

"Speaking of uncertainty," said Elizabeth, "what did you decide about my furniture?"

Her question caught me off guard. I hadn't exactly forgotten, but I had been rather distracted. "Uh . . ."

It was a welcome interruption when Raphael the waiter appeared with my usual—a glass of red wine, grilled cheese, plus a tiny little burger ball for Jackhammer. Chuck ordered another beer, Elizabeth asked for coffee with anisette.

When Raphael left, Elizabeth rested her chin on her hands and stared at me. "You were about to say . . ."

The answer to that, of course, was nothing. I'd thought quite a lot about whether I should take Elizabeth's furniture, even dreamed about it in wide-screen Technicolor holographic 3-D. I'd done every damned thing but made up my mind about it. From the look on Elizabeth's face, I knew the deadline for decision had come. "Well," I said, "I like your furniture a lot. I guess, that is, the thing is, uh . . . I don't know what to do with my furniture."

While the two of them pondered that, I was struck with

a brilliant idea. "How about you, Chuck?" I asked. "Why don't you take my furniture?"

He almost spit his beer out. "You've gotta be kidding. Get rid of my beanbags to make room for that clunky, dark, depressing crap?"

"If you ask me," said Elizabeth, "you should put your furniture out on the street. Someone will take it in and give it a good home. It's nice enough, if you like that style."

"Which none of us do," added Chuck.

"Come on," said Elizabeth. "It'll be fun. Early tomorrow morning we'll take your stuff to the street and shove my stuff over to your place. Then I'll have enough space to bring in the lumber. You'll help, right, Chuck?"

Chuck grunted.

"Tomorrow?" I said.

"The sooner I get started on the built-ins, the better," said Elizabeth. "Before I know it, Dude Bob will be here. I want the apartment to be perfect."

That was the first mention of Dude Bob. I glanced across the table at Chuck. He gripped his beer mug tight. His knuckles turned white. He started to say something.

That's why I was there, to stop him from saying something he'd be sorry for. I gave him a hard kick on the shin.

"Ouch. What the hell?"

"Oh, so sorry," I said. "Was that your leg, Chuck? I thought it was the table."

"What's going on with you two?" asked Elizabeth.

"Nothing," I said.

Chuck behaved after that. He and Elizabeth went over the drawings for her built-ins. I tuned them out and thought about the daunting job before me. I'd be up all night getting stuff out of drawers to prepare for the big furniture switch.

Raphael came by. "Drinks on the house."

He put our drinks on the table and gave Jackhammer a doggie treat. Then he kind of hovered around like he had something more to say.

We all looked at him expectantly. Finally he said, "I

want to tell you I'm very sorry about Johnny.'' He left
before I could say anything.

The cat was now officially out of the bag. I was positive
Chuck and Elizabeth hadn't heard about Johnny's engagement. Chuck had been immersed in a virtual Vietnam; Elizabeth had banned all media from her life decades ago.

"What about Johnny?" said Chuck.

"What happened? Is Johnny all right?" said Elizabeth.

"He's fine," I said. "Got himself engaged to the guest
starlet from the *Tod Trueman* special."

"Damn," said Chuck. "I forgot to watch that."

"You must feel terrible," said Elizabeth. "If there's anything I can do, just give a holler."

"Thanks, but it's okay. Really. I'm extremely happy for
Johnny. Delighted. I'll bet she's a lovely girl."

"Wanta know what I think?" asked Chuck.

"No."

"I think you should stop chasing after murderers and lost
ex-husbands. Stop trying to solve everybody else's problems. Get your own house in order. Go after Johnny."

"Good advice," said Elizabeth.

It was lousy advice. I had no intention of doing any such
thing.

I went home, made a pot of coffee, and got to work. I
yanked the drawers out of the bureaus, dumped the contents
into a pile in the corner of the room. Jackhammer hopped
up on the pile, burrowed beneath it, and dragged garments
around. He had a blast. I did not. For me, the process was
painful. When my friend had been killed, I inherited her
apartment and everything in it. Many times I'd tried to get
rid of her clothing and failed. I'd finally shoved her stuff
to the corners of the closets and the bottoms of the drawers.
Now all our stuff was mixed together. I figured I'd sort it
out later.

Then, as if I didn't feel rotten enough already, I was
overcome by the desire to hear Johnny's voice. I called his

Bleecker Street apartment and listened to his recording promise that if I left my name and number, he'd get right back to me.

Around four in the morning the phone rang. It was Johnny's agent Lemmy Crenshaw, calling from LA.

"You gotta help me out here, Brenda. Johnny is just about to flush his entire goddamn career down the toilet. Here I am, working my friggin' ass off, in a selfless effort to get our boy into the movies. So he gets this offer, a fantastic once-in-a-lifetime four-picture multimillion-dollar deal. You know what? He won't sign on the dotted line. Absolutely refuses. Can you believe that?"

"He must have a reason," I said, trying to fathom what it might be.

"Reason? Oh sure, he's got reasons up the ass. He's being a prima freaking donna. You see, Brenda, it's like this: The deal hinges on a few changes, you know, *necessary* changes, a tweak here, a twizzle there."

"Tweaks? Twizzles? What kind of tweaks and twizzles?"

"Slight change in locale, no big deal."

"Do they want him to transfer to another precinct? Midtown South wouldn't be bad." I could see that.

"Not exactly," said Lemmy. "The high concept is to move Tod to a rural town in Iowa. Tod's still in law enforcement, only he's a sheriff. A family man."

"That's a mighty big tweak, Lemmy."

"It's a tweak that could get our boy into the big-time. Call him. Try to talk some sense into his hard-as-a-rock head. He respects your opinion."

"No. I won't do that. It sounds to me as if Johnny's made the right decision."

"But—"

"Night, Lemmy."

After I hung up I realized I hadn't told Lemmy about the murder, and he hadn't told me about Johnny's engagement.

13

I slept like a rock for a couple of hours. No dreams about chairs, no more telephone calls from the hotheaded agent of my possibly engaged ex-boyfriend, nothing but plain old much-needed deep sleep. I awakened to a call-in talk show on the radio. A caller complained about a rude sock vender at a street fair, the host made a smart remark. I hit the off button, sat up, and looked around at the apartment. It looked like the aftermath of a natural disaster. Furniture-moving day. Like I didn't have enough to do already.

Chuck showed up on time, red-eyed, bushy-haired, and cranky.

"I take it you've got bad news about Dude Bob?"

"What I have is no news, which in this case is bad news. All I know for sure about Dude Bob 43 is that he's a lying sack of shit."

"Why don't you just call Dude Bob and ask who he really is? Confront him."

"You know, Brenda, that's not a bad idea. I'll think about it. But now we've got furniture to move. Let me take a look at what you've got here." With his hands clasped behind his back and Jackhammer at his heels, Chuck walked around the apartment and eyeballed the furniture. "Lotta heavy shit here."

He sure had that right. In more ways than one. While he looked, I thought. I remembered my friend Carla, whose furniture I was about to trash. The more I thought, the more I felt I couldn't go through with it. "Uh, Chuck, I think maybe I changed my mind."

Chuck whirled around. He looked like he was about to call me a jerk or worse, but when he saw the expression on my face he softened. "I understand," he said. He sat me down on the couch, offered words of comfort, *then* he called me a jerk. "You're not gonna cry like some jerky girl, are you?"

"No, I'm not."

"Okay then. Are you ready to rock and roll?"

I nodded my less-than-hearty assent.

"Great. I figure after we curbside your crap, we'll stoke up with some chow, then push Liz's stuff across the hall to your place. How's that sound?"

"I'm not hungry."

"Believe me, by the time we've lugged this load, you will be."

Elizabeth was raring to go. I knew how Chuck felt. It was difficult to look her in the eye, knowing what I knew about Dude Bob.

Together, the three of us moved my stuff. For the most part Chuck pushed, I pulled, and Elizabeth guided. It was pretty slow going, but we got each piece into the elevator, through the lobby, out the door, and around the corner to the curb. Elizabeth insisted we take the time to arrange it nicely. "Proper presentation is very important," said Elizabeth. "Right, Brenda?"

"Yeah," I mumbled, looking at the furniture for the final time. My throat caught and my eyes filled.

"I can't believe it," said Elizabeth. "You're crying, aren't you?"

"I am not. A speck of dust blew in my eye."

Elizabeth patted me on the back. "It's only furniture."
"Let's eat," said Chuck.

We went to the coffee shop across the street. It was known
for being fast, cheap, and really sort of not bad for a greasy
spoon, plus, as Elizabeth said, the booth by the window
was empty. "We'll sit here and keep an eye on the street.
You'll feel much better, Brenda, once you see how quickly
your furniture gets adopted and how happy it makes its new
family."

Elizabeth made rapid headway through a huge spinach
salad. Chuck bolted down a western omelet, a side of fries,
and an extra-thick chocolate milkshake. I picked at a blue-
berry muffin and focused on the scene across the street.

The first person to stop, a runner dressed in light pink
nylon sweatgear, jogged in place for several minutes and
stared at the furniture. She looked like a nice sort, the kind
of person who'd give the furniture a good home. Just as I
got used to the idea of her having my furniture, she ran off
into the distance. I continued to watch. A Dalmatian on one
of those mile-long retractable leashes dashed around the
corner and lifted his leg on one of the dressers; its owner
pretended not to notice. Next, a young couple stopped. The
man slid the drawers open, patted the sofa. He smiled,
seemed delighted with the find. The woman stood back a
ways, crossed her arms, and shook her head no.

For a while, nobody stopped. Then a tall, thin, pale man
with dyed-black, slicked-back hair popped up out of nowhere and glided over to the furniture. He was dressed in
all black, hardly uncommon for this part of town, but somehow on him the black looked different. He ran his blue-
white hand lovingly over the dark wood.

"Cool," said Chuck. "A vampire."

The color drained out of *my* face.

Elizabeth looked at me. "Oh, stop it, Chuck. You've
upset Brenda."

"She's too sensitive," said Chuck. "Besides, I'm merely

reporting what I see, and what I see is a vampire scoping out Brenda's furniture.''

''I don't believe in vampires,'' said Elizabeth, ''at least not in the West Village. Anyway, everybody knows vampires don't come out in the daytime. The sun makes them shrivel up and die or something.''

''First off,'' said Chuck, ''vampires are already dead, so they can't die. And as to the sunlight thing, perhaps they've evolved. They've had centuries to learn how to deal with the sun. I mean, what else do they have to think about while sleeping it off?''

While Chuck and Elizabeth yakked about the possibility of vampire evolution, I watched the pale man. He stretched his arms out wide, stepped back, tilted his head to the side. He removed all the dresser drawers and stacked them up on the sidewalk. He sat on the sofa, bounced up and down. I was relieved when he hailed a cab, but when it pulled up to the curb, he didn't get in. Instead, he conversed with the driver and handed over a wad of bills. Then he hailed another cab and took off.

''Smart vampire,'' said Chuck. ''He paid the first driver to stand watch over the furniture.''

I hoped Chuck was wrong, but a short time later the man returned, this time with a yardstick and several people, all of whom looked like him, all of whom dressed like him, and all of whom pushed brand-new shiny silver blue hand trucks.

''I tell you,'' said Chuck, ''they're a tribe of vampires.''

I don't believe in vampires, evolved or unevolved, but this was a weird crew. They flitted all over, measured the furniture, then, working together like an efficient team of ants on a gumdrop, loaded it up and rolled my furniture down the street. They left one dresser behind—the one with the bottom drawer that still smelled of my friend's perfume. It looked sad and lonely.

Traumatized, I didn't know which bothered me more: the strange strangers who'd claimed the furniture, or the fact they'd left the dresser behind. My distress must have shown.

Elizabeth patted my hand. "I'm sure they're wonderful people."

"Don't sweat it," said Chuck. "Somebody'll snag that dresser in a flash."

He was close. About a flash and a half later, someone approached.

"Oh no," said Elizabeth. "Julia."

We watched in horror as Julia Pond, dressed in her usual flowery muumuu, stopped and ran her hand over the dresser, nodded to herself, and ran back into the building.

Elizabeth and I looked at each other. No more communication was needed. We threw down our napkins, flew out of the restaurant, and across the street, leaving Chuck behind.

They say people can perform incredible feats of strength in an emergency. They know what they're talking about. Elizabeth and I dragged that sucker back into the building all by ourselves.

In the lobby we ran smack into Julia, who was on her way back out. Behind her, the building superintendent wheeled his hand truck.

"Halt," she yelled. "That dresser is mine. I saw it first."

"Go to hell in a handbucket," said Elizabeth. That pretty well summed up my feelings too.

"That's hand*basket,* you idiot," said Julia.

"Whatever suits you," said Elizabeth.

The super turned his back on all of us and wheeled the hand truck down the corridor.

Elizabeth and I wrestled the dresser into the elevator. As the doors closed, Julia shook her fist at us. "I won't let you get away with this."

"So how come you guys stuck me with the goddamned bill?" asked Chuck after he'd rejoined us in Elizabeth's apartment.

"We couldn't let Julia take that dresser," said Elizabeth.

"We didn't have time to explain," I said.

"So who's this Julia person?"

"She's the pompous witch whose cat bloodied Jackhammer's nose," said Elizabeth. "She moved into the Randolph apartment."

"Figures," said Chuck.

"She owns Julia's Trick Shoppe, the plastic vomit store that opened on Eighth Avenue."

Chuck perked up. "I was gonna stop in there later to see if they've got any of that fart-in-a-can stuff."

Elizabeth and I had put my old dresser back in my apartment. Once we'd shoved her furniture across the hall into my apartment, it became obvious there was no room for the dresser. Something had to go.

Too pooped to pop and damned depressed to boot, I sprawled out on Elizabeth's biomorphic banana-shaped couch, which was now mine, and contemplated the plaster peeling from my ceiling. I allowed myself two minutes of self-indulgent gloominess. Then I had an idea. "Here's what we'll do," I said. "We can store the dresser in Nado's van in Lance's parking space. I've got the garage-door opener, so I won't have to bother Lance."

I checked the hallway. No sign of Julia Pond. So, for the third time that day, the dresser got moved. Being the strongest, Chuck got stuck with the bulk of the weight. He grumbled all the way to the Hudson Shadow's garage.

I aimed the opener, the garage door lifted, we slid the dresser down the incline, then pushed it over to Nado's van. Chuck and Elizabeth both seemed impressed when I kicked the van door open. I climbed in, unlocked the side door. Together, we heaved the dresser into the van. I covered it with a blanket.

"Will you two do me a favor," I said, "and take a look through the van? See if there's something I missed, something that might indicate where Nado ran off to.''

They poked around, then Chuck wandered off. "Gotta check out the garage," he said. "It's a guy thing."

Elizabeth rifled through Nado's duffel bag. She held up a yellow shirt. "One hundred percent pure unadulterated polyester. I can't believe you were married to this guy."

"It travels well," I said.

She found the stack of flyers and read out loud. " 'Sharpe's Hiway Haute Doggerie, the home of Belup's Creek's best hot dogs.' Is this for real?''

"Yes."

"You, Miss Vegetable USA, were married to a purveyor of hot dogs? I can't believe it. You think you know a person, then all of a sudden they're not who you think they are."

If only she knew what Chuck and I knew about her Dude Bob 43.

Chuck bopped over to the van. "You know what this place is? I mean, besides the obvious?"

"Yes. It's a clandestine rendezvous point for drug dealers."

"More," said Chuck. He pointed to a car in the far corner of the garage. "That's a stolen car."

"How do you know?" asked Elizabeth.

"Because yesterday I saw a neighbor of mine steal it from Avenue B."

"You sure it's the same car?"

"Yep. Same make, same model, same paint job, same HONK IF YOU THINK EINSTEIN WAS BENT OUT OF SHAPE bumper sticker."

14

Somewhere, the phone rang. It took a moment to find it. In the big furniture exchange it got shoved into the corner underneath an end table. I picked up. It was Dweena.

"I made some inquiries about that hooker raid. The bomb threat was definitely a new twist. Nobody's ever heard of such a thing before. Most of the hooker roundups in this neighborhood are preplanned, politically motivated, highly visible biannual sweeps. Everybody benefits: cops look like they're doing their job, the girls get some publicity and if they're lucky a shot on TV, the community feels all warm and cozy. Next day, things go back to normal."

"Thanks, Dweena. You've pretty much confirmed my hunch about Maris Montmyer."

"Glad I could be of help. Does this mean the widow did it?"

"Could be, but there are other possibilities. Montmyer had plenty of enemies. Plus, that Hudson Shadow parking garage is a veritable hotbed of illicit activity. I witnessed a drug deal and Chuck spotted a stolen car."

Dweena sighed. "A car theft ring is operating in my very own backyard and I didn't know? Oh me, oh my. Such news makes Dweena feel very out of it."

"Don't sweat it. You can't be expected to be on top of

everything. Besides, Chuck didn't say it was a car theft ring. It was only one car.''

"Stolen cars are like cockroaches," said Dweena. "For every one carousing on the kitchen counter, there's a thousand more screwing around behind the wall in the dark."

"That reminds me," I said. "Ever heard of any vampires in this part of town?

"Vampires? Not here. They're strictly East Village."

I stopped by Midnight Millinery. No new Nado calls. Damn. I must have been crazy to think all I had to do to find him was stick up a bunch of missing person posters. Nothing was ever that easy. I tried to convince myself it didn't matter, that Nado wasn't really in danger, that even if he had seen anything, whomever he'd seen probably hadn't seen him. But what if I was wrong and something had happened to Nado?

I couldn't just sit around and do nothing. I decided to follow up on Maris Montmyer and take a look at the scene of the alibi, the rapidly gentrifying meat market. If I managed to expose her as the killer, it would help Lance and it would be on TV and in the papers. Nado might see and realize he had nothing to fear from the cops and resurface on his own. Stranger things have happened.

To ease my guilt about once again putting my summer line on the back burner, I put on a light blue organdy bowed visor. I might as well take it out for a little test drive.

Jackhammer and I headed west to the fringes of the West Village, a place where butchers in blood-smeared white aprons rub shoulders with models, club kids, designers, and latté-sipping yuppies.

And then there were the hookers.

A gaggle loitered in the shadows in front of a building where sides of beef swung on hooks. Their extremely brief ensembles made Dweena's getups look downright dowdy. If I could only get them to talk to me about the raid. What was I gonna do? Go up to them and say, "How about that raid?'' That was absurd. I was busy thinking they'd never give me the time of day, when one of them called out to me.

"Fabulous hat," she said. "Love that baby blue."

"I'll trade for information," I said.

She sashayed across the street to where I stood with Jack-hammer. "What kind of information?"

"About the raid the other night."

"You one of *them*?"

"I don't think so. Who do you mean?"

"Gang of upscale rival hookers. They reported a bomb to get us"—she gestured toward her friends—"off the street. Fat lot of good it did."

"No, I'm not one of them. Are you sure that's who reported the bomb? I kinda thought it might be—"

"Sure I'm sure. Now, if you'll excuse me, I've got to get back to work, so if you'll just give me my hat."

It didn't really count as a sale, but my bowed visor was, as they say, out there. And, I must admit, it looked great on her. My summer line was officially launched.

Rival hooker gang? I guess it could be true, but I still wasn't convinced it hadn't been Maris Montmyer setting up her alibi. Mulling that over in my mind, I'm afraid I forgot to detour around Julia's Trick Shoppe.

She lounged on a plastic lawn chair on the sidewalk in front of her purple-painted storefront, face turned toward the sun. She had on big plastic sunglasses shaped like daisies and a T-shirt printed with a scattering of bloody gunshot wounds. GREETINGS FROM NEW YORK it said in letters that looked like dripping blood. Didn't she know violent crime in New York had plummeted?

She looked over the top of the sunglasses. "Well, well, well. Will you look who's here to apologize. Gee, Brenda, if I'd a knowed you was a-comin' I'd a made a call to the Sixth Precinct. Yep, that's what I'd a done. See what the boys in blue have to say about that dresser you stole. The super is a witness.''

''That dresser is mine,'' I said. ''It got put out on the street by mistake.''

''Oh, give me a break. You don't expect me to believe that crap, do you?'' With that, she pushed herself out of the lawn chair, folded it up, and stormed into her store. When she passed through the door she triggered a loud belching sound.

Midnight Millinery has jangling bells on the door, some stores have electronic devices that bing-bong when a customer enters or leaves, Julia's Trick Shoppe burped.

I went by the apartment just to look at the furniture. A blobby blue amoeba-like chair was temporarily located in the center of the room alongside a kidney-bean-shaped coffee table. The banana-shaped couch and other chairs were pushed against the walls, as were a couple of odd storage devices. It'd take a day or two of living with the new furniture to decide what should go where. For now, the haphazard arrangement was fine. I tried not to think about the dresser in Nado's van.

Inspired by seeing my hat on someone else, I planned to work hard the rest of the day, make a dozen fancy visors, grab a salad at the deli for dinner, go home, get to sleep early, get up at dawn the next morning, and redo Midnight Millinery's window display. Then I'd worry about Nado and murder and all that. From the get-go, nothing went according to plan.

First off, I had too many customers to get much work done. I don't know where they all came from. It must have had something to do with the wonderful weather. They streamed in all afternoon and evening. Those who didn't buy hats ordered hats. This was good.

Then my dinner plans changed. Pete put a small table out on the sidewalk in front of his café and asked me to join him. With Jackhammer on my lap, on a perfect spring evening, on a charming cobblestone street, I feasted on Pete's cream of carrot soup and cracked Julia Pond jokes.

I'm afraid what happened to mess up the last part of my plan wasn't nearly so pleasant.

Ralph the doorman stood in front of the apartment building watching passersby. "Nice night," he said.

"Gorgeous."

He tilted his head toward the lobby. "Somebody waiting to see you."

"That's odd, I'm not expecting anyone."

"You said it, not me," said Ralph.

"What do you mean?"

"Odd," he said, rolling his eyes. "Very, very odd."

Curious, I went into the lobby.

There, surrounded by a set of matching pink and green paisley luggage, sat Kathilynda Annamarie Cooper Sharpe. Her waist-length straight blond hair was no longer. She had instead a close-cropped helmet of light brown curls.

Over the years, safe in the thought I'd never see her again, I'd indulged in a harmless little game of gracelessly aging the Kathilynda in my mind. I didn't think of her often, but whenever I did, I added another ten pounds, etched in a new laugh line, or sagged a jowl. After our last conversation, the one in which she'd mentioned that she told Vinnie I was a drug addict who turned tricks, I'd piled an additional thirty pounds onto the make-believe Kathilynda.

The Kathilynda sitting in my lobby, the real Kathilynda, hadn't done nearly so badly for herself. A bit older, sure, and a tiny bit heavier, but the weight had fallen nicely over her small frame. She was, however, dressed head to toe in pastels, which must be what Ralph, who never leaves Manhattan, meant by odd.

"Kathilynda?"

"Brenda Sue?"

She jumped up out of the chair, ran over to me, gave me a quick hug, buzzed my cheek. Then she pushed me back at arm's length and said, "Why, Brenda Sue, I swear you haven't aged a day."

15

Kathilynda's collection of paisley luggage took up most of the floor space in the elevator. Jackhammer had to ride on top of her largest bag. He looked up at her and wagged his tail stub.

"What's it's name?" she asked.

"*His* name is Jackhammer," I said.

"Well," she said, "at least Jackhammer is happy to see me."

A mile-wide opening. I resisted the urge.

When I didn't respond, she said, "Well, you *do* seem surprised to see me."

"I *am* surprised to see you." Actually, surprised was too mild a word to describe the bad feelings that churned within. I seethed, I burned. What a lot of nerve she had, to show up like this, unannounced, especially after our last conversation. Unlike Nado, it looked like she planned to stay with me. We'd see about that. Mrs. Sharpe might be in for an unpleasant surprise.

"Didn't you get my phone message? I told you when I'd be here."

The garbled message.

"No, Kathilynda. I didn't get your message. My machine—" I cut myself off. I didn't owe her any explanation. "Why are you here?"

"To look for Nado, of course. You lost him. I came to find him."

The elevator jerked to a stop at my floor. With Jackhammer still on top, I pushed the large suitcase around the corner to my apartment. Kathilynda struggled with the smaller bags. She watched in amazement as I unlocked the door. "It's just like on TV," she said.

"What are you talking about?"

"You know those comedy shows that take place in New York? All the apartments have two locks. Back in Belup's Creek, we wonder why."

"One's a deadbolt."

I flicked on the light switch inside the door, stood back, and let Kathilynda go in first.

Her hand clutched her chest. "Oh my," she gasped.

I couldn't tell if it was the sight of Elizabeth's furniture or the apartment itself that so astounded her. Nor could I determine whether her exclamation was positive or negative. "It takes some getting used to," I said.

"I should think it would," she said. She walked through the foyer into the room. "If you'll just point me in the direction of your spare bedroom, I want to unpack, freshen up, and then maybe have a bite to eat before I crash. You wouldn't believe how little they feed you on airplanes these days."

Kathilynda had a lot to learn. I sat her down and explained the facts of life, New York style.

"You're kidding," she said.

I shook my head.

"You really don't have a spare bedroom?"

"I not only don't have a spare bedroom, I have no bedroom at all. This is a studio apartment." I started to tell her how my couch made into a bed, but then I remembered the vampires took that couch. I'd kept the mattress, of course, and stored it in the closet.

"Boy, did you ever have us fooled," said Kathilynda.

"Back home in Belup's Creek everybody thinks you're some big-time la-ti-da hat designer."

"Everybody except Vinnie T," I said. "You told him I was a drug addict who occasionally turns tricks. Remember?"

"That was a joke, Brenda Sue, a joke. Get it? I thought it was pretty funny."

I glared my opinion.

"You know what's wrong with you, Brenda Sue? New York has made you hard. You've got no sense of humor."

I kept going with the glare.

Kathilynda continued, "I should have known all that stuff about you being a success was a crock. You're destitute, aren't you? Don't worry, Brenda Sue, your little secret's perfectly safe with me. I won't tell a soul."

"I am not destitute."

I thrust a super-fluffy nondestitute guest towel at her and told her to take a shower. While she belted out a ten-year-old Broadway show tune, I called a woman I knew who ran a bed-and-breakfast on Jane Street. Her place was full up. And no, she didn't know of anyone who might have a vacancy. "Crime's down," she said. "Tourism's up. Most of the B and Bs are booked a year in advance."

Great. It boiled down to two choices: I could sleep at Midnight Millinery and let Kathilynda stay in my apartment, or I could toss her and her paisley luggage out on the street and hope that a band of roving vampires carted her off. I liked the latter choice best, but since I hadn't been raised by wolves, felt obligated to go with the first. True, I couldn't stand Kathilynda's lying, cheating, deceiving, selfish guts. However, since we'd both married Nado, we were kind of like family. I had to let her stay. However, I promised myself that before Kathilynda went back to Belup's Creek, we'd have it out about the time she'd called me in high school and pretended to be Vinnie T.

*   *   *

Kathilynda plopped down on one of my new chairs and towel-dried her hair. "You got anything to eat besides rabbit food?"

Cursing under my breath, I disappeared into the kitchen and made her a cheese sandwich.

She wrinkled her little pig nose and poked at the dark seeded bread, then lifted the top slice and sniffed the twelve-dollar-a-pound cheddar. "Looks weird," she said. Then she wolfed it down and asked for another. That one she ate at a more leisurely pace, which allowed her to ramble on about life in Belup's Creek. "When Vinnie T came into the Haute Doggerie, I told him Nado had run off to New York to shack up with you."

If looks could kill, I'd have been figuring out how to get rid of Kathilynda's body, not where to let her sleep. My emotions must have leaked out onto my face.

"You don't have to get so hot and bothered," she said. "You'd have thought the exact same thing. I mean, how does it look? Nado and I have a fight. He runs off and tells me he's going to stay with you, his ex-wife. Believe it or not, I actually hated you there for a spell, Brenda Sue. Anyway, Vinnie T looked at me with those gorgeous eyes— did I mention he just got a divorce? has a great job? and he looks as good as ever?—and he tells me, 'Go after your man.' At the time I was too mad at Nado. I didn't care if he ever came home, but once you set me straight about him and you, I started thinking maybe I should come to New York and look for my husband. Your search hasn't amounted to a hill of beans, now, has it?"

"I have to admit, response to the missing person posters has been rather disappointing."

"What else are you doing?"

"I'm taking a two-pronged approach. Somebody killed Royce Montmyer. So, I figure if I find out who did it, it'll be on the news, Nado will find out he's not a suspect. Then he'll come out of hiding."

Kathilynda frowned. "Instead of looking for your fright-

ened lost ex-husband, who wouldn't be in the predicament
he's in if you hadn't arranged for him to park at the scene
of a murder, you go after a vicious killer. That's downright
stupid. You're a milliner, not a detective. But if that's what
you want to do, fine. However, it's my wifely duty to find
my husband and that's exactly what I'm going to do."

"Your chances of finding Nado in New York City are
next to nothing."

"That's where you're wrong, Brenda. *Your* chances of
finding Nado in New York City are next to nothing because
you don't know Nado anymore. I know my man. There's
like this psychic connection or something. It's hard to explain, especially to someone like you who never stayed
married to anybody very long."

"You might have noticed on your ride from the airport,
New York's a tad bigger than Belup's Creek."

"I thought maybe you would help me find my way
around."

I began to see the bright side of Kathilynda's uninvited,
unannounced, unwelcome visit. She could do the legwork
on the search for Nado. All I had to do was provide a New
York City map, a Metrocard, and a stack of posters.

While Kathilynda babbled on about the record-breaking
spring rains in Belup's Creek, how it cost a fortune to be
in business these days, and Vinnie T's recent divorce, I
pulled my mattress out of the closet and put fresh bedding
on it. "You can sleep here," I said.

"On the floor? Don't you have one of those pull-out
couch contraptions?"

"A bunch of vampires carried it off this morning."

"New York has done some mighty strange things to your
head, Brenda Sue."

I dug out a Midnight Millinery business card. "In case
you need me, this is where I'll be tonight."

"You can't leave me here all alone."

"Unless you want to sleep in shifts, or in the chair you're

in, that's exactly what I'm going to do. The shop's only a couple of minutes away. I'll be back first thing tomorrow morning.''

I stopped at the deli for a giant-sized cup of their strong coffee. ''Black,'' I said.

''Pulling an all-nighter?'' asked the guy behind the counter.

''Gonna try.''

As I worked, the electric New York buzz gradually ebbed. Around three in the morning I got up to stretch and looked out the window. No one walked by. The windows in the buildings across the street were darkened. Somewhere in the city thousands of lobster-shifters toiled, thousands of others stayed up, plotting, planning, drinking, dancing. But not on West Fourth Street. Here it was dead silence. Even Jackhammer was sound asleep, curled up into a tight doughnut shape on his pile of fabric. It was odd, peaceful and lonely at the same time.

I shook off the feeling and got back to work. By the time the sun poked up over the buildings, I had one dozen completed summer hats. I was too tired to hang them up, but too excited not to. I climbed in the window, dismantled the spring display, and got busy. I tend not to get too wrapped up in sentiment, but I've got to say it: The experience of hanging up the new hats as the day brightened and the city came alive was truly magnificent.

I had a summer line.

16

I poked at my sleeping bag with a broomstick. It was stuck on the high shelf in my storage closet, wedged in tightly between a roll of buckram and the wall. I finally jarred it loose and it tumbled down along with the buckram and an antique five-part wooden hat block, which landed with a clatter. No damage as far as I could tell.

I dragged the sleeping bag to the old spot beneath my blocking table, rolled it out, and crawled in. Cozy. Just like the old days when I'd lived at Midnight Millinery.

I wanted to get a couple hours of sleep before I had to deal with Kathilynda again. If I got lucky, maybe this would all turn out to be a bad dream. When I woke up she'd be back where she belonged, slinging hot dogs in Belup's Creek. If I could control things to that extent, maybe I could roll back the old nightmare machine to include Nado's visit as well. And Johnny's engagement. What the hell, maybe even Royce Montmyer's murder was a nightmare. The guy sounded like a creep. That didn't mean he deserved to die.

I'd wake up from the dream and it would be the day of Johnny's party. Or maybe long before. Thoughts of Kathilynda rolled around my mind. An unruly bunch, they bumped into and unleashed old memories of Belup's Creek and high school and Nado and Vinnie T. What if Kathilynda had not played that mean trick back in high school? What if I'd had that date with Vinnie T? What if I'd married Vinnie T instead of Nado?

I envisioned myself still in Belup's Creek, with Vinnie T for a husband. According to Kathilynda he had a prestigious job as project engineer for Belup Development. "They do all the really expensive subdivisions." I pictured us together, madly in love, having breakfast in our beautiful ten-thousand-square-foot fully basemented home. Our charming sunny breakfast nook overlooks a vast yard. Tree leaves rustle in the breeze. Birds tweet, squirrels scamper, rabbits frolic. A passionate kiss, and Vinnie T leaves for work. I clear away the breakfast dishes, put them in the dishwasher. Time to relax. I flip on the large-screen TV, surf through dozens of channels. Hold on a minute. What was that? Something familiar flickered by. A place, a face. Desperate, I surf back. With an electronic crackle the screen fills with a syndicated *Tod Trueman* rerun.

Suddenly my little "what if" game turned very sad. I was engulfed by an overwhelming sense of loss. Midnight Millinery did not exist in this version of reality. I didn't know Johnny. Or Chuck, or Elizabeth, or Jackhammer. My heart pounded. Terrified, I woke up. Jackhammer was curled up next to me. What a relief.

The phone rang.

It was Kathilynda. Complaining. "I didn't sleep a wink last night."

"Homesick?"

"Don't be silly. I'm not a six-year-old at summer camp. It's this crazy furniture of yours. I don't know who could sleep in the same room with it. It's a nightmare, like being in the middle of one of those weirdo paintings by that Picasso guy. I finally got smart and found a nice quilt in your closet. I pulled it over my head and pretended I was back home in Belup's Creek, safe in a normal bed, in a normal bedroom, with normal furniture. From what I can see, the only normal thing in your entire apartment is your quilt.''

"My grandmother made it for my sixteenth birthday.''

"Well, it's beautiful. I love the luxurious satin and velvet, the rich colors—''

"It's casket lining.''

Five seconds of dead silence, then Kathilynda shrieked,
"It's what?''

"Casket lining,'' I repeated. "My grandmother was good
friends with the funeral director in her town. He loved her
date-nut bread. She needed his casket lining scraps. They
worked out a deal.''

"Excuse me while I puke. Are you telling me I spent
the night underneath the undertaker's casket lining? That
the other people sleeping under the fabric woven from the
same cloth are like *permanently* asleep?''

"I suppose you could look at it that way.''

"Ohmygod. It's like I shared a quilt with a hundred dead
people. In bed with the dead. You're a ghoul, Brenda Sue.''

"Settle down, Kathilynda. It's only fabric. I can assure
you nobody dead ever slept under those particular scraps.''

"A destitute New York ghoul. . . .''

"Stop it.''

"All right. But I'll tell you one thing, Brenda Sue, I'm
gonna find me something else to cover my little bod with
tonight, thank you very much.''

"Whatever you want, Kathilynda.''

"Now, all this weirdness almost made me forget why I
called in the first place. I thought you'd want to know about
the harassing telephone call you got late last night.''

"Was it a heavy breather?''

"No. It was some jokester, kept saying he was Johnny
Verlane, you know, that guy who plays Tod Trueman, Urban Detective on TV.''

"Johnny called?''

"You know Johnny Verlane?''

"Yes.''

"Get out of here. Johnny Verlane is big, big, big. All

the girls at the Haute Doggerie are wild about him. We've got a TV in the restaurant and you should see when his show comes on. My female employees are totally useless for the entire hour. They burn the hot dogs, or serve them raw. And I'm right beside them, drooling.''

"Johnny and I . . . were . . . he's my . . . uh . . . he's like a neighbor. Lives a couple of blocks away on Bleecker Street. Except now he's in LA. Looking into a film deal.''

"Sure, Brenda Sue. I get the picture. He dumped you, right?''

"Wrong, Kathilynda. It was mutual.''

"Yeah. I think you're making it all up. In any event, you'll be pleased to know I played along with whomever it was. I told him you were out on a hot date and that I didn't expect you home until morning.''

"You did what?''

"I was merely protecting your reputation. I didn't want anybody, not even a prank caller, to know you were at your millinery store late on a Saturday night. He might get the notion you were hard at work. I wanted him to think you were out on the town, partying. It was the right thing to do, wasn't it?''

"No, Kathilynda, it wasn't. Please, the next time Johnny, or anybody pretending to be Johnny, calls, refer them to Midnight Millinery.''

"Well, if that's really what you want.''

"Yes, Kathilynda. It really is what I really want.''

"You don't have to get so huffy.''

"Put on a pot of coffee," I ordered. "I'll be by in half an hour with some muffins for breakfast.''

"Yes. One thing, Brenda Sue, before I hang up: Where the hell is your microwave? I can't seem to find it anywhere.''

To try to repair the damage Kathilynda had done, I dialed Johnny at the LA number Lemmy had given me. Engagement be damned. After two rings I realized it was the middle of the night in California. I hung up before anyone answered.

Okay. Against my better judgment, I'd decided to let Kathilynda stay in my apartment. I figured I might as well try to make it easier on both of us. On the way to my apartment I worked on my attitude. I put on my best smile and tried it out on Jackhammer. "What do you think, little guy?"

He was too busy staring down a chow who was urinating on a fire hydrant across the street to look at me. By the time the chow moseyed on down the street, my smile was gone.

Kathilynda was up and already dressed in an acid-washed denim miniskirt and matching vest, her turned-up little nose stuck in a New York City guidebook.

"Here, take a look at this," I said. "Better than any guidebook." I dumped the Sunday *Times* on a boomerang-shaped end table and went into the kitchen. Then, remembering my manners, I stuck my head out the door and flashed a grin.

I poured a mug of coffee and put the muffins on a plate. When I came back out Kathilynda said, "Big paper."

"You should see it in December." I cracked it open, sorted out the slippery advertising inserts, and gave Kathilynda the Arts and Leisure section.

I settled down with real estate. I figured with Royce Montmyer dead, and no one around to screw up apartment sales, some of the owners he'd kept from selling would rush their apartments on the market. I stopped counting at three open houses. The doorman would have a complete list.

Kathilynda slowly turned through the entertainment pages, making *tsk-tsk* sounds. "There's so much to spend your money on. No wonder you can't afford the finer things in life."

"What are you talking about? I'm not rich, but I have all the stuff I need." And then some, I thought, as I looked around the room. It'd be better once I had a chance to arrange the furniture.

"Well," said Kathilynda, ticking off points on her fingers, "you don't have a microwave. I mean, come on, get with it, girl. Then you've got this old piece-of-garbage black and white TV and the sound doesn't work, no VCR, no cable, and this weird pile of bright-colored marshmallows you call furniture. What a joke. You know what I think? Nobody wears hats anymore. Milliner Brenda Midnight can't make ends meet. I think the repo man's been snooping around your place, took all the good stuff with him. I'll bet he got your car too."

It wasn't worth my breath to set her straight on the car situation. However, I was sick and tired already of hearing her insults to me and my apartment. I'd show her a thing or two about the value of New York space; I'd take her with me to the Hudson Shadow open houses. I opened my mouth to tell her, but her attention was elsewhere. Her eyes were closed. She sat stone still with her palms pressed against her head. "What's the matter?" I asked.

Her eyelids flickered open, and she said, "Take me to Times Square."

"What the hell for?"

"To find Nado, of course."

"What makes you think Nado is in Times Square?"

"I don't think he *is* in Times Square, not right this minute. I just flashed on it, you know, like a feeling. I know he *was* in Times Square. See, Brenda Sue, it's like this. I've never been to New York before. Neither has Nado. When I thought about all the possible places to go, the first thing that popped into my head was Times Square. Nado and I think exactly alike. Therefore, Times Square would be the first place Nado would have headed. Once I go to Times Square and see what he saw, feel what he felt, I'll know where he went next, and so on, until eventually I find him."

"That's the nuttiest thing I've ever heard," I said.

"Nado is not sightseeing; he's on the run. He thinks the cops are after him." And maybe the killer, I thought. I didn't want Kathilynda to know about that possibility.

"If you were married, you'd understand."

In the end, I agreed to take her to Times Square. "But later in the afternoon," I said. "First I want to show you Midnight Millinery, then we'll go apartment shopping. After that we'll do the Deuce."

"I don't want to go apartment shopping."

"Look," I said, "the apartments are in the building where Nado stayed. The van is still parked in the garage. Maybe you'll pick up another vibe."

I figured as soon as Kathilynda saw Midnight Millinery, she'd be forced to eat her words about nobody wearing hats anymore. We rounded the corner to West Fourth Street. I swelled with pride when I saw my hot-off-the-block summer line displayed in the window. The hats swung enticingly on monofilament fishing line. The sun glinted off the gold-leaf-outlined M of the word MIDNIGHT. "Over there," I said. "That's my shop, Midnight Millinery."

But Kathilynda was looking across the street. "Ohmygod," she said. "There's a bum asleep on the sidewalk."

I crossed the street to investigate. "Elliot," I said softly, "is that you?"

The blanket wiggled, a hand came out, two eyes and a nose were revealed. It was Elliot.

"Welcome back," I said.

"I can't believe you actually know a bum," said Kathilynda.

"He's not really a bum. He helps out, does odd jobs."

"Then why does he sleep on the street?"

It was hard to explain to someone from Belup's Creek.

I showed her around the shop, but Elliot's presence distracted her. She frequently looked out the door and shook her head. She asked, "Why doesn't he have a home?"

"I don't know. Some people don't. It's a fact of life."

"Is he a drunk?"

"I don't think so."

"I don't get it. Why is he there?"

"Because he is. I never asked."

"Well, Brenda Sue, maybe you should."

She finally sat down at the vanity and tried on hats. No matter what I put on her head, or how good it looked, her response was the same. She'd frown into the mirror and say, "I don't know. I guess I am just not a hat type."

"It takes attitude and practice," I said.

At noon we left for the open houses. When we passed by Pete's Café, Pete waved us inside. I made the introductions. Since Kathilynda owned a restaurant in Belup's Creek, Pete showed her the kitchen. While she oohed and aahed over his shiny new stainless steel implements, Pete told me Elliot was back.

"I know, I saw him."

"I'm worried about him," said Pete. "I asked him straight out who gave him that hundred to get lost. I wanted to find out if it was one of our business association members. Know what he said? He said it was some bum. That's nuts. I don't get it. Elliot usually tells the truth. Do you think he was sucking on wacky weed over in the East Village?"

Another possibility occurred to me.

"I know what happened. Remember that other homeless guy who showed up about the same time Elliot went away?" I'd felt bad for him the time Nado pulled away from Midnight Millinery, leaving him in a cloud of exhaust.

"How could I forget?" said Pete. "It was his presence that so riled some of our business association's less tolerant members."

"He's the one who gave Elliot the money."

"You're starting to sound as nutty as Elliot," said Pete. "What's a bum doing with a hundred-dollar bill?"

"What if he wasn't a bum?"

"He looked like a bum, acted like a bum."

"It was an act. I bet that guy was really a writer. He was probably doing one of those *I've-been-there-walked-in-his-newspaper-shoes* kind of articles about the homeless. He needed the street to himself, gave Elliot the hundred, told him to scram. You wait and see. The story will end up in *New York* magazine.

"You know, Brenda," said Pete, "you just may have something there."

At least that was settled.

17

"He's cute," said Kathilynda. "Face of an angel, body of a god. He keeps a very nice kitchen too."

Pete? I'd never thought of Pete in terms of cute. "He makes a killer cream of carrot soup."

"Think he'll give me the recipe? I'd like to introduce a soup or two. Carrot 'n' dog might get some of those health food fanatics into the Haute Doggerie. They look down their noses at us now."

"I don't know, Kathilynda. Pete guards his recipes closely."

"It's not like we're in competition or anything."

I took a roundabout path to the Hudson Shadow. I wanted to show Kathilynda the high points of the neighborhood. "Greenwich Village is steeped in history," I said.

She was neither intrigued nor charmed. She didn't care where Bob Dylan sang or where Dylan Thomas drank. Kathilynda wanted to window-shop. She cut me off in the middle of what I thought was a fascinating story about pilfered cobblestones. "That's nice, Brenda Sue, but right now I've gotta check this place out." Before I had a chance to react, she darted into a store. The store belched its welcome.

I'd been so caught up in the cobblestone story I hadn't realized we were in front of Julia's Trick Shoppe. I followed Kathilynda in. The store belched again.

Perched on a high stool behind a glass counter was Julia herself. She had on a cheap mass-produced straw hat with a hatband of miniature beer cans. The smile she'd pasted on to greet Kathilynda quickly inverted when she saw me.

The store assaulted all five of my senses and maybe a couple I didn't know about. Thousands of cheaply manufactured off-color products and bad jokes lined row after row of shelves, swung from the ceiling, and festered in every cubic inch of space.

By way of an overhead mirror cleverly rigged to show the entire store, Julia watched Kathilynda peruse the geegaw-laden aisles.

I tried to make the best of an uncomfortable situation. "I've never been in here before." A waste of breath.

Julia took her eyes off the mirror long enough to scowl at me.

Kathilynda finished her spin through the store and joined us at the counter. She pointed to a revolving display. "Let me see those."

Without a word, Julia handed her a pair of bulging bloodshot eyeball holographic earrings. Kathilynda pushed back her hair, dangled one of the eyeballs in front of her ear, and looked into a distorting mirror on the wall. "What do you think, Brenda Sue?"

I cleared my throat.

"Well, I think they're super. I'll take three pair."

The store belched our exit and we continued our walk to the Hudson Shadow.

"You don't much like that lady, do you?"

"No, I don't."

"She sure has a cool store. It's really cute how it burps."

A long, long limousine, ice-white with blue trim, double-parked in front of the Hudson Shadow. Maris Montmyer was striding toward it, dressed head to toe in all-white designer duds. A uniformed man in wraparound mirrored sunglasses followed a few steps behind. He carried three matched pieces of light tan leather luggage.

Kathilynda was transfixed by the scene. "She must be somebody famous."

"Believe it or not," I said, "that's none other than Maris Montmyer, grieving widow of Royce Montmyer."

"The guy in the garage when Nado—"

"Yes. She's probably on her way to her face-lift."

"Shouldn't she still be mourning?"

"She couldn't reschedule. Her plastic surgeon is booked solid."

Kathilynda turned that over in her brain. "Well, it's as plain as the nose on your face. She's the one who did it, she murdered her husband. I bet she's using the insurance money to pay for her face-lift. Everybody knows the spouse is almost always the guilty one. I can understand that. There's been plenty of times I could have wrung Nado's skinny little neck, and we have a good marriage. Except for that last fight. Once I find him, we'll kiss and make up."

As we watched, the limousine glided off, spiriting Maris Montmyer away.

"Maris Montmyer might have killed her husband," I said, "or else hired someone to do it for her. I've got a lead that may blow apart her ironclad alibi. I'm still not totally convinced she did it. There are other possibilities. The open houses might answer some of my questions."

Kathilynda and I spun through the revolving door into the Hudson Shadow's lobby and were confronted with hundreds of images of ourselves. I'd forgotten about the excess of mirrored surfaces. True to form, anything I hated, Kathilynda loved. She traipsed through the lobby and admired many variations of herself.

I approached the doorman's desk. He recognized me from the other day. "How's that project going?"

"Fine," I said, "but right now, I'm here for the open houses."

The doorman handed me a flyer. I scanned the list of apartments and recognized two of the names from the board minutes, owners who hadn't been able to sell thanks to Royce Montmyer.

"Have any of these been on the market before?" I asked.

He looked me up and down, frowned, and shrugged. "I dunno."

"I heard that some of them were."

He shrugged again. "I wouldn't know anything about that."

I felt his eyes on me as I crossed the lobby, headed for the elevators. I gestured for Kathilynda to join me. She was no longer looking at herself in the mirrors. She sat stiffly on a chrome and leather bench. She had an odd look on her face. She shot the doorman a furtive glance, got up, and kind of sidestepped her way around the perimeter of the lobby.

"What the hell is the matter with you?" I asked. Her sudden peculiar behavior made me uneasy. She could be, for all I knew, seriously wacko.

She whispered in my ear. "New York is decadent beyond belief." She refused to say more until the elevator door shut and we were headed up. Then she explained. "You know that super-shiny floor? It works exactly like a jumbo patent leather shoe. The doorman, or any of the other deviants who live in this city of yours, can see straight up your skirt."

"That's ridiculous," I said.

"If you don't believe me, sit yourself down in that lobby and watch. You should have seen that doorman check you out, little Miss Black Panties."

Black? I thought for a moment. "Lucky guess, Kathilynda. Now grow up."

*   *   *

"Holy cow," said Kathilynda. "This apartment is worse than yours."

"It's loftlike," I read from the impressive brochure I'd picked up on our way in.

"What's that mean?"

"In this case, not a thing. It's a buzzword, a bald-faced and"—I looked again at the brochure—"bold-faced lie. Guess how much?"

She made a guess.

"Not even close." I showed her the price in the brochure. "In a bidding war it could go higher."

Kathilynda shook her head in disbelief. "In Belup's Creek you could get four bedrooms and a four-car garage on four acres for this kind of money."

"It wouldn't have a doorman," I pointed out.

If I remembered correctly, the co-op board, under Royce Montmyer's leadership, had rejected at least two buyers for this particular apartment. Unfortunately, the owner did not seem to be in attendance. Not that it would have made any difference. What did I expect anyway? A deranged person muttering about Royce Montmyer? The smoking gun on the coffee table? From the cozy overstuffed furniture, crocheted doilies, and multitude of family pictures, I'd guess the owner was a little old lady—an unlikely suspect. Of course, the little old lady might have an anxious heir or two.

A broker dressed in Sunday-casual khakis scurried over and thrust a clipboard in my face. "Please sign in," he said. He had a deep tan and an insincere smile that revealed a mouthful of too-white teeth. A cap job, probably from when he thought he could make it as a model.

I scribbled something on the line. "I think I've been here before. Wasn't this apartment on the market a few months ago?"

"I think not," said the broker.

"Guess I'm déjà vuing."

*　　*　　*

It was the same story at the next apartment, a one-bedroom with a river view and the world's smallest closet. Another broker—this time a woman in a bright red suit with heavy-duty shoulder pads—assured that I must be mistaken. "Hmmm," I said. "I could have sworn."

She started to comment further, but got distracted, flashed a smile, and tore into the bedroom. "Goddamn it, Rita," she said. "How'd you sneak in here without me seeing you?"

The source of her anger was a short stocky woman in her fifties. She—Rita—possessed a perfectly round moon face, further enhanced by a choppy bowl-type haircut. Rita snarled at the broker. "I got as much right to be here as any of these others."

"You are not a serious buyer," said the broker. "You're a nosy, thieving witch." The broker turned to the presumably serious buyers who by now had edged over to soak up an earful. "It's all right, folks. Nothing to get excited about. This is no reflection on the apartment or the building."

"This is bullshit," said Rita. She left the apartment, pulling behind her a large laundry cart full of dirty clothes.

"Does that woman live in the building?" asked one of the serious buyers, a seriously pregnant woman.

"Of course not," said the broker. She extracted a cellular phone from her chain-strapped quilted knock-off Chanel purse. "I'm calling security right this instant."

Brokers often lie, sometimes out of necessity, sometimes for sport, and sometimes to keep up their chops. As it turned out, Rita did in fact live in the building, as Kathilynda and I soon discovered. We were in the elevator on the way to another apartment on the list. Rita pushed her way on, rode a couple of floors, then got off.

"That woman is a menace," said a fastidiously dressed man who'd been forced to hug the wall to make room on the elevator for Rita's laundry cart. "The board would love to throw her out."

"So she does live here?" I said, casually, like I had every right to know.

"Oh yes," he said. "She's one of the original renters. A noneviction plan; we'll never get rid of her."

"What's she do?" asked Kathilynda.

"Rita is into laundry for fun and profit," he said.

"What did he mean by that?" asked Kathilynda. "Is it some kind of secret New York code?"

"Not that I know of."

We went to the next apartment on the list and I rang the doorbell. When the door opened I got a major surprise. Frowning at me was Susan Chapoppel, Lance's ex-wife-to-be. Susan and I had never seen eye to eye, and it showed. "What are *you* doing here?" she asked, a nasty edge to her voice.

All I could come up with on the spur of the moment was, "My friend Kathilynda came here from out of town to look for an apartment in the Village. I'm helping her."

"Is that so?" Susan's dirty look included both me and Kathilynda and Kathilynda's acid-washed outfit. "And where is Katha-what's-it from?"

Kathilynda opened her mouth to answer. I elbowed her to shut up and said, "Queens."

"She's wasting her time here. This apartment is not for sale."

I waved the paper the doorman had given me in front of her face. "Then why is it on the list?"

"A mistake."

Her snobby uppity ways got me so angry, I refused to let it go. "I'm afraid I don't understand, Susan."

"It's on the list because Maris Montmyer put it on the list, and Maris Montmyer put it on the list to harass me. Her husband, who happened to be my lover, owned the apartment. She killed him and now she thinks she can do whatever she damn well pleases. There, are you satisfied now?'' She slammed the door.

''What's queens?'' asked Kathilynda.

After that, the rest of the apartments we tramped through that afternoon, and the brokers who tried to sell us those apartments, blurred together in my mind. Did the two-bedroom have the river view or was it the other one, and did the one with the wood-burning fireplace also have the eat-in kitchen? Somewhere a broker in a light blue shirt and a bright red bow tie gave a highly entertaining and informative Murphy bed demonstration to a roomful of potential purchasers.

At each stop I asked if the apartment had been on the market before. I thought that such information would identify owners and brokers who would have loved to speak of Royce Montmyer in the past tense. But if I thought anybody was going to tell me, I was dead wrong. Each time I asked, a broker assured me this was a brand-new listing and if I wanted to make an offer I'd better hurry because such a desirable apartment would get snapped up fast. ''You've gotta be quick in this market.''

''I can't take much more of this,'' said Kathilynda.

''All we have left is the garage. You do want to see the garage, don't you?''

I had Lance's garage-door controller, but since we were already in the building we went via the basement. That led us by the laundry room, which, according to the man in the elevator, was Rita territory. And Rita barreled toward it full speed, cart first. ''Outta my way,'' she grumbled. The cart missed Kathilynda's toe by a half inch.

I started to say something, but thought better of it. I might want to talk to Rita later.

Kathilynda peeked in the window of Nado's van. ''What's a dresser doing in here?''

"It's mine," I explained. "I needed to store it."

"You're a strange one, Brenda Sue. The only normal stick of furniture you've got is stashed in your ex-husband's van, which is parked several blocks away from your apartment. I swear, they must put something weird in the water in New York. Remind me to pick up some bottled stuff."

"Do you have keys to the van?" I asked.

"Nope."

I'd left all the doors locked except the driver's. That I kicked open. Kathilynda was impressed. "I never did learn how to do that."

We both climbed in. She sifted through some papers in the glove compartment, felt under the seats, looked in Nado's duffel bag. "Poor Nado," she said.

"Getting a vibe?" I asked.

I don't think she picked up on my sarcasm. "No."

On the way out of the garage Kathilynda grabbed my arm. "Ohmygod," she said.

"What is it?"

She pointed to a light blue station wagon. "Over there. See? Those two people? Brenda Sue, I think they're doing it."

18

"What kind of ex-wife are you, Brenda Sue? How could you let our Nado stay in a bordello?"

"One instance does not a bordello make. Also, if you remember, I didn't know he was staying there. Besides, think of the alternative. If Lance hadn't offered up his space for free, Nado would have been forced to park on the street." The words were no sooner out of my mouth than I realized it would have been better for everyone if Nado had parked on the street.

"Now I understand why your friend Lance let Nado use his parking space. He was probably afraid to park there himself."

"Wrong, Kathilynda. Lance doesn't park anywhere because Lance doesn't own a car."

As it had been for Nado, that was a difficult concept for Kathilynda to grasp. She scratched her head and gave me a puzzled look. "But you told me Lance had money."

"Yes, I did. Lance has gobs of money, but he doesn't own a car. Nobody I know owns a car. In New York City, cars are more trouble than they're worth."

"Weird," said Kathilynda.

Moments later, with unfortunate timing, a late-model luxury sedan, dark green with heavily tinted windows, screeched to the curb a few feet in front of us. Diplomat plates. That could mean only one thing: Dweena. How would I ever explain Dweena to Kathilynda?

Dweena powered down the window and stuck her head out. Today's wig was a perky side-parted strawberry blond flip. "Yo, Brenda," she said. "Hop in, I'll take you home."

"I thought your friends didn't have cars," whispered Kathilynda.

"Dweena is an exception to that rule." And a whole bunch of other rules.

"Come on," said Dweena. "It's not like I've got all day."

Kathilynda got in the front. "You're a lifesaver," she said. "My feet are killing me."

While she and Dweena introduced themselves, I got into the backseat. After I got situated I heard Dweena say, "Oh. You must be the wife. I helped Brenda plaster your husband's missing person posters all over town." She whirled her head around and asked me, "Did he turn up yet?"

"Buncha crank calls is all."

"That's too bad," said Dweena. "Perhaps you should have been more specific about the reward money. 'Generous' is too ambiguous to attract your normal reward-seeking rat. You should have advertised an outlandish amount."

"Yeah, maybe."

I had to change the subject before Dweena said something about the possible danger to Nado.

"Kathilynda had the pleasure of meeting Susan Chapoppel today."

"Fabulous introduction to New York," said Dweena.

"She's a bitch," said Kathilynda.

Dweena braked in front of my building. "Here you are."

"Your friend Dweena dresses good," said Kathilynda. "Those pink-and-orange-striped capri pants were too much. What do you call that thing she had on top?"

"Bustier," I said.

"How do you think I'd look in one?"

A fully loaded question that deserved a half-baked answer. "I don't know. Okay, I guess."

"If I had one now, I'd wear it to Times Square."

While Kathilynda got dressed up for the big Times Square trip, I took Jackhammer out and over to West Fourth Street, where I stood outside Midnight Millinery, admired my new window display, and promised myself that real soon I'd try to keep the shop open more regular hours.

On the way back in I ran into Chuck. He had a large canvas bag slung over his shoulder. He walked lopsided under its weight.

"What's in the bag?"

"Power tools. I'm loaning them to Elizabeth for her goddamn built-ins."

"Did you call Dude Bob yet?"

"Not yet. Soon, though. Maybe tonight."

"Are you helping Elizabeth today?"

"No way. I can't face her now, knowing what I know. Soon as I drop the tools off, I'm going straight home to worry, fret, and knock back a few cold ones."

"Come along with us," I said.

"Who's us, and where to?"

"Nado's wife, Kathilynda, is in town. She insists I take her to Times Square."

"What the hell for?"

"My words exactly."

"The first thing I want to see," said Kathilynda, "once we get to Times Square, is that great big sign with the guy blowing smoke rings."

"Gone," said Chuck.

"Gone?"

"Hasn't been there for years," I said.

We were headed uptown, zipping beneath Seventh Avenue on a number one train, which was packed with an interesting assortment of young, old, fat, skinny, tall, short, rich, poor New Yorkers of all colors, races, religions, sexual persuasions, and, for good measure, a couple of possible alien life-forms. We all jostled for position. Chuck and I stood on either side of Kathilynda—just in case—and, shouting over the racket, tried to explain the metamorphosis of the Times Square area.

"Gone," said Chuck, "is absolutely everything that made Times Square, Times Square."

"How come?" asked Kathilynda.

"Sleaze implosion," said Chuck.

"Now," I said, "Times Square has been repurposed. Bits and pieces of the sleaze like Julia's Trick Shoppe slithered into other neighborhoods."

"I don't care what you say," said Kathilynda. "I liked that Julia person's store." She showed Chuck the bulging eyeball earrings she'd bought.

"Cool," he said. "Did you happen to notice if she had any of that fart-in-a-can stuff in stock?"

"Not that I remember."

With a metallic squeal the train stopped at the newly renovated Forty-second Street station. We got off and ascended to the new Times Square.

"Oh look," said Kathilynda. "A poster of Nado. He looks so handsome with a mustache."

Somebody had also added a set of devil horns to Nado's picture.

"I'm surprised it's still up," said Chuck. "They keep this place clean as a whistle these days."

I'd never cared much for the old Times Square, but it did have soul, even if it was a dirty old perverted soul on its way to hell. The new Times Square was a hideous reminder that, despite everything, New York City really was part of the rest of the country.

"Basically," said Chuck, "it sucks."

"Oooh," said Kathilynda. "It sparkles." She held her

arms away from her body, dramatically beholding the lights, the sights, the theme stores.

I was afraid she'd burst into song.

Chuck stopped dead in his tracks and pointed. "Look up above. Johnny's on the Jumbotron!"

Ten stories above my head, in color more real than real, a forty-foot-high image of Johnny passionately kissed his guest starlet bride-to-be. My heart stopped. I did not move, or breathe, or process the eight zillion candlepower of information that beamed into my brain.

Chuck grabbed my elbow. "You all right? You look pale."

I had an important decision to make. I could die on the spot or not. I thought of Jackhammer and Midnight Millinery. I took a deep breath. "I'm okay."

"I can't believe Brenda Sue really knows Johnny Verlane," said Kathilynda. "He's so dreamy."

"Oh, she knows him, all right," said Chuck. "Get this: She broke up with him because she didn't like his shag rug."

"You've got to be kidding," said Kathilynda. "*She* broke up with *him* over a *rug*?"

I'd recovered enough to try to defend myself about that stupid rug. "It was orange and yellow and—never mind. There was a lot more to it than that rug."

"You know," said Kathilynda, "Johnny Verlane looks a little like Vinnie T. Don't you think? Around the eyes?"

"I see no resemblance."

"Who's Vinnie T?" asked Chuck.

"Nobody," I said.

"Not true," said Kathilynda. "Back in high school, Brenda Sue had like this huge crush on Vinnie T. When he asked her out she got so nervous she stood him up."

"You, of all people, know that's not true, Kathilynda."

"Me? What are you talking about?"

"Look, Kathilynda, cut the innocent act. Okay? I've got a good mind to—"

Were we finally going to have it out right in the middle of Times Square? I was willing. I'd waited a long time for this moment.

Chuck stepped between us. "Girls, girls, girls," he said. "Cut it out. Whatever happened, happened. It's in the past. In the present, I think I feel a pizza coming on. The goddess of pepperoni beckons."

He grabbed Kathilynda's hand, and did a quick right turn into a filthy hole-in-the-wall storefront, miraculously untouched by the Times Square cleanup. "Come on, I'll treat you both to a slice."

"What's a slice?" asked Kathilynda.

Chuck rolled his eyes and pulled her the rest of the way inside, ordered three slices, and instructed Kathilynda that the proper way to eat New York pizza was to fold it in half lengthwise. I climbed up on a stool and stared out a grimy window at passersby, none of whom looked like New Yorkers.

"Well, what do you think?" asked Chuck.

"It's okay," said Kathilynda, "except it doesn't taste much like pizza. We've got this place back in Belup's Creek that makes an island-mix pizza. It comes with those little bitty shrimps and chunks of pineapple. Now, that's what I call good pizza."

Chuck shrugged his shoulders. "Can't say I didn't try."

Back on the street, Kathilynda stood motionless on the crowded sidewalk, and soaked up atmosphere. She put her hands to her head and closed her eyes.

"So, are you picking up Nado's vibe?"

"You don't have to be so sarcastic, Brenda Sue. This is no joke. I want to find my husband. My method is scientific, based on knowing Nado every bit as well as I know myself. I know he came to Times Square. He would have seen that billboard." She pointed at a jeans ad that covered most of a building. It showed the backside of a model, who glanced enticingly over her shoulder.

"Great buns," said Chuck.

"Exactly what Nado would have thought," said Kathilynda. "Therefore, his next stop would have been Bloomingdale's."

"I seem to be missing part of the equation," said Chuck.

Under my breath I said, "I think it's Kathilynda who's a few variables short. She left her brain back in Belup's Creek."

"I heard that, Brenda Sue. Say what you want. You'll eat those words when I find Nado. You see, Chuck, unlike most men, Nado owns a hot dog restaurant. To him, a nice set of buns has a double meaning. A nice set of buns also means bread."

"I see," said Chuck. He put his hand over his mouth to suppress a laugh.

"And of course bread means Bloomingdale's," I said.

"No, silly. Bread means money. Bloomingdale's is where I always said I'd go if I had money. Nado knows that. So he went to Bloomingdale's to buy me a present to make up after our fight. That's where I'll go tomorrow."

"That certainly is what I'd do," said Chuck, "if I'd had a fight with my wife, was on the run from big-city cops, owned a hot dog joint, and had just seen denim stretched over the butt of a gorgeous model. Yep, I'd head straight for Bloomingdale's."

Later that evening Chuck called. "They grow them mighty weird in Belup's Creek," he said.

"Not everybody in Belup's Creek is like Kathilynda," I said.

"Who's this Vinnie? You should have seen your face when Kathilynda mentioned him. You almost slugged her, didn't you?"

"No I didn't."

"Not very ladylike. You're a disgrace to the millinery tradition. Now, tell me about Vinnie."

"There's nothing to tell."

"Then let's talk about Johnny and how you're being a goddamned fool."

"I don't want to talk about Johnny. Did you make that call to Dude Bob?"

"Yeah. I told him I knew he wasn't who he said he was. He said he could explain, then that low-down piece of garbage hung up. I called right back. No answer. I wish I were a goddamned electron. I'd slip into the phone system, zip through the wires, and be at Dude Bob's Montana spread in the blink of an eye. I'd find that lying bastard and punch him in the nose."

"As an electron, you'd punch him?"

"Well, it's a stretch. Someday, though . . ."

Absurd, but it gave me an idea. Chuck. Phones. Wires. Why hadn't I thought of this before? "Chuck, do they save tapes of nine-one-one calls?"

"I guess. Sure. They play them back on the TV news sometimes, so they must."

"Fantastic. I need you to access them with your computer. I can't think of a better way to find out who called in that bomb-scare hooker raid. If it was Maris Montmyer—"

"I can't believe what I hear," said Chuck. "You, Brenda Midnight, you want me to break the law? Remember what happened the last time?"

"Oh yeah, that. Right." I remembered only too well. I'd once had Chuck hack into some stuff for me with near-disastrous results.

"Look, Brenda, even if I were crazy enough to do something like that again, a computer won't help. Contrary to what the popular media would have you believe, computers are not magic. Those tapes don't exist as blips on some hard drive somewhere. They're physical, probably in a file cabinet. What you need is someone with access who owes you a big favor. You know, like Turner or McKinley.''

So much for that idea.

19

In a way I felt negligent. I should have been more worried about Elizabeth and Dude Bob. However, I was fully confident that Chuck would worry more than enough for both of us, which left me time to worry about everything else.

I didn't sleep well. I tossed and turned in my sleeping bag and enumerated my problems. Not counting Elizabeth, I counted four major problems: finding Nado, clearing Lance, solving the Royce Montmyer murder, and dealing with Johnny. The first three were related; at least the solution to one might provide solution to one or both of the others. Johnny stood alone. Actually he didn't stand alone, and that *was* the problem. It seemed pretty definite that he was engaged. That Jumbotron kiss looked like the real thing to me.

Way too soon it was the next day. I lay there grumpy until Jackhammer cold-nosed my arm. I sat up and saw my hats in the window, which cheered me up. It was a good strong summer line. Unfortunately that reminded me of yet another problem: keeping Midnight Millinery open long enough to sell some hats.

Already I had a full morning ahead of me—away from the shop. I wanted to go back to the Hudson Shadow and

look for that woman Rita. I had a feeling not much happened in that building without her knowing about it.

"Why do you want to talk to Rita?" asked Kathilynda.
"She's creepy. That guy in the elevator called her a menace."
    "Because she lives in the Hudson Shadow, she's nosy,
and the co-op board doesn't like her. That's a pretty good
pedigree."
    "Good luck."
    "You too. I hope you find Nado at Bloomingdale's.
Don't forget to take some posters with you."

Elizabeth pulled her collapsible wire shopping cart from out
of a tight space in her foyer closet. "You ought to get
yourself one of these."
    "Never," I said.
    "They're not just for old ladies, you know."
    "It's not that. . . ." They were so . . . I don't know what,
so terminally uncool. I didn't want to insult Elizabeth, so I
changed the subject. "What's that wonderful odor wafting
out of your kitchen? Cinnamon?"
    "Cookies, of course. Would you like to come in?"
    "Thought you'd never ask."
    "You and Jackhammer pull up a piece of floor," she
said, and disappeared into her kitchen.
    Jackhammer trotted around and sniffed at all the newly
exposed areas. I sat in the middle of the room next to a big
pile of lumber, surrounded by bare white walls, and pondered the emptiness.
    Elizabeth returned with coffee and a plate piled high with
cookies.
    I took a small experimental bite. "Hmmm. Interesting.
Cinnamon and what?"
    "Can't you tell?" asked Elizabeth.
    I took another bite, chewed it slowly. "No."
    "Garlic. I'm still working on the recipe. I think they need

more punch up front, then a smoother aftertaste." She
popped one in her mouth.

"I never would have thought of that."

"No offense, Brenda, but you're not much of a cook.
On the other hand, Johnny—"

I held up my hand. "Stop."

"Sorry. How's your house pest?"

I laughed. "I like that. 'House pest' pretty much sums
up the situation. Today Kathilynda went to Bloomingdale's
in pursuit of Nado."

"That's kind of an odd place to look, isn't it? Which
department?"

"I'm afraid I can't do justice to the theory behind Kathilynda's search. Perhaps when you meet her, she'll explain.
It's all bullshit, of course. The hunt for Nado is a lame
excuse for her to shop and sightsee and spend a lot of
money to get back at him."

"What's she getting back at him for?"

"They had a big fight about something; I'm not sure
what."

All the time we talked, I gazed around her apartment.
The bare walls unnerved me.

Elizabeth apparently felt the same. She gestured toward
the walls. "Weird, isn't it?"

"Yes. I can't figure out why the apartment seems smaller
without your furniture. You'd think it would be just the
opposite."

"I thought about that for a long time," said Elizabeth.
"I believe it has to do with the fact that there's nothing
that recedes. If you put a dark painting on a plain white
wall, it punches a hole in the whiteness and fools your
mind. Here, with nothing to focus on, the white comes forward and imposes itself on us."

"The white wall as aggressor."

"Exactly. It makes me crazy, which is why I've got to
forge ahead on the built-ins. Chuck dropped off his power
tools yesterday. I thought he'd help out, but he made an

excuse and split. Alone, I couldn't get inspired. Have you seen Chuck around lately?"

"I ran into him yesterday on his way to see you," I said. A deceptive statement, I know, but I could hardly tell her Chuck went to Times Square with Kathilynda and me, or about his call to Dude Bob.

"Did he seem a little, uh, different?"

"Chuck? Different? That's a good one, Elizabeth." I laughed. "Actually, he is different. I asked him to hack into something for me. He said he couldn't. I got the impression that even if he could, he wouldn't. All of a sudden he's got respect for the law."

"Good," said Elizabeth. "The law no longer considers hacking amusing. They prosecute to the full extent and all that rot."

I glanced at my watch. "Well, I'd better get going."

Elizabeth walked me to the door. "I suppose I should ask where you're going with my cart."

"I'm taking my laundry over to the Hudson Shadow."

"What's wrong with our laundry room? I hope they're not painting that floor again. Remember the last time when the super goofed and got cheap paint that wouldn't dry and we couldn't do our laundry for days?"

"As far as I know our laundry room is intact. I want to talk to a woman who hangs out in the Hudson Shadow's laundry room. Dirty laundry is my entrée."

Elizabeth shook her head. "Chuck's right, you know. You should stop with this sleuthing crap already. Nado is probably perfectly safe, and if Lance were a suspect, you'd think the cops would have arrested him by now. You're wasting your time. You should find out what's up with Johnny."

"What's up with Johnny is that he's a good friend who got himself engaged to a lovely girl. I finally saw what she looked like yesterday. She and Johnny were on the Jumbotron at Times Square."

"Whatever were you doing in Times Square?"

"Kathilynda wanted to go."
"What the hell for?"

As far as collapsible carts went, Elizabeth's was definitely a cut above. She'd souped it up with hot pink spray paint, a set of fuzzy dice, a rearview mirror, and one very loud bicycle bell. I sounded that bell three times on the way to the Hudson Shadow—once in the hallway to scare Julia Pond's mean cat Irving, then when a crazed pizza delivery guy raced his bicycle down the sidewalk straight at me, and half a block later to warn the driver of a station wagon with New Jersey plates, who was trying to sneak an illegal right on red. "Look around," I said. "This ain't Jersey."

The driver completed his turn and sneered at me. "You ain't no cop, honey."

I used Lance's remote control to open the garage door. For a change, I saw no crimes committed in the minute or so it took me to walk through the garage and to unlock the door to the basement.

I pushed Elizabeth's cart through the long corridor and stopped outside the laundry room. From within I heard a rhythmic banging. I peeked in the room. Rita stood, hands on hips, before clothes dryer number two and watched a pair of red high-top sneakers flop around.

"Shit," she muttered to herself.

Her light brown hair was wound around tiny pink plastic rollers and topped with a red and white bandanna. She wasn't so much overweight as out of shape. A pair of cut-off overalls exposed pale legs and flabby knees. An unlit cigarette dangled from the side of her mouth.

She yanked open the door of dryer number two and threw in a red-and-white-striped beach towel. "Now shut the hell up," she said, apparently to the sneakers. She slammed the door shut and restarted the dryer. The sneakers still banged against the sides of the dryer. "Shit."

"Some racket, huh?" I said.

Rita spun her head around, jerked the cigarette out of her mouth, and stuck it in her pocket. "Who the hell are you?"

"I'm Brenda Midnight," I said. "We sort of met—"

"Yeah, yeah, yeah. I remember. You were at that open house. Goddamned uptight broker has got a lot of nerve, insinuating I'm a thief. Between you, me, and the lamppost, I'm thinking maybe I should sue that bitch for slander." She wrinkled her nose at my laundry. "I suppose you think that because you went to an open house or two, you have a right to use our laundry facilities?"

"I was hoping—"

"Yeah, yeah, yeah. You can hope all you want. What will get you into this laundry room is me, myself, and I." She thumped her chest with her forefinger three times.

I smiled and nodded.

"So come on, babe," she said. "Cough it up."

A little slow on the uptake, I asked, "Cough what up?"

Rita rubbed her thumb and forefinger together. "Money. M. O. N. E. Y. Mucho dinero."

"Oh. How much is mucho?"

"Depends." She jiggled the cart. "How many loads you got?"

"Two, a dark and a light."

She jutted her chin toward a price list on the wall. "Buck a load. Seeing hows you don't live here, the price to you is two bucks."

I handed over four dollars.

She frowned at the bills in her hand. "That is, two bucks a load after the five-dollar nonresident entry fee."

I added a five. She rolled it up with the singles and tucked it into the same pocket the cigarette had gone in. She handed me two slugs and said, "You are assigned washers six and seven. Later we'll negotiate for dryers."

"So what exactly is it you do down here?" I asked.

"Who wants to know?"

"I was just curious. Does the building pay you to run the laundry room?"

"Get real. You could say I'm an independent entrepreneur. I see an opportunity to make some dough, I grab it. Don't you know when you've been shook down?"

I chuckled and tossed my clothes into the designated washers.

Rita had outfitted a large Formica table with the comforts of home: coffee machine, popcorn maker, and an old color television set adjusted to garish green. She settled into a folding chair in front of the TV, aimed a remote control, and switched channels. Multiple signals flickered across the small screen. The actors, locked in passionate embrace, had three noses each. Rita slapped the top of the TV. "Shit."

"Not coming in too well, is it?" I said, to make polite conversation.

Rita shook her head, cursed again, and said, "Used to have cable rigged up down here. Then the friggin' cable company found out and jerked out my goddamned wires. Ever since, I haven't been able to pick up shit." She hit the TV again, this time with her fist. The scene shifted to what looked like a hospital room, filled with distraught three-nosed six-eyed actors weeping at someone's bedside.

I shook my head in sympathy.

"So why you here, anyway? Your building doesn't have a laundry room?"

"I'm interested in one of the apartments I saw at the open house, but you know how those real estate guys are. Can't believe a word they say."

"You can say that again. Assholes, every last one of them."

"So I figured what better place to get the real lowdown dirt on a building than in the laundry room?"

Rita beamed at me. "You know something, you're all right. One cool cookie. I shoulda charged you less, but I never go back on a deal. Go ahead and take a gander around."

While I took the suggested gander, Rita waylaid someone who wanted to do "just one little bitty load."

"These machines are all reserved," said Rita. "However . . ."

I moved out of range over to a bulletin board plastered with advertising flyers, snapshots of furniture for sale, cats for adoption, and a plea from a man who wanted "desperately" to buy a parking space. I wondered if he was a drug dealer, car thief, or pimp.

Rita completed her transaction and ambled over to the bulletin board. "I see the Martins have their king-sized platform bed for sale. That is big news."

"How so?"

"You're a little slow, aren't you? Course that's not fair; you don't have all the information. The service entrance to the building is down here. Nothing big comes in or out of here that I don't see. So, here's the other piece of the puzzle: Last week the Martins had twin mattresses delivered. Get it now?"

"I guess the Martins' marriage is on the rocks."

"You get an A-plus. Here's something else you didn't know: Mrs. Martin caught the mister with the lady down the hall, who's no lady, if you know what I mean. No lady at all." On that note, Rita walked over to the bank of dryers. "Shit," she said as she took items out of one dryer and stuffed them into another.

I took down the phone number of someone who was offering to sell a "gently used" air conditioner. The one in my apartment was on its last legs last year. It might not make it through another summer. Rita, meanwhile, had finished with the dryer and was back pounding on the television.

I joined her. "Seems like a nice building," I said, "but I can't help but be concerned about the murder that happened here."

"Don't be. If ever a guy deserved to die it was that Royce Montmyer. I saw it coming a mile away. Bold as daylight Montmyer's screwing around with some little chicky right under her husband's nose, not to mention his own wife's nose job. Then he goes and sets the chicky up in her own apartment in the building. I mean, what did he expect? I figure one of those wronged spouses plugged the bastard. Can't say as I blame them.''

"They say it's usually the spouse," I said. "Although I heard a couple of real estate brokers talking, and they said Montmyer used his power as president to screw people, that he manipulated sales, rejected buyers for no good reason, and then snapped up apartments at a bargain. Any truth to that?''

"Could be. Twenty-two B's been trying to sell for months," said Rita. ''The poor old bat. She can't even separate her darks from her lights anymore. Then there's Fourteen P, same story. I never saw prettier underwear in my life. All lace, and she throws them in with her jeans. You saying one of them blew him away?''

"Not really," I said. "It probably was one of the spouses.''

I was tempted to ask Rita about the illegal doings in the garage, but it seemed wise to keep my mouth shut. For all I knew, Rita had a piece of that action. She sure seemed the type.

''Better get your crap out of the washers,'' she said. ''The spin dry is over.''

I took my wet clothes out, piled them in Elizabeth's cart, and rolled out the door.

Rita shouted after me, ''Aren't you gonna dry that stuff? I'll give you a good deal.''

''No thanks,'' I said.

20

I rolled my cart of wet laundry onto the elevator. I was pleased that Rita thought Maris Montmyer had "plugged the bastard." To be fair, Rita had said *one* of the wronged spouses, but I knew Lance hadn't plugged anybody, so that left Maris.

Or someone else. There were far too many someone elses.

What had I actually learned from Rita? Not much. Elizabeth was probably right. I was wasting my time.

As to my theory that Montmyer had been killed because he'd messed with the wrong person in a self-serving real estate scheme—it was hard to tell what Rita thought. The apartments she'd mentioned—Twenty-two B and Fourteen P—I already knew about from the board minutes. I'd paid special attention to them at the open houses. Not that it had done any good.

Then there was the garage. What the hell was going on there and who knew it? I was scared to ask Rita or, for that matter, anybody else.

The elevator stopped at the lobby level. I started to get off, but it occurred to me that the owners of those two apartments might be home. It wouldn't hurt to ring their bells. I even had an excuse to drop by. I'd say I found something in the laundry room that Rita said might be theirs. I took the elevator up to Twenty-two B.

I hesitated for a moment to get my lost-laundry story straight, then rang Twenty-two B's bell. That would be the little old lady with the crocheted doilies. She either wasn't home or wasn't answering.

I never found out if Fourteen P, the woman with fancy lace underwear, was home or not. On the way down to fourteen, without the excitement of the open houses or Kathilynda to distract me, I realized that was Lance's floor. I chickened out and left. I didn't want to run into him until I had good news. Or at least some news.

When I got back to my apartment, I draped the wet clothes over the shower rod, towel racks, and doorknobs. They'd dry neither fast nor fluffy, but I'd had enough of laundry rooms for one day. Besides, I had more important things to do.

I opened up Midnight Millinery and tried to get some work done. While I cut and stitched and steamed, I thought about Maris Montmyer. Even though there were other possibilities, I liked her as the doer. If I could only find a way to prove she'd engineered the bomb-scare hooker raid, I might be able to light a fire under Turner and McKinley. Of course, I could always find the hit man or woman she'd hired and beat a confession out of him or her. Yeah, right.

The phone rang. It was just as well. I was not exactly lost in constructive thought. I let the machine answer in case it was someone responding to Nado's poster. It wasn't. It was Kathilynda. I picked up. "I'm here," I said.

"What's with all the wet clothes in the bathroom?" she asked.

You'd think it was her apartment or something.

"Saving money," I said. "The dryers in the laundry room downstairs are way overpriced."

"Oh, Brenda Sue, who'd have thought you'd end up destitute? I feel absolutely terrible about the way your life has turned out. But guess what, that's all about to change. You will not believe what happened."

"Did you find Nado?" I crossed my fingers.

"No, but I picked up the most beautiful all-silk turquoise teddy at fifty percent off. I also determined where he went next—the Empire State Building, so I'm headed to the observation deck tomorrow. However, that's not why I called. I hope you're sitting down, Brenda Sue, because you won't believe what I did for you."

"If you don't tell me what it is that I won't believe, I won't have a chance not to believe it."

"Okay, here goes. Thanks to your old pal—that's me—you have a golden opportunity to make your life once again worth living even after you so foolishly broke up with dreamy heartthrob Johnny Verlane over a shag rug."

"What have you done, Kathilynda?"

"You're gonna love it," she said. "Vinnie T will be in New York for a big meeting with this firm Belup Development might buy, or who might buy them. I can't remember which. But who cares? The important thing is that he'll be here. Fabulous timing, don't you think?"

I didn't say anything.

"Didn't you hear me?" she said. "Vinnie T. Here. New York. And get this: The three of us have a date tomorrow night for dinner. After that, girl, you are on your own."

I still didn't say anything.

"I suppose you're wondering how this all came to be. I've still got a business to run, you know. After I got back from Bloomingdale's, I called back home and talked to our Haute Doggerie manager. She had the usual messages about the hike in the price of mustard and other condiments, a new contract with the trash removers, the grease people, that kinda bullshit. I delegated all that crap. I'm a much better delegator than Nado. As you know, he's more a hands-on type. Anyway, there was also a message from Vinnie T. That callback I handled all by my sweet self. Naturally, I told Vinnie I was staying with you in New York. He said he'd sure like to see little Brenda Sue after all these years. Now, don't you worry, I didn't tell him that in order for me to stay at your place, you had to sleep at your shop under your blocking table. For all he knows you've got a penthouse with lots of bedrooms, so we'd best meet him at the restaurant.''

''Tomorrow?''

''Yes. The first day of the rest of your life. I told him I'd leave a message at his hotel to let him know where to meet us. He said he'd treat. Guess he's on an expense account. Belup Development's got the bucks. We can go anywhere we want. How about a romantic dinner at one of those high-up restaurants that spin around? Surely New York has got one of those.''

I did not appreciate Kathilynda's fixing me up with Vinnie T. It was a too little, too late attempt to make amends for what she did in high school, without admitting what she'd done. I should have said no. I should have said I had other plans. I should have said anything but what I said, which was, ''Yes.'' Then I said, ''I don't know if New York has a restaurant that spins, but if it does, I wouldn't go.''

''Why not?''

''Vertigo.''

''You're no fun, Brenda Sue. What's the most romantic stationary restaurant you know?''

Romantic was hardly appropriate for dinner with my ex-husband's estranged wife and someone I'd never actually dated and hadn't seen for a million years. ''On second thought, maybe this isn't such a good idea.''

''I should have known you'd chicken out, just like you did that night you were supposed to meet Vinnie T at the drive-in.''

If this hadn't been a phone call, if I had a weapon, and if I knew how to use that weapon . . .

''I'll go,'' I said. ''The most romantic restaurant in all of New York? You're talking La Reverie, but it's impossible to get a reservation on a one-day notice, especially for a threesome.''

"There's always more room," said Kathilynda. "Believe me, I know my way around restaurants. I own one, remember? Give me the phone number of this La Reverie. I'll get us a reservation."

Technically, I supposed, Sharpe's Hiway Haute Doggerie was a restaurant, though I'd never thought of it as such. Neither would the snobby staff at La Reverie. I gave Kathilynda the number. Later, if I got a spare moment, I would examine my motive for even mentioning La Reverie. I suspected I wanted to humble Kathilynda. The crew of people who handled La Reverie's reservation desk would take care of that.

Regarding Vinnie T: Why not? What was one more disruption? I was getting good at thrashing from one to another.

Later that night Chuck called. Yet another disruption.

It was almost midnight when the cab dropped me in front of Chuck's. When Chuck let me in I asked if Dude Bob had really come all the way from Montana.

"He sure did," said Chuck.

I got myself situated in the beanbag chair. Chuck leaned up against his refrigerator, crossed his arms, and glared at Dude Bob. Dude Bob avoided Chuck's eyes. He raised his eyebrows at me in greeting. I nodded back.

I'd met Dude Bob 43 the first time he came to New York for a face-to-face meeting with Elizabeth, aka Luscious Liz, his cyber soul mate and now wife-to-be. He looked the same, handsome and soft-eyed, a little scholarly maybe, not at all like the Vietnam hero he had claimed to be. In retrospect, I guessed that made sense.

"Dude Bob was about to explain," said Chuck, "why he's a lying sack of—"

"Stop," I said. "If Dude Bob came all this way, in person, to explain why he did what he did, we owe it to him to listen politely. Let him say what he came to say."

"Okay," said Chuck. "But I reserve the right to call

him any goddamn name I want after he says it.''

"Fair enough," said Dude Bob.

"So," said Chuck, "why'd you tell Elizabeth you'd done three tours of Vietnam?"

"That's simple. I lied to impress her."

"You sure messed that up, didn't you?" I said.

Dude Bob nodded. "You can say that again. It was pretty goddamned stupid of me. At the time, I had no idea Elizabeth had given up her painting to protest our Vietnam involvement. The lie kind of backfired."

"I remember," I said. "You two had a big fight over politics."

"I faked the whole story about going over there. I never left the country and, to tell you the truth, I never cared much about that war one way or the other. But once I'd lied, I couldn't take it back. Elizabeth would get even madder. So, I kept the debate—and the lie—going. True love triumphed. Elizabeth decided she liked me just as I was."

"Except you weren't what you said you were," said Chuck.

"I guess I've got to tell her."

"Damn right you do," said Chuck.

Chuck blew off some steam, called Dude Bob a few choice names. And then a few more, even choicer.

Dude Bob took it all quite well. When Chuck calmed down, the Dude promised he would tell Elizabeth the truth.

I left the two of them to figure out the whens and wheres this truth session would take place.

21

I'd made sure that Kathilynda always took Nado posters with her on her shopping trips. The results were immediately apparent by an increase in the number of crank calls on Midnight Millinery's answering machine. Three more had come in while I'd been at Chuck's. I played back the tape. The first two messages were the usual bullshit, but the last call sounded legit: "Few days ago," the caller said, "I saw the guy with the goofy hair chomping down a hot dog in Times Square."

Was it possible Kathilynda actually knew what she was doing?

Early the next morning Lance Chapoppel called. He didn't sound any too happy.

"Why do I get the feeling you're avoiding me?" he asked.

I tried to put some zip in my groggy voice. "Me? Why would you think that?"

"I haven't heard a peep out of you. You know how important it is to find Nado."

"I just didn't want to bother you with inessential details of my search."

"Please, Brenda, keep me in the loop."

"Okay. I guess the biggest and best news is that Nado's wife Kathilynda came to New York to help search for

Nado. She's got ideas and strategies I never would have come up with. It's freed me to pursue other aspects of the case.''

''Oh?''

''You wouldn't believe some of the stuff going on in your building. For instance, the garage—''

''If Nado doesn't turn up soon, I'll be thrown out of the building.''

I could tell from the tension in his voice that Lance was less than pleased with my progress. I didn't blame him one bit. I felt lousy that I had not yet come through for him. Lance Chapoppel was a good friend, and it saddened me to think that this mess could destroy our friendship.

Kathilynda was thrilled when I told her about the message. ''I told you he'd go to Times Square.''

I was walking her to the bus stop on Sixth Avenue because it was quicker than drawing a map. Jackhammer went along. He didn't particularly care where he got his morning walk as long as the route had the requisite number of fire hydrants along the way. The downside was that I had to listen to Kathilynda gloat.

''You also couldn't have been more wrong about that La Reverie place,'' she said. ''I had no problem getting a reservation for tonight.''

''What did you do, tell them you were the Queen of England?''

''Of course not, silly. They'd never believe that. I told them I was the executive assistant to that big director Sal Stumpford, and that Mr. Stumpford would be in town this evening.''

''Are you nuts? Johnny has worked with Stumpford. Stumpford spent a month shooting in the Village. They _know_ Stumpford at La Reverie.''

''Give me some credit. I didn't actually come right out and say that Mr. Stumpford would be there himself. You could say I was a bit vague on that issue.''

"That's just great, Kathilynda. This is my neighborhood. I don't lie and deceive my way into restaurants. I've got my reputation to protect."

"I thought everybody in New York City was anonymous and lost in the hustle-bustle, alone in the crowd."

"I'm not anonymous, not in the Village. Down here, everybody pretty much knows everybody's business. In some ways it's worse than Belup's Creek."

Kathilynda brushed off my concern. "So hide behind a big pair of sunglasses," she said. "They'll think you're from Hollywood. It'll fit right in with the Stumpford bit."

I groaned. "Of all people, why'd you have to use Stumpford's name? I'm surprised you even know of Sal Stumpford. His name is not exactly a household word."

"Just because I live in Belup's Creek doesn't mean I don't read the credits at the end of TV shows. Then, when I saw Stumpford's name in that little book you keep by the phone—"

"What were you doing in my book?"

Kathilynda got lucky. Before I inflicted damage to her person, a bus shuddered to a stop in front of us. Its doors whooshed open. I gritted my teeth, squelched my anger, and told Kathilynda, "Take this to Thirty-fourth. Walk one block east. You can't miss it."

She mounted the steps, turned, and flashed a smile over her shoulder. "Don't forget, Brenda. Dinner's at eight."

The bells on the door jangled. I looked up from my work. "Margo!"

She looked great. Tall and thin, with photogenic cheekbones and great taste, it was impossible for her not to. I hadn't seen Margo since she'd closed her Soho boutique and run off with her good-for-nothing Euro-trash boyfriend.

"What brings you to New York?"

"I'm back."

"To live?"

"Yes. Alone. And don't ask."

"Well, it's wonderful to have you back."

"Thank you. It's good to be back and on the verge of a brand-new stupendous career."

"Which is?"

"Stylist. Can you imagine a better job for me?"

I couldn't.

"And you, if you will, are about to help me with my launch."

"Anything you need."

"I knew you'd say that."

Margo borrowed five hats for her first stylist gig. A soon-to-be-famous photographer was shooting the fall fashions of a soon-to-be-famous designer for a spread in a trendy soon-to-be-famous new magazine. She promised my name would be in the credits alongside the pictures and also in a list at the end.

I'd just got back to work when the bells on my door jangled again. I recognized my hat first, then its wearer. It was the hooker from the meat market. Both she and the woman with her were dressed in jeans and sweatshirts. I figured they were off duty.

"This hat gets a ton of compliments," said the hooker. She jerked her thumb at the other woman. "Taffy here wants one. I told her you'd give her a hat for information."

"That's right," I said.

"Great. I'll leave her here with you, then, but I'm afraid I must run. Pressing engagement."

"Thank you," I said. "Come by when you have more time, pick out another hat."

"I'll do that. 'Bye now." With a wave she was gone.

I gestured for Taffy to sit down at the vanity. "You have information about the raid?" I asked.

"I was there," said Taffy. "You see, I'm a location scout."

That was a new twist on an old profession. I bit my tongue to hold back a sarcastic comment that was just itching to come out. If Taffy really had information, I didn't want to insult her.

Taffy went on. "I was scoping out the meat market. I thought it might be a cool place to shoot a perfume ad. You know, teeming with sex and violence, yet understated, not overt. It's not PC to do overt these days. I got picked up in the bust along with everybody else. It was one chaotic mess—dogs sniffing, cops yelling. Everybody got searched for explosives. Of course they didn't find any bombs, but they ran us all in anyway. Once we got to the station they sorted everybody out."

"Do you remember an older woman, fiftyish, maybe sixty, grayish blond hair?"

"You must mean the lady with the bad 'tude."

"Sounds like Maris Montmyer, all right."

"Yeah, that's her. I recognize the name. She kept screaming, 'You can't do this to me. I'm Maris Montmyer.' She went into a heads-will-roll-I-have-friends-in-high-places kind of riff."

"Did you happen to notice her before the raid? Maybe making a call from a pay phone or cell phone?"

"I saw her wander the streets, but that's all. If she made any calls, I didn't see. She might show up in some of my photos, though.

"Photos? You've got photos?"

"Of course. I'm a location scout."

I was one happy milliner. This could be the big break I'd been hoping for. Unfortunately, Taffy's film was still at the lab. She promised that as soon as she got her negatives back, she'd make contact sheets and bring them over.

The rest of the day whizzed by. Before I knew it, it was seven o'clock, time to dress for dinner. Despite Kathilynda's insinuations, I had no romantic interest in Vinnie T. Even if we were to hit it off, the last thing in the world I needed was a boyfriend who lived in Belup's Creek. However, I thought it would be interesting to see how Vinnie T had turned out.

I wasn't really all that worried about blowing my reputation at La Reverie. It was doubtful anyone on the staff would recognize me with or without sunglasses, though I'd never admit this to Kathilynda.

I went back to the apartment to shower and change. Kathilynda hadn't gotten back from the Empire State Building and wherever else she'd gone to shop. Jackhammer and I both appreciated having the apartment to ourselves even though Kathilynda's junk was strewn all over the place.

Kathilynda had left her makeup on the shelf over my sink. Blue eye shadow? I put a dab on my hand and marveled at the fact that she actually wore the stuff. I heard her let herself into the apartment.

"You here, Brenda Sue?"

"In the bathroom," I said.

"Wait'll you see what I got to wear tonight."

"I've only been in the Big Apple a short time," said Kathilynda, "but already I've noticed that everybody wears black, everywhere, all the time. Why is that, Brenda Sue?"

"I don't know."

"Well, you should. You are in the fashion business."

"You might as well ask me, 'what is art?'"

"You're too profound. Now, are you ready for this?" Kathilynda pulled a tissue-wrapped parcel from a generic plastic I LOVE NY shopping bag. She tore off the tissue, unfolded the garment, and swung it back and forth in front of her body. "Well, what do you think?"

It was a dress, a black dress, knee-length with a fitted bodice and an A-line skirt. Stiff prim ruffles circled the edge of the neck, the armholes, and the hem. Kathilynda had done the impossible. She'd found the only black dress in all of New York City that didn't look the least bit black.

*   *   *

I put on my long black dress.

"You're wearing that?" she asked.

"Yes."

"It's so plain."

"I accessorize," I said, and proceeded to do so. I plunked a little straw cocktail hat on my head.

We walked along Bleecker Street to La Reverie, a route that took us by Johnny's building. I looked up at his window. Pure habit. The blinds were down, as they'd been ever since he'd gone to LA. I wondered if he'd give up his place when he got married. People would kill to get his apartment, a rent-stabilized one-bedroom.

Kathilynda babbled about her tour of the Empire State Building. "You know, Brenda, from the observation deck the people look exactly like little bitty ants."

"Uh-huh."

"And the streets are filled with yellow from all the cabs."

La Reverie was known as *the* place to pop *the* question. A fantasyland where engagement rings bobble in champagne flutes, swim in the sauce of poached pears, and rest atop tall pyramids of baby lettuces. They probably sell stand-in zirconium rings in vending machines in the men's restroom, for that unforeseen romantic emergency.

I'd been to La Reverie a few times, always under ridiculous circumstances, never once to get proposed to. Chalk up yet another ridiculous situation. As we walked through the heavy etched-glass door I wondered whatever had possessed me to agree to go.

We were supposed to meet Vinnie T in the entrance-level bar. It was very sophisticated, very shiny black lacquer, with touches of silver. A tuxedo-clad man played requests at a white baby grand.

"There he is," said Kathilynda, pointing. "There's Vinnie T. Yoo-hoo, Vinnie, over here."

Kathilynda had told the truth about one thing: Vinnie T did look a little like Johnny, especially around the eyes. The rest wasn't bad either.

"Brenda."

"Vinnie."

Kathilynda told the hostess we were the Sal Stumpford party. The hostess gave us an odd look, shrugged her shoulders, and had someone escort us downstairs to the only table in the entire establishment set up for three.

As we descended the curved staircase, Kathilynda elbowed me, winked, and mouthed the words, "What did I tell you?"

In contrast to the hard-edged bar, the restaurant was soft-lit. Everything was peach-colored. The wait staff swooped down on our table. Apparently they, every last one an actor- or singer- or dancer-in-waiting, had been clued in that this was big-deal director Sal Stumpford's table.

Dinner happened. A lot of small talk. Kathilynda regaled us with descriptions of the weird method she used to search for Nado. Vinnie told Kathilynda that yes, it was still raining like crazy back in Belup's Creek, a fact that had slowed a major construction project, so it was a good time to be in New York anyway and if this deal went through it would be a feather in his cap, which led the talk around to millinery, and Vinnie T said he'd like to see the shop sometime while he was in New York, and I, of course, said sure. At the end of the meal the entire wait staff brought out a cake because Kathilynda had told them it was Sal Stumpford's birthday. We were treated to a creatively arranged, choreographed, on-key, totally professional, emotive rendition of "Happy Birthday, Dear Mr. Stumpford."

Much later, as I drifted off to sleep, I thought about how Vinnie T looked like Johnny, around the eyes. I realized I had it all backward. Since I'd known Vinnie T first, it was Johnny who resembled Vinnie T. It followed, then, that my attraction to Johnny was based on nothing more than a teen-age fantasy. I found this thought extremely comforting, especially in light of the fact that Johnny appeared to be engaged to someone else.

22

In my nightmare the Hudson Shadow grew taller and taller, piled on floor after floor, until it was over a hundred stories high. Its shadow reached all the way to West Fourth Street, where it hovered over Midnight Millinery, shrouding it in darkness. Along came a state-of-the-art special dream effects generator to save the day. With one giant whoosh the shadow blew away and I was back to dreaming about Johnny and Vinnie T. Whoosh. Johnny transformed into Vinnie T. Whoosh, whoosh. Vinnie T transformed into Johnny. Whoosh, whoosh, whoosh. An add-on feature enabled the generator to filter out all appearances by guest starlets and Kathilynda Annamarie Cooper Sharpe.

Midway through a double whoosh, a sound from the real world pierced through the haze—the telephone.

I fought hard to keep the dream going. Johnny, Vinnie T, Johnny, Vinnie T, but Chuck's voice came out of the speaker. "Pick up, Brenda."

I stuck my head under the pillow.

"Come on, Brenda, I know you're there. Yo. Get that pillow off your head and answer the goddamned phone."

Chuck Riley knew me too well. The special effects generator sputtered and ground to a halt in a puff of neon smoke. No more Johnny, no more Vinnie T. Chuck continued to nag. "Rise and shine, Brenda. Up and at 'em."

I picked up the phone. "You messed up a good dream."

"You'll have another," said Chuck. "Now listen up. I just got off the phone with our good buddy Mr. Dude Bob 43. The slimeball claims he spent all day yesterday in his hotel room trying to get up the nerve to tell Elizabeth that he's a lying sack of shit. He's finally ready to fess up. Get this—he wants me to go with him."

"What for?"

"Moral support. Guess I'm the closest thing he's got to a friend in this town."

"With friends like you—"

"Right. Who needs enemies? However, it's okay by me. I'll make sure he comes through with the truth. It also means I'll be there in case Elizabeth needs me."

"Good idea, Chuck."

"I'm so glad you think so. I told the Dude I'd do it as long as you agreed to come too."

Jackhammer and I went over to the apartment to wait for Chuck and Dude Bob. Kathilynda had already made a pot of coffee. I helped myself to a cup and felt like a guest making myself at home—weird because I was in my own home.

I took the coffee into the room, sat on the banana-shaped couch, and wished Kathilynda would go away. I needed that special effects generator in real life. I took a sip of coffee and forced a smile.

She sat cross-legged on my mattress, and looked at me expectantly. "Well?"

"Well, what?"

"I'm dying to hear. What'd you think about Vinnie T?"

"He was okay, I guess. Dinner was nice, except for the Stumpford stuff."

"Okay? That's all you can say? Come on, I was there, remember? I saw the way you looked at Vinnie T and, I might add, the way Vinnie T looked at you."

"Of course I looked at him. I wanted to see if you were

right, and you know, he does look like Johnny. A little. Around the eyes.''

''You can't fool me, Brenda Sue. I think the two of you are cute together. I can't wait to tell everybody back in Belup's Creek. This is *so* romantic.''

''Cut it out,'' I said. I felt myself blush.

''Here's how you get to the boat that goes to the Statue of Liberty.'' Kathilynda watched as I traced my finger along the subway route on the map.

When Chuck showed up he told her she should take the Staten Island Ferry instead. ''It's free,'' he said. ''It floats right by the statue.''

''Does it stop?''

''Only at Staten Island.''

She closed her eyes and put her hands to her head. My eyes met Chuck's, and we both held back laughs.

After a minute or so, Kathilynda opened her eyes and shook her head. ''I'd like to save money, but I have to do exactly what Nado would have done. I know he went all the way up in the statue's crown. Besides, I want to see the full range of souvenir items.''

''Whatever,'' said Chuck with a shrug.

''Did Brenda Sue tell you where we went last night?'' asked Kathilynda.

Chuck shook his head no.

''To this very fancy restaurant, La Reverie. Romantic as all getout and *tres* gourmet. They had stuff like arugula and salmon and crème brulée. You'll never guess who we went with.''

''Then tell me,'' said Chuck.

''Vinnie T.''

''That guy Brenda used to have a crush on?'' Chuck looked at me for some reaction.

I quelled a rising blush.

''None other,'' said Kathilynda. ''He came to New York to put together a business deal. It was really cool. The people at the restaurant thought he was that big director, Sal Stumpford, and we got a free birthday cake and everything.''

Once she'd thoroughly embarrassed me, Kathilynda grabbed a stack of posters and hurried off for the Statue of Liberty. "I want to beat those silly tourists."

I started to tell Chuck that the posters had netted one possibly legit message about a Nado sighting but was cut short by Dude Bob's arrival. Poor Dude Bob. He looked like he hadn't slept since the last time I'd seen him and he'd looked pretty awful then.

"Coffee?" I asked.

"No thanks," he said grimly. "I want to get this over."

"Let's do it," said Chuck.

In the time it took to open my door, walk into the hallway, and over to Elizabeth's, the expression on Dude Bob's face changed from wary to flat-out petrified. His forefinger hovered in the vicinity of Elizabeth's doorbell, touched down for a second, then jerked back as if the bell were on fire. "On second thought," he said, "I think it's too early. Elizabeth might not be up yet. Sometimes she likes to sleep—"

"Push the goddamned bell," ordered Chuck.

The Dude pushed, then slunk off to the side.

"A totally chickenshit move," said Chuck.

Elizabeth cracked the door open a few inches. When she saw us, all the color drained out of her face. "Oh my," she said.

We waited for her to invite us in. She didn't. Dude Bob cleared his throat a couple of times. Chuck shifted his weight from one foot to the other. I stood there, holding squirmy little Jackhammer, embarrassed.

After what seemed like hours, Elizabeth spoke, her voice taut. "Maybe you could come back later, uh, for breakfast or something. It's kinda early, and"—she lowered her voice to a whisper—"I have company."

Dude Bob aged ten years in that moment. His face crumpled, his body drooped.

"Go," said Elizabeth. Then she closed the door firmly.

For one very long minute, no one said a word. Then finally Chuck squeaked out with, "I'll be goddamned."

We crossed the hall to my apartment. The Dude slumped on the banana couch that used to be Elizabeth's. He refused to speak. I offered him a graham cracker. He bit into it halfheartedly and gave the rest to Jackhammer. Jackhammer sensed something was wrong. He actually chewed before swallowing, then ambled over to his spot beside the radiator and lay down with his back turned to us.

In a surprise turnaround, Chuck rose to the occasion. He slapped Dude Bob on the back. "Come on, man, I know what you need."

Dude Bob didn't respond.

"Let's go." He pulled Dude Bob off the couch.

"Where are you taking him?"

"Angie's."

"At ten o'clock in the morning?"

"This is a very special ten o'clock in the morning," said Chuck. "The Dude just got dumped. Wanna come with?"

"No thanks. I've got work to do."

"Later, then."

Dude Bob shuffled along. He didn't look up or say goodbye.

What a way to start the day.

I should have known better. When Chuck told me what Dude Bob planned, I should have put a stop to it. I'd led Dude Bob astray, set him up, let him down.

Maybe it's different in Montana, but in New York you don't drop in unannounced. Since Elizabeth and I live across the hall from each other, we frequently break that rule. Dropping by with Chuck and the Dude was a whole different deal. I felt terrible.

*   *   *

While the boys bonded and tied one on at Angie's, I opened
Midnight Millinery, straightened up, filled in some gaps in
the window display, then settled down to work on a great
batch of denim I'd gotten my hands on at a liquidation sale
in the garment district. Under steam it totally relaxed and
molded smoothly around impossibly tight corners. If only
I could do the same, I thought. I was admiring a perfect lip
on a tricky brim when the phone rang.

I halfway expected a call from Vinnie T. This could be
it. Or not. Too many thoughts all at once, flash-flood fast,
dumped into my brain. Should I pick up or not? What
would it mean if I did? If I didn't? If I monitored and then
picked up? Did I want to talk to him? If he asked me out,
did I want to go? What would I wear?

"Hello."

"Brenda."

"Vinnie." I tried to sound detached.

"I enjoyed last night," he said.

"Me too," I said, somewhat less than eloquent.

"Seeing you again after—"

"After such a long time," I said.

"I'd like to see you again before I leave."

Decision time. Yes? No? Maybe so?

"Without Kathilynda," he added.

Yes? No? Johnny on the Jumbotron. "Sure," I said. And
it was done.

We decided on tomorrow. Once we got that out of the
way, conversation flowed. I told him that Kathilynda's
search strategy may have actually paid off and we laughed
at the thought of her scarfing up souvenir Statue of Liberty
hats. He told me how much Belup's Creek had changed.

"Ever consider moving back?"

"No."

"Oh."

Another lull in the conversation.

After an uncomfortable silence, I said, "I'm looking forward to tomorrow night."

"So am I, but you've gotta promise me one thing."

"What's that?"

"Don't stand me up like that time at the drive-in."

Elizabeth, wild-eyed and frantic, cannonballed into Midnight Millinery. "Where's Dude Bob? Where's Chuck?"

Jackhammer trotted over to greet her. She scooped him up, gave him a quick hug.

"They went to Angie's," I said. "The Dude was devastated. I guess Chuck thought a little—"

She was out the door before I could finish.

I wanted to follow her, but held back. I'd done enough already to screw up that relationship.

23

A little later I glanced out the window and thought I saw Elizabeth zoom past in a cab. By the time I got outside, the cab had disappeared around the corner.

Elliot was weeding out the cigarette butts from Pete's flower box of pansies. "Did you see who was in that cab?" I asked.

"A lady from the neighborhood. I don't know her name."

"Anybody with her?"

"No."

Except for a couple of quick trips around the block with Jackhammer, I spent the entire day at Midnight Millinery. I had some customers, sold a few hats. On the downside, I had a few surprise visitors. It seemed that every time I looked up somebody I didn't want to see was coming through the door.

First, the landlord. I couldn't imagine what he wanted. The rent wasn't due yet, so it couldn't possibly be late.

This time when his limousine pulled up in front of the shop it was to buy a chapeau (his word) for his niece (also his word). She, preceded and followed by various silicone enhancements, wiggled into the shop behind his cloud of foul cigar smoke. I knew she was no niece. However, I played along and didn't even inquire after the landlord's wife's health.

I was still airing out the place when Turner and McKinley strode through the door, marched over to my worktable, stood a little too close, and looked down at my work. "What is that?" said Turner.

"It's a hat, or almost a hat." I held it up so they both could get a better look. "It's like the ones in the window, only different. A variation in denim, a bit casual, a bit more toward fall, which is coming, you know, right after summer, which is almost here." I babbled; they glared.

Finally Turner said, "I am well aware of the order of the seasons, Ms. Midnight."

Uh-oh. I did not like the edge in his voice. Keep it light, I thought. "So, Detectives, what brings you to Midnight Millinery on such a lovely, uh, spring day?"

"This," boomed McKinley. He stuck a Nado missing person poster under my nose.

I knew pasting up posters was illegal, although due to the public service nature of the message, I was sure it would be overlooked. Since detectives didn't go around busting people for posters, I figured they were angry that I'd gone behind their back after they'd told me to stay out of it.

"I was only trying to find Nado," I said in my defense. "You said yourselves Nado wasn't a suspect, so how could hanging a few posters in any way interfere with the investigation you so rightly told me to stay out of?" I was in treacherous verbal territory, but I think I managed to stay on the side of truth with that carefully worded statement.

"She really doesn't get it," said Turner to McKinley.

"You don't get it," said McKinley to me. And he was off. "When you put up posters such as these"—he rattled it under my nose once again—"you attracted the attention of our cronies in other precincts. Those astute individuals wondered at the circumstances of your ex-husband's disappearance, something Detective Turner and I had been trying to keep low-key for rather obvious reasons. From the poster, our cronies learned that Mr. Sharpe was 'Last seen in the East Village,' so, being investigators, they call the Ninth Precinct to inquire. The Ninth refers them to the Sixth and the assholes there bend their ears with the story of Nado. To get to the point, Ms. Midnight, Detective Turner and I look like Class A fools, not only in our own precinct, but now, thanks to you, your goddamned ex-husband, and your goddamned poster, throughout the entire goddamned metropolitan area.''

McKinley stood over me to deliver this tirade. When he finished, he paced. His legs were too long for the amount of floor space, so he spent much of the time executing tight turns.

I didn't know what to say, so I watched him pace.

Turner, meanwhile, had seated himself at the vanity. I checked to make sure he hadn't disturbed Jackhammer, who was pretending to be asleep beneath the vanity, then I turned my attention back to McKinley. Who paced. As he did so, he looked down at the floor. This went on for far too long. Then suddenly McKinley stopped on a dime. He looked at Turner and said, ''What in holy hell are you doing?''

I too looked at Turner, and cracked up. I couldn't help myself. I felt a little less guilty when I heard McKinley's deep ho-ho-ho join in.

What we were looking at and laughing at was Turner, sitting pretty as a picture, trying on a hat. This was a side of Turner I'd not been exposed to. From McKinley's reaction, I'd guessed he hadn't either.

What a tension-breaker.

Turner picked up a piece of veiling and twisted it around the hat and down over his left eye. I thought it was nice that he felt so secure in his masculinity.

McKinley stopped laughing long enough to say, ''It's definitely you.''

Turner growled, "It's for my sister's birthday. We kinda look alike."

I piped up with, "How about a gift certificate?"

"Now, that's a great idea." Turner unwound the veiling and eased the hat off his head.

I filled out a gift certificate, folded it over several times, wrapped it in bright blue tissue paper, and put it into a miniature hatbox.

"Cute," said Turner.

That hat helped. The detectives were in a slightly better mood when at long last they headed for the door. They weren't quite smiling, but they weren't yelling or glowering either. I breathed a sigh of relief. Then, damned if Turner didn't pull an oh-by-the-way on me. He paused in the doorway. "Wasn't that you we saw last night at La Reverie?"

Talk about your small worlds.

"Moonlighting," explained Turner. "Owner hired us to watch the room. There had been some pilfering, possibly a staff member in collusion with a patron."

"Where were you, behind a smoked mirror?" I asked.

"A little more sophisticated," said McKinley.

"Right," said Turner. "A series of peepholes."

"You're kidding." With the two of them, I could never be sure.

"So, who was that you were with?" asked Turner.

"Kathilynda Annamarie Cooper Sharpe, Nado's wife. She's here to look for Nado. If she finds him, rest assured the very first thing I'll do is—"

"And the guy?"

"Nobody, an old friend, an acquaintance, actually."

"A rather close acquaintance, yes?" said Turner.

"No."

"Don't give me that crap. We saw the way he looked at you. We saw the way you looked at him. We also know he's not Sal Stumpford even though the reservation was in Stumpford's name.''

"Is that what this is all about? I can explain. You see, Kathilynda used Stumpford's name to get a reservation. I had no idea—''

But no, that wasn't what it was about.

"Can't say as I blame you, Ms. Midnight,'' said Turner. "Making eyes at some other guy, what with your boyfriend Johnny Verlane getting engaged and all.''

"I was not making eyes. Johnny is not my boyfriend. Johnny is my ex-boyfriend. I am very happy for him.''

"So, is he really getting married?'' asked McKinley.

"I haven't spoken to Johnny,'' I said.

"Think the wedding will be in New York?'' asked Turner.

"I haven't the foggiest.''

"If you do happen to hear anything, Ms. Midnight,'' said McKinley, "do us a favor and let us know. Maybe you could put in a good word for us with Lemon B. Crenshaw. I assume he's handling the guest list?''

"I don't know.''

"We'd sure hate to miss out on the wedding on account of some silly misunderstanding,'' said Turner.

I would have loved to ask Turner and McKinley how their investigation on the Royce Montmyer murder was going. I would have loved to ask what they thought of Maris Montmyer's alibi, or if they knew what I knew about the garage or the real estate. I would have loved to sit down and shoot the breeze with them about the case and share information. That kind of stuff didn't even happen in a *Tod Trueman* episode.

I was sweeping up scraps of denim when Lance Chapoppel stormed into the shop. Great. This was all I needed to complete my day. Our friendship was destroyed. I made a futile attempt to save the situation. "I'm following up on a lead—"

"Never mind about that now, Brenda. I've got something great to show you."

Then I noticed the triumphant smile that lit up Lance's face. He radiated high energy. This was the old Lance, the before-Nado Lance, the Lance who was my friend. It was good to have that Lance back. I hoped he stuck around.

"Remember that noodle I told you about?"

"The one that makes less sauce seem like more?"

"Uh-huh. Finished it, sold it, and Brenda, it's a beautiful sight to behold. Sculpturally speaking, this noodle's a masterpiece. It's by far the best noodle of my career." He dropped a handful of prototype noodles on my blocking table.

Now I understood his change of mood. It was a simple case of creative frenzy. Art was all. Nothing else mattered. I bent down to get a closer look. The noodles were beautiful—gentle curves, intersecting in three-dimensional space. "Nice," I said.

While I admired his noodles, he looked around the shop. After a while he said, "Brenda?"

"Yeah?"

"What's this?" His voice sounded tense. He pointed to a black-velvet-brimmed hat behind the counter.

"That's from last fall," I said. "You remember. I wore it to that party where—"

He pounded the counter with his fist. "Shit. I can't believe it. I'm ruined. Lance Chapoppel is over, washed up."

"What's wrong?"

"That hat! I swear to you, Brenda. I had no idea."

"What are you talking about?"

"Look at the noodle. Look at the hat. It's the same goddamned shape. I copied you, Brenda. I've lost my creative soul."

I tried to make him feel better. I pointed out subtle differences between the shape of the hat and the shape of the

noodle. I told him I knew that he hadn't copied intentionally. "This kind of stuff happens. Another milliner and I
once came up with almost exactly the same hat. It's no big
deal. Really."

"This is different. I saw your hat last year. Face it,
Brenda, I ripped you off. I have to go now, think about
how to handle this. I'll call my attorney. I promise to make
it all right."

"It's already all right, Lance."

For him it wasn't. I understood. Lance had more artistic
integrity than anyone I knew. He brooded, said he was a
total failure. He'd failed at his marriage to Susan, and now
he'd failed at his art. I tried to make him feel better by
changing the subject to my own failure to find Nado.

"None of that matters anymore, Brenda."

With that, he pocketed his noodles and walked out the
door.

I didn't go after him. He needed to be alone.

A sign of how lousy a day it had been: I was actually happy
later that evening to see Kathilynda. She bustled into the
shop carrying several shopping bags. Obviously she hadn't
found Nado.

"I never noticed how much alike they look," she said.

"Who, Johnny and Vinnie T?"

"No, silly, that's only around the eyes. I'm talking about
the Statue of Liberty and Elvis."

24

I crawled into my sleeping bag way too early for an adult. It had been a bad day and I'd had quite enough of it. Besides, I fully expected to be jolted awake by a call in the middle of the night from Chuck or Elizabeth to fill me in on the Dude Bob situation. I also thought Lance might call once he calmed down.

As it turned out, no one called, and I got in a full eight hours. I felt great when I woke up, until I realized that no one had called, and then I felt negligent. These were friends in trouble. I should have followed up myself.

Better late than never, I thought, and speed-dialed Chuck's number.

"What happened yesterday with you and Dude Bob?" I asked.

"We went to Angie's, tossed back a couple, then the Dude said he could do with a good dose of Hank Williams. That jukebox at Angie's didn't cut it; plenty of Frank, and jazz, and blues, but not exactly robust in the twang realm. We split and I took him to this East Village bar where they've got a box full of Hank and Patsy."

"Not that hideous new theme restaurant where the guy in a cowboy costume stands outside and spins a rope?"

"No way. I took him to a joint that's been on Avenue

B for like seventy-five years or something. An authentic East Village country western bar.''

"Odd location.''

"They've got a screen door that bangs, a lady bartender with a twelve-inch-high bleached-blond beehive hairdo that's got a chewed-up pencil stuck in it, old guys with sideburns who hoot and holler. All that's missing is a dog with a litter of puppies asleep under the front porch. They've got no porch, so the dogs kind of wander around. They fart and beg for dried beef swizzle sticks.''

"Not long after I opened the shop," I said, "Elizabeth burst in looking for Dude Bob. She was crazed. I sent her to Angie's. A little later I thought I saw her go by in a cab.''

"That was her. I thought she might be looking for me and the Dude, so before we left Angie's I told Tommy where we were headed.''

"Good thinking.''

"Elizabeth caught up with us a few minutes before Dude Bob passed out. He told her he was a lying sack of shit, although he phrased it differently. She explained why she slammed the door on us, which was to protect me.''

"Huh? Protect you? From what?''

"A long story. If Elmo hadn't gotten sick—''

"The precinct captain's bulldog?''

"Uh-huh. Elizabeth was dog-sitting. In the middle of the night Elmo knocked over her cookie jar and ate seventeen banana-chili-pepper cookies. When Elizabeth woke up, Elmo was having a puke fest, spewing all over the place. He was still erupting when the captain came by to pick him up. The dog wasn't seriously ill, but they thought he'd be too much of a handful to transport in the captain's brand-new car with its custom leather interior. Elizabeth made breakfast while they waited for Elmo's stomach to quiet down.''

"I still don't understand why Elizabeth shut us out.'' Then again, maybe I did understand after all. "Are you saying that Elizabeth and the precinct captain, uh—''

"For chrissakes, Brenda, get your mind out of the gutter. The captain's wife was with the captain. In fact, she was the reason Elizabeth acted so weird.''

"I must have missed a vital part of this story," I said.

"The captain's wife's is some big muckety-muck with the Feds," said Chuck, as if that made things clear.

"So?"

"Do you remember telling Elizabeth that you'd requested my services hacking into a computer?"

"Yes. I told her exactly what you said, that you couldn't and even if you could, you wouldn't.''

"Well, Elizabeth figured that me being me, I went right ahead and did it anyway. Then we show up yesterday with Dude Bob at the exact time she had a federal agent in her apartment watching her dog puke. Elizabeth did what came naturally: She reverted to her sixties fear of authority and panicked. She thought the captain's wife might be after me.''

"That's absurd.''

"It is, but it sounded pretty good when Elizabeth told the story. I like the fact that she protected me.''

"What about Dude Bob and her?"

"That situation is currently up in the air.''

I was thinking about Elizabeth and coaxing some of that pliable denim into a flower shape when a bicycle messenger dropped off the hats Margo had borrowed. Inside the box she'd enclosed a set of photos and a note. "These are great, no?''

They were great, yes. Every season I take a few snapshots to document the current collection, but I've never had professional fashion shots before. The photos were contrasty black and whites. The hats looked dramatic and sculptural and even though they were last year's fall hats they went well with the clothes of the soon-to-be-famous designer. I couldn't wait to see the final magazine layout.

Seeing my old fall hats served as a reminder that although I'd managed to get summer hats up in the window by spring, which was the selling season for summer, I wasn't exactly ahead of the game. Fashionwise, fall was charging full steam around the corner. For many designers, fall was over months ago, but the nature of my business allowed me to work a bit closer to the actual season.

Not that it wasn't confusing. I was always thinking ahead or behind, designing one line, selling another, making yet another. I've been known to lose track of the real world. When I shiver, I have to look out the window to know if it's summer and the air conditioner is on too high, or if it's winter and the radiator isn't radiating.

Vinnie called midafternoon. "We still on for tonight?"

"Sure," I said. "Why don't you come by and see my shop? After that we can go to this great little Italian place I know."

"I'd like that, Brenda, really, but this deal is coming to a head and I've got a late meeting, so I thought maybe we could meet at my hotel. Around sevenish?"

An alarm went off in my head. A man. A hotel. I paid it no mind. It wasn't like Vinnie T was a stranger. "See you at seven."

About four o'clock Taffy came by with the contact sheets of the meat market hooker raid and bomb scare, proving that she really was a location scout.

"Look around," I said. "You can have any hat in the shop."

While she looked through my collection, I sat down at my worktable and studied the photos with a magnifying glass. They emphasized building exteriors, but there were incidental hookers and other people hanging out, including Maris Montmyer. She was in two of the early shots. After the cops came on the scene, Taffy recorded the raid. Maris was in most of those shots, looking really angry. I was more interested in the two early photos, the ones Taffy took before the raid. I studied them carefully and was disappointed that neither showed Maris using the telephone at the corner or a cellular. One showed her as she first arrived in the area. The other showed her standing in front of one of the new restaurants. As I looked at that picture, all of a sudden I wasn't so disappointed anymore. Sitting in the window of that restaurant, sipping a cocktail, was Susan Chapoppel.

I didn't know if that was significant or not, but it sure gave me something to think about.

Taffy chose a bright orange bowed visor. On her way out she asked if she could take some pictures of Midnight Millinery. "Your space has real potential as a location. I'll put it in my database."

For someone who doesn't like to travel, I like hotels. I associate them with glamour gleaned from old movies, an image that has very little to do with reality. When I envision room service, I see a rolling cart covered with fresh white linen, a single fresh flower in a crystal vase, domed covers on platters, rare wines, silvery champagne buckets, elaborate coffee services, and four-star food lovingly prepared by a toqued chef. In reality the cart won't fit into the cramped room, the food is straight out of the microwave and served on Styrofoam, and the halls are littered with plastic trays full of rancid garbage and cigarette butts awaiting pickup from the service crew, who are always late.

And this was a nice hotel.

I gingerly stepped around someone's lunch, possibly Vinnie's, and knocked on his door. Vinnie opened up right away, greeted me with a small hug and a big smile. I was halfway across the room before I noticed he wasn't alone.

"Brenda, this is Richard. Richard and I are working together on the deal I told you about."

"Pleased to meet you, Richard." He was a pleasant-looking man with a friendly open smile and a nice handshake. He looked vaguely familiar. "Are you from Belup's Creek?"

Richard laughed. "Born-and-bred Brooklynite. I represent the other company."

"I see."

"I better get out of here now. Two's company and all that. I get the distinct impression that Vinnie would like to be alone with you. I can't say as I blame him. See you tomorrow, Vinnie?"

"Sure."

"Hope to see you again too, Brenda."

With a wink he was gone.

So, after all these years Vinnie T and I finally had our date. We were at a classy restaurant, and not the drive-in, but you can't have everything.

We waited in the bar for our table. The place was filled with a trendy, fashionable crowd. I was appropriately attired in my short black dress. I spotted one of my hats across the room on the head of a stylish woman and pointed it out to Vinnie with great pride.

Soon we were escorted into the large dining area. Dinner went by in a swirl of conversation. We talked about people, places, and things I hadn't thought about in years. I brought him up to date on Kathilynda's search for Nado. We had yet another good laugh at her expense. He told me about his job for Belup Development and the proposed merger, which, from what he could tell, was moving along quite nicely.

Over dessert Vinnie T dropped a bomb. "If this deal goes through and I play my cards right, there's a damned good chance they'll want me to run things from this end."

"Does that mean you'd move to New York?"

He nodded. "Since my divorce I've got no reason to stick around Belup's Creek." He touched my fingertips. "I can think of at least one good reason to be here."

*   *   *

I wished I'd left Jackhammer at Midnight Millinery instead of the apartment, so I could avoid Kathilynda. To tell the truth, I felt positively swoony. All I wanted to do was get into bed, tune in the oldies station on the radio, listen to sappy love songs all night, and think about Vinnie T. Or Johnny.

I could hear the television blasting from out in the hallway. Kathilynda must have figured out how to run the sound through the stereo. I let myself in.

She was sprawled out on my mattress; the TV was perched next to her on a pillow. When I entered the room, she flicked it off. "Where've you been so late? I've been calling Midnight Millinery all evening."

I could have made it easier on myself by lying, but it would have been short-term. Like my grandfather used to say, "A lie'll always sneak back and bite you." So I told the truth. "Dinner with Vinnie."

She clapped her hands together. "Oooh Brenda Sue. What did I tell you? The two of you were meant to be. I bet you were together in a previous life."

The only previous life I knew was the one where Kathilynda sabotaged my drive-in date with Vinnie T. "We went out to dinner, that's all. I doubt I'll ever see him again." Unless, of course, he called me, or I called him.

Kathilynda giggled. "I can't wait to tell everybody back in Belup's Creek."

"Nothing to tell. Nothing happened. Nothing at all."

She bent her lip down in an exaggerated pout. "That's too bad. You know, Brenda Sue, you could do a lot worse than Vinnie."

A note from Pete was stuck under the door of Midnight Millinery. The business group had scheduled an emergency meeting for tomorrow afternoon. "Whatever you do, don't let Julia Pond catch wind of this." Like I talked to Julia. I made a note of the meeting time, then did exactly what I'd wanted: dozed off listening to love songs of a quaint time that seemed very long gone.

A half hour of that crap and I was bored to death. I'd been wrong. That quaint time wasn't long gone at all; it had never been. I turned the radio off. I had real thinking to do, about real stuff, in the real world, like what the hell did it mean that Susan Chapoppel had been in that restaurant on the night her lover was murdered.

Vinnie T meant nothing to me. Besides, the last thing in the world I needed was another distraction. On that note I was out like a light.

25

The very first thing I did after I woke up was think about Vinnie T. The second thing I did was to resolve not to think about Vinnie T, which was next to impossible, because the third thing I did was answer the phone. Speak of the devil.

"I just wanted to hear your voice," said Vinnie. Once he had, he said he'd like to see me again.

Before I could bite my tongue, "I'd love to" slid out of my mouth and into the receiver.

"Tonight?" he asked.

By then, I'd gathered my wits. "Tomorrow would be better."

That way, I rationalized, I'd have some time to get these crazy thoughts out of my head.

I hadn't checked the answering machine the night before. Four new calls about Nado had come in. The loonies: a woman who claimed to have seen Nado in her dreams every night for the last twenty years, and a man who said Nado was the reincarnation of his evil uncle. And then possible paydirt: A lady had spotted Nado in the lingerie department at Bloomingdale's, and someone else had seen him eating a hot dog in front of the Empire State Building. Much as it pained me to admit it, and as absurd as it seemed, Kathilynda really was on to something.

Later that morning, Kathilynda dropped by to get directions to the Museum of Modern Art. "I much prefer the old masters," she said, "but I must remember this isn't about me, it's about Nado, and he's got a thing for the abstract."

I found myself encouraging her. "Be sure to take lots of posters. They're getting results."

"Hardly surprising," she said. "I know my man. Speaking of men, are you seeing Vinnie T tonight?"

"No, Kathilynda. I told you, there's absolutely nothing going on between me and Vinnie T."

"Whatever you say, Brenda, but remember the refrain."

"What refrain?"

"Johnny on the Jumbotron."

Elizabeth wheeled her collapsible shopping cart into Midnight Millinery. "I wanted to let you know everything's hunky-dory with me and Dude Bob." She needn't have said a word; it was obvious from the way she glowed. "I freaked out when I saw Chuck. I thought maybe you'd talked him into hacking again. It's not every day I have a federal agent and a police captain standing in the middle of my apartment watching their bulldog throw up."

"How is Elmo?"

"I talked to the captain earlier this morning. Elmo's back to normal."

"Did the captain happen to mention the Royce Montmyer case?"

"No. Are you still on that?"

"Yes. Lance is in a bad way. In addition to everything else, he's having an artistic crisis."

"Oh my, I've been there before," said Elizabeth. "Tell him he has my deepest sympathy."

"I'll do that."

"Well, I must go. I'm meeting the Dude at the paint store. Today we decide on colors."

The cart was halfway out the door when she stopped.

"This misunderstanding with Dude Bob was all my fault, wasn't it? I never should have put on that widow veil."

Later that morning I looked out the window as Elizabeth and Dude Bob passed by. Elizabeth's collapsible shopping cart, now filled to the brim with paint cans, weaved back and forth on the sidewalk in front of them. They seemed very happy, very much in their own little world, very much like two peas in the same pod.

A little after three o'clock I went next door to Pete's Café for the business association's emergency meeting. I assumed the subject was the homeless situation and the return of Elliot. But I was wrong. The subject was once again Julia. They'd already started when I got there, so I made myself a watercress and tomato sandwich, grabbed a seat near the front, and listened.

They wanted to force Julia's Trick Shoppe out of the neighborhood.

"She's gone way too far this time."

"You can say that again," said Anna of the bakery. "That goddamned talking casket is absolutely the last straw."

Had I heard right? "Excuse me," I said. "What's a talking casket?"

"Exactly that," said Barry, the publisher. "It's a life-sized casket that talks."

I burst out laughing. "You've gotta be kidding."

"I wish," said Anna.

"It's true," said Pete. "It's a black wooden casket rigged up on a wheeled platform, and damned if the thing doesn't talk. I guess it's got a tape recorder inside."

"Julia hung out in front of the bakery with it and scared my customers away," said Anna. "The casket makes rude suggestive obscene comments in a loud raspy voice. I don't see how you could have missed it. She pulled it all over the Village last night. She offended hundreds of people, thousands maybe."

"I had a dinner date in midtown."

"Well, excuse me. You're not wasting any time, are you?"

"What do you mean?"

"Johnny Verlane. Everybody knows he dumped you for that movie star."

I was at a loss for words.

Pete held up his hands and stopped that conversation. "I believe the subject is Julia."

Those assembled had plenty to say about Julia and her talking casket. Someone wondered if she needed a license. The consensus was that there probably never had been a talking casket in Greenwich Village, and therefore no one had authority over it.

"So we're stuck with Julia and her goddamned Trick Shoppe and her goddamned talking casket? Is that what you're saying?" said Anna.

A man I'd never seen at one of our meetings before stood up and said, "It's obvious that Julia Pond will not listen to reason. I'd say it's time we took action ourselves."

His words, and the way he spat them, sounded a tad extreme for my taste. "What exactly do you mean by that?" I asked. It came out much louder than I expected.

"What I mean is, there's lots of ways to get rid of freaks like Julia. Damn cops are useless. Landmarks Commission is a joke. It's time we get serious. I've got plenty of action ideas."

"Action ideas? Like what?" I said, this time much louder, and intentionally so.

Everyone stopped their little side conversations. There was dead silence as we waited for the man to answer.

He shrugged. "Hey, we don't have to take this, right? We'll drive Julia out." He looked out into the crowd of shopkeepers. "Come on, guys, you with me on this?"

Heads bobbed up and down. Somebody stuck a fist into the air. "Right on."

I stood up. "Now, you all wait just a minute."

Later Pete told me that I climbed up on a table to deliver my full tirade. I have no memory of such a thing.

"I can't believe what my ears are hearing," I said. "I don't like Julia Pond's stupid store. Personally, I don't like Julia Pond, but you guys have an attitude worse than two tons of plastic vomit."

"We're only thinking of the good of all," said Anna.

"And the children."

"Save our children."

"You're misguided." I launched into an impassioned speech in defense of Julia. I defended her right to be in the Village, I defended her right to be obnoxious and arrogant, I defended the right of her store to belch, and I defended her talking casket. I ended with a rousing reminder of what the Village had always been, and if I had anything to do with it, what it would always be—a neighborhood known for its tolerance, a place where anything and everything goes. "We are not the aesthetic police."

When I was done and looked out into the crowd, everyone was staring. Pete started to applaud. Others joined in.

The man with the action plan looked angry. "So why don't we just kidnap the friggin' Statue of Liberty and sit her ass on a bench in Abingdon Square?"

Pete told me that except for that guy, there wasn't a dry eye in the place. "The only thing missing," he said, "was patriotic music swelling in the background. I think 'YMCA' by the Village People would have been appropriate."

The worst part about doing good and being right was that later Julia herself came by Midnight Millinery and thanked me.

"Who's the snitch?" I asked.

"In this neighborhood, gossip travels at the speed of light."

She brought me a present, one of those green foam rubber hats that look like the Statue of Liberty's crown.

Not even Kathilynda had purchased one of those.

"I'll bet you don't have any hats like this," she said.

"No I don't. Thank you."

"It's the least I can do. I heard some mighty nasty things were said at that meeting. Buncha asshole blowhards, if you ask me, but until this settles down, I think I better park my casket at the apartment at night. It might not be safe alone in the shop."

"Not a bad idea," I said. Of course, I regretted that immediately.

She'd brought her fat mean yellow cat Irving with her, except now he wasn't mean. He made nice to Jackhammer. They chased each other and frolicked around the shop, knocking over displays. Julia and I either half glowered or half smiled at each other; I couldn't tell which.

On her way out, Julia thanked me again effusively.

I'd created a monster.

I called Kathilynda to warn her that she might run into a talking casket in the hallway.

"That's just great, Brenda Sue. Somehow I'm not surprised."

"So, how did your day go? Did you find Nado at the Museum of Modern Art?"

"Nope, but I came back with a fistful of postcards, a new respect for Picasso, and a lovely nylon tote bag."

I took Jackhammer for a long walk. We wound around the Village and ended up in the meat market—the scene of Maris Montmyer's alibi.

Too bad Taffy's photos didn't show Maris calling in the bomb scare. That didn't mean she hadn't, but I didn't know how to prove that she had, which left me pretty much nowhere.

I walked by the restaurant where Susan Chapoppel had been that night. She sure had herself a ringside seat to the hooker raid. And, come to think of it, an alibi for the time Royce Montmyer was killed. She was the one person who didn't need an alibi. Susan wasn't the type to bite the hand that fed her and Royce Montmyer had been feeding her quite nicely.

On the way home a car slowed down beside me. The driver looked exactly like one of those drug dealers I'd seen in the garage. He rolled his window down, gave me a once-over, then sped off. I was starting to get nervous when I noticed New Jersey plates on the car. What a relief. The guy was looking for a hooker.

26

Bright and early Kathilynda came by
Midnight Millinery.

"Where're you off to today?" I asked.

"Well," said Kathilynda, "I'm picking up definite vibes
about Central Park. Nado's not used to being surrounded
by cement and tall buildings. My guess is about now he'll
be needing a tree fix."

It was a beautiful day for the park. To my knowledge
Nado was never the outdoorsy type, but who was I to argue
Kathilynda's methods?

"Any more calls about Nado?" she asked.

"He was spotted at the Statue of Liberty."

"I'm closing in, Brenda Sue. I can feel it in my bones."

"I hope so."

I called Lance. I didn't expect him to answer, not in the
middle of an artistic crisis, and he didn't. However, I left
a message, figuring he was monitoring. "Hope you're feeling better. Here's some news to cheer you: Kathilynda is
closing in on Nado and I'm about to blow Maris Montmyer's alibi sky high." That last was an exaggeration, or
perhaps an out-and-out fib, but I figured once Kathilynda
found Nado it wouldn't matter. Lance would be off the
hook with the cops and with his co-op board.

* * *

That done, I allowed my mind to stray. What to wear to dinner with Vinnie? He'd already seen my long black dress and my short black dress. I decided on a deep brown sheath I'd made last year when I fell for the proclamations in the fashion press that brown was the new black, and decided to see for myself. It wasn't, but I liked the dress anyway. This year they claimed navy was the new black. I say, not if I have anything to do with it.

I rooted through previous collections to see if I could find a hat to go with the brown dress. I came up with the perfect shiny black straw. A little squished, but a shot of steam perked it up.

I heard loud angry familiar voices outside on the street. A car door slammed shut, then another, then a string of curse words filled the air.

I looked up to see Johnny roll his suitcase over my transom. Did he look engaged? I couldn't tell. Mostly he looked mad.

Lemmy chugged in behind him, red-faced, spewing goddamns. Goddamn this, goddamn that, goddamn everything in between. From what I could tell he was mad at Johnny, the cab driver, and the world.

Outside, the cab idled at the curb. The driver stuck his arm out the window, middle finger held high. He waved it around for several seconds, then peeled out, leaving long black tire marks on West Fourth Street.

Lemmy looked first at Johnny, then at me. "You wanna know why I didn't tip the bastard?" he shouted. "I got this personal policy regarding gratuities. I don't tip assholes who pull over to the side of the road, shake a slimeball fist at me, and threaten to toss me out of the cab if I don't shut the hell up."

Johnny sat down on my vanity bench. He sighed as if he had the weight of the world on his shoulders. "Lemmy's been like this all the way from Los Angeles," he explained. "He's picked fights with me and anybody else foolish enough to cross his path." He turned to Lemmy. "You've got to spout off, don't you?"

"You'd spout off too," said Lemmy. He stamped his feet, his arms batted up and down like he was trying to fly. "Do you fully understand that Johnny here, our very own Mr. Tod Trueman, Urban Detective, plunged his entire freaking career down the toilet?"

"I will not compromise the Tod Trueman character," said Johnny. "Brenda, you won't believe what Lemmy wants me to do."

"I know," I said. "Lemmy told me."

"It's no big deal," said Lemmy. "Just a little tweak is all."

"Tweak this." Johnny made an obscene gesture that involved his entire forearm. "An Iowa setting, an apple-pie-baking wife, a station wagon, two-point-five kids, two cats, one dog, and a herd of pigs—that is a very big deal, not a tweak."

Johnny, born and bred in New York, couldn't be expected to know that pigs didn't gather in herds. Later I'd set him straight on proper pig lingo and tell him about the hysteria over the proposed pig farm on Charles Street. Later I'd ask if he was engaged. For now, pigs and fiancées were not the point. Johnny's artistic integrity was at stake.

Lemmy flung his hand in the air, vaguely toward New Jersey and the rest of the country. "Out there. That's where all the good crime is. I'm bored as a gourd already thinking about New York crime. We're washed up as a crime capital. If our boy's gonna get in the movies, we've got to repurpose Tod Trueman, get him to the boonies, where, if the good lord's willing and the creek don't rise, crime still runs rampant."

I hit them with a cold, hard fact. "We had a murder in the neighborhood while you were gone."

Johnny said, "I know all about that. Over in the Hudson Shadow, right? I hear you're right smack in the middle of it."

"Where'd you hear that?" I asked. I doubted that Royce Montmyer's murder got any play in LA.

"Your houseguest—Kathilynda, I think—she's been keeping me updated on that, and a lot of other things."

"When did you talk to Kathilynda?" Kathilynda hadn't breathed a word about any calls after the one she thought was somebody pretending to be Johnny.

"Many times," said Johnny. "Every time I called you were out with some guy, so I talked to her."

"Why didn't you try calling the shop?"

"Because I tried you at home first, and Kathilynda told me you were out."

"Well, she lied."

"Back up a minute," said Lemmy. "What's going on? How come nobody tells me nothin'?"

" 'Cause telling you something," said Johnny, "would mean talking to you, and I'm not talking to you."

Lemmy held out his hands. "See what crapola I have to deal with? So, Brenda, what's with this murder? Give me the scoop."

I did the condensed version.

Lemmy shook his head and rolled his eyes. "As high concept, it's a stinkeroo. Misuse of power. Dead guy in a parking garage. Burnout living in his van. Comedic relief by inept cops. A little hanky-panky on the side. Been done hundreds of times, thousands."

"This is real," I said.

"Reality, as you should know by now, often sucks. It doesn't make the first cut."

They were off again, arguing about Johnny's career.

I was fed up. "That's enough. Out. Both of you. I've got hats to make and a shop to run." And a date to get ready for, an ex-husband to find, and a murder to solve.

Neither said another word. Johnny stormed out the door and walked toward Bleecker Street. He pulled his suitcase behind him. Lemmy, who lived uptown, hailed a cab.

What a pair. I preferred Lemmy in small doses. Johnny . . .

well, he was another story, the denouement of which would depend on his marital status.

I settled back down to work. Three stitches later Johnny showed up again. "Now that Lemmy's gone—" He stopped short, because Lemmy wasn't gone.

Lemmy's cab pulled up to the curb. Lemmy hopped out, marched into the store, and confronted Johnny. "I knew you were gonna do that."

And so they resumed their fight. Jackhammer joined in. He banged his front paws against his pile of fabric and made weird synthesizer-type sounds. I didn't want to take sides, but in the end, as he knew I would, I defended Johnny.

Lemon B. Crenshaw will probably never understand the concept of artistic integrity. However, he shut up and listened, nodded, and left. This time for good.

I was alone with Johnny for the first time in a long time.

"Thanks, Brenda."

"It was nothing." I looked at him, around the eyes, wondering.

"It's good to be back. I could use some New York food. Want to go to Angie's tonight?"

"Tonight? Uh . . ."

"We have to talk."

"All right."

I told myself it wasn't really such a creepy low-down thing to do to Vinnie. In fact, it was because of Vinnie that I agreed to see Johnny. I'd be better able to assess how I felt about Vinnie once I was clear about Johnny's situation.

I called Vinnie. "About tonight," I said. "Something came up." I didn't want to elaborate myself in to a lie.

He was fine with that and even made a joke. "Don't tell me," he said, "Kathilynda, on a tour of Radio City Music Hall, stumbled across Nado dressed as a Rockette."

"No such luck," I said, "but she is getting close."

We rescheduled for the next night. He had another late meeting that evening with Richard, which meant another trip uptown for me, and again Vinnie wouldn't get to see Midnight Millinery. But what the hell, if things worked out, there'd be plenty of time for that in the future.

I couldn't believe it when a limousine pulled up outside. I thought it was the landlord again, but this time it was Maris Montmyer. The last time I'd seen her she was dressed in all white and getting into a white limo, presumably on her way to her face-lift. Now she was getting out of a black limo, dressed in all black, her face covered by the widow's veil.

"I'm so glad you're here," she said. "Be a dear and make sure this hat is properly anchored. I'm on my way to put in an appearance at Royce's memorial shindig. I wouldn't want any slippage. I'm afraid even Dr. Ruggetay can't speed up the healing process. Underneath it all, I'm still a mess."

I was dying to see how much of a mess. My successful design thwarted my efforts to see through the veil.

Maris sat at the vanity. The hat and veil were rock-solid secure. I made a couple of adjustments anyway to make her feel that she'd not wasted her time. "How'd the surgery go?" I hoped she'd let me take a peek.

"Wonderful. Dr. Ruggetay is a true artist, a regular Leonardo." She twisted her head around and up toward me. Although I couldn't see in, I felt her penetrating stare. "You know," she said, "girl to girl, it's *never* too early."

It took a moment for her meaning to sink in. I made a conscious decision not to be offended.

She went on. "An early pinch, a little fat injected, can save a heap of trouble, pain, and money in the future."

"Really," I said.

"Absolutely. I should go now, mustn't be late or people will talk. Not that they're not already talking. Half of Royce's relations think I killed him. Can you imagine?"

I laughed. "Any news on the police investigation?"

"No. I don't know what's taking them so long. They must be incredibly incompetent. It's obvious to me who did it."

"Really? Who?"

"Royce's sweetie's husband, Lance something or other."

27

I didn't wear the brown sheath after all. Angie's was a jeans and T-shirt kind of place. Besides, it was only Johnny. Yeah right, only Johnny.

I stopped outside Angie's and put Jackhammer in his canvas bag and told him to keep his head down. Then I paused to check my reflection in the plate-glass window. I figured I looked okay. At any rate I looked like me.

Tommy waved from behind the bar. He lifted his eyes toward the back room to let me know Johnny had already arrived. As I pushed my way through the crowd, I thought about how I'd much rather not be here, not be meeting Johnny, not be steeling myself to hear live and in person, straight from the horse's mouth, that he was engaged to the guest starlet.

I thought back to the night of Johnny's bon voyage party. I'd assumed too much when Johnny said he wanted to talk about this "just friends crap." Now it looked like the signal I'd picked up on wasn't the one he'd meant to send, but then Johnny and I never had been too good at communicating. If we had been, things would have been different long ago.

Johnny was hunched over a dark beer at what used to be our table, the one where if I held my head exactly right I could still make out the initials we'd carved back when we were more than just friends, before that incident with the orange and yellow shag rug.

"Hey," he said.

I slid into the booth across from him. Jackhammer crawled out of his bag. When he stood on the seat, he was tall enough to rest his chin on the table.

Johnny reached across and scratched Jackhammer between the ears. "Hey, little doggy. Sorry about the ruckus this afternoon. Thanks to my hothead agent, I didn't take time to say hi."

Jackhammer wagged his stub. He liked Johnny a lot.

Johnny leaned back and said, "You're looking at one happy guy. I am thrilled to be back in New York."

"Does that mean you'll be staying in New York?"

"You don't think I gave that Iowa pig gig serious thought, do you?"

"Not Iowa, but I thought maybe . . ." Actually I didn't know what I thought. Or more precisely, I didn't want to think about what I thought, which was that the guest starlet, his probable fiancée, might prefer the climate in Los Angeles. I searched for the right words.

"I'm a New Yorker," said Johnny. "We don't transplant well."

Raphael the waiter came by. "The usual?"

I nodded. "And one of your special burger balls for Jackhammer."

Raphael left and I continued my search for the right words to say what was on my mind. Or for Johnny to say something.

This was not one of those comfortable silences that good friends sometimes share. This particular silence was horrendous. Why didn't he tell me about his engagement? Was he waiting for me to come right out and ask?

I studied his face. Did he look like Vinnie T? A little, maybe. Like Kathilynda said, it was around the eyes. Then again, it could be the lack of light in Angie's back room.

Tommy kept the place dark enough to hide decades of dirt and dried puddles of beer.

"So," said Johnny, breaking through the silence, "here we are." His eyes focused on mine.

"We certainly are," I said. "Here."

I just loved the free flow of conversation.

Raphael brought our food, a welcome interruption. Jack-hammer downed his burger ball in one gulp. I, exercising restraint, chewed each bite of my grilled cheese one hundred times. That gave me a good excuse not to talk. Johnny too seemed to linger over his cheeseburger.

As happens, we inevitably finished our food. Johnny signaled to Raphael for more drinks, another dark beer for him, a red wine for me. When his beer came, he took a big swallow, then leveled his gaze at me. "Who's this guy you've been seeing?"

That hit me like a ton of head blocks. "Guy? What guy?"

"Come on, Brenda. We've known each other a long time. Your friend Kathilynda—"

"First off, Kathilynda is not my friend. She is my first ex-husband's estranged wife. Second, she made all that stuff up. Back in Belup's Creek it looks bad not to have a date, especially on a Saturday night, so she lied when you called. Like I told you earlier, I wasn't home because I was at Midnight Millinery. At work. Alone."

Johnny took another swig of beer, then, very serious, said, "Oh."

Not that I owed him an explanation or anything, but I felt obligated to tell him about Vinnie T. "Kathilynda and I had dinner with this guy we both used to know back in high school. He's in town on business. Then I met him again, for old times' sake."

Another swig. "I see."

"He looks like you."

The right side of Johnny's bottom lip twitched. It might have been a smile. "Really?"

"Yeah. A little. Around the eyes."

Another conversation used up, exhausted. I still hadn't asked the question. He still hadn't volunteered the answer.

Jackhammer curled up and went to sleep.

What seemed like five minutes went by before Johnny cleared his throat and said, "If Kathilynda's not your friend, why did you let her stay in your apartment? Were you friends before she married your ex?"

"No. In fact, long before she married Nado I couldn't stand her. The reason I let her stay has to do with Nado and Lance, not her. Despite her wacky methods, she's closing in on Nado."

"So this guy and you—"

I cut him off and told him how well my hats were doing and about Margo and the upcoming magazine spread and about the neighborhood business association and Julia and her stupid talking casket and Elliot and Pete and Dude Bob and Elizabeth and finally I couldn't stand the suspense anymore. "Turner and McKinley are mad at you because they weren't invited to your bon voyage party and now they're afraid they won't get invited to your wedding."

There. I'd said it. It was done. The die was cast. I downed half a glass of wine, sighed, and slumped against the wall of the booth.

Johnny looked utterly perplexed. He stared at me. Finally he said, "Are you proposing to me, Brenda?"

I came very close to spitting out the last half of that glass of wine I just poured down my throat. "No."

"Oh."

"What is this, you think because you're engaged to that guest starlet that all of a sudden everybody wants to marry you?"

"You think I'm—"

"Well, aren't you? I saw you with her on the Jumbotron at Times Square."

"Times Square? You went to Times Square?"

"Yes I did."

"What the hell for?"

"Oh for chrissakes. The question is not why I was in Times Square. The question is why when I was in Times Square did I look up and see you in a passionate forty-foot-high lip lock with your guest starlet fiancée. That is the question."

I waited for the answer.

"I can't believe you think I'd get engaged to anyone. That engagement was a publicity stunt, something Lemmy dreamed up in one of his jerkier moments. He didn't spring it on me until it was too late to back out. He promised me they wouldn't broadcast it outside of LA. He said he'd call you so that in case somebody got wind of it, you could tell everybody it wasn't for real."

"The only time Lemmy called, he tried to get me to convince you to do the Iowa pig thing."

"Damn his shiny bald head."

"Why didn't you call me yourself?"

"I did. Remember?"

"So you're not—"

"No. And you're not—"

Glad we got that all straightened out.

Johnny walked me back to Midnight Millinery, gave Jackhammer a pat on the head, me a peck on the cheek, and said he was jet-lagged and exhausted and that he'd call tomorrow.

Like Johnny, I was exhausted, but not too exhausted to call Lemmy Crenshaw and give him a piece of my mind.

"Goddammit, Lemmy," I said.

"Hey, Brenda. Hang on a sec. I've got Brew Winfield on the other line. Believe it or not, we were just talking about you."

Brewster Winfield, doting snake owner and lawyer, had once helped Lemmy out of a pickle that I was partially responsible for getting him into. They sometimes teamed up to work on various moneymaking schemes.

Lemmy came back on the line. "Sorry about that, Brenda. Brew says that once you find that ex-husband of yours, he oughta sue the city, the police department, and my two least favorite detectives in the world, Turner and McKinley. Teach those assholes a lesson. Get 'em fined and fired."

"They love you too," I said, "especially after they didn't get invited to Johnny's bon voyage party."

"Gee, I wonder how that could have happened," said Lemmy. "My database must have malfunctioned."

"Look, Lemmy, right now I don't care about my ex, or Turner and McKinley. I want to know why you didn't tell me Johnny wasn't really engaged."

"Oversight," he said. "Oops, somebody's beeping in. Back in a flash."

Oversight? He had a lot of nerve.

Lemmy was back. "Brenda, I've gotta go. Johnny's on the other line. Boy, is he ever pissed."

"Tell him—"

But Lemmy was already gone.

Once I calmed down, I felt a great relief. Johnny wasn't engaged. Johnny had never been engaged. And to think I'd been seriously wondering how life would be if Vinnie T moved to New York and . . .

I must have been out of my mind, flipped one of my lids. I mean, Vinnie T? I barely knew the guy. Deep down inside, even though I hadn't admitted it to myself, I'd been pretty shook up when I thought Johnny was engaged.

I had to break that date with Vinnie T. It wasn't fair to lead him on. On second thought, I owed it to Vinnie T, for old times' sake, to tell him in person. I would explain over dinner.

I'd just settled down in my sleeping bag when the phone rang. I let the machine pick up. It was another call about Nado. A woman had seen him at the Museum of Modern

Art. And then a couple of minutes later another call. Nado had been seen in Central Park. Amazing, fantastic. Everywhere Kathilynda went, Nado had gone before. She was catching up to him. It was too good to be true.

Oh. Too good to be true. Suddenly I had a really bad thought. What if it was literally too good to be true? What if, as she'd done in high school when she pretended to be Vinnie T, Kathilynda had disguised her voice and made those calls about Nado? Damn her. She just had to prove to me that she knew her man.

I felt sick, foolish, and guilty all at the same time. I'd gone from complete skepticism in Kathilynda's stupid search methods to total belief that she'd find Nado. As a consequence, I'd slacked off on my own search for Nado. Not only that, I'd downplayed the fact that he could be in danger. If anything happened to him . . .

And Lance. What good had I done him? Had I found Nado for him? No. Had I found out who killed Royce Montmyer? No. I'd come up with some plausible motives, uncovered a couple of crimes. I'd proved nothing.

I'd show that Kathilynda Annamarie Cooper Sharpe. I'd expose her search for the sham it was.

I called Dweena and explained what I needed. "How would you like to tail Kathilynda, see where she goes, what she does, and if she makes any telephone calls write down the exact time?"

"Sounds like fun to me."

"I'll call you tomorrow as soon as I know where she's headed."

28

Kathilynda smiled sweetly. "Of course, Brenda Sue, I understand completely. Now that Johnny Verlane is back in town, you want your apartment back so you can get your life together."

The tall thin pale vampire narrowed his eyes. "Of course, Miss Midnight, I understand completely. Now that Johnny Verlane is back in town, you want your furniture back so you can get your apartment together."

Vinnie T touched my cheek softly. "Of course, Brenda, I understand completely. Now that Johnny Verlane is back in town, you want . . ."

A car alarm blurted and wailed and hiccuped and rudely ripped me out of the dream before Vinnie T finished his sentence.

The meaning of that dream was clear: I wanted my apartment back, and I wanted it now. I'd had enough of Kathilynda. She wasn't doing me any good, or Nado, or anybody. The time had come to have it out with her and throw her the hell out.

Full of resolve, I crawled out from beneath my blocking table, grabbed Jackhammer, and headed home.

"Kathilynda, we have to talk."

She glanced at the clock on the wall—my clock, my wall, in my apartment, where she'd been for far too long.

"Will it take long?" she asked. "I'm signed up for a ten-thirty tour of the UN."

I copped out. My resolve dissolved and flew out the window. I was stuck being me, Brenda Midnight, who always bends over backward to avoid conflict. Instead of confronting her about the calls, I said, "Well, Kathilynda, now that Johnny Verlane is back in town—"

"Ohmygod," she shrieked. "Johnny Verlane is in New York, and you didn't tell me! Brenda, how could you? You know I'm dying to meet him."

My resolve surged back.

"You did a rotten thing, Kathilynda. Johnny told me he talked to you many times on the phone. You told me about one call. Why didn't you tell me about the rest?"

" 'Cause you got all hot and bothered."

"So you lied, once, twice, how many times did you tell him I was out on a date? You can't imagine how much trouble your lies caused me. Or maybe you can. You're a good liar, aren't you, especially on the phone?"

"What are you getting at, Brenda?"

"Those calls about Nado."

"What calls about Nado?"

"You know damn well what I'm talking about, Kathilynda. Then there was my date with Vinnie."

"Last night?"

"No, not last night. I canceled that. I'm talking high school, Kathilynda." At last. I erupted, I screamed, I cursed, I said all the things I'd wanted to say for years.

Throughout, Kathilynda remained calm. When I finished with an impressive burst of expletives, she had the nerve to plead innocent, claimed she had never pretended to be Vinnie T or made those calls about Nado. "Disguised my voice? How?"

"There's a million ways. You could have talked through a hair-dryer tube, or put cellophane over the mouthpiece."

"Oh Brenda Sue, get real." She laughed. "I better take your umbrella to the UN. I think it might rain."

* * *

I called Dweena and told her Kathilynda was headed for the UN.

"I'm on my way," said Dweena.

To walk off my anger, I took Jackhammer over to West Street and looked across the Hudson River at New Jersey. It did me good to confirm that yes, I really did live on a teeny-tiny island chockablock full of people, places, and things.

A Circle Line boat full of tourists passed by. Then a garbage barge. I studied the rotted piers, the busy highway, and realized it would be a real bitch to dump Kathilynda's body in the river. There were too many obstacles to overcome. I had to come up with a more elegant solution to my housing problem.

On the way back I stopped and sat on the stoop across from the Hudson Shadow parking garage. Jackhammer marked the area. I watched and waited for something. Whatever, it never happened.

What was I going to do? Trusting Kathilynda to find Nado had cost way too much time. I needed to regroup, rethink, and take action. Quickly.

I went to the shop. No reason I couldn't make some more bowed visors while figuring out what to do.

Vinnie T called to confirm our date for that night. I let the machine swallow his call. Maybe I shouldn't go.

I could take the easy way out and keep breaking dates until he went back to Belup's Creek, or I could do the right thing and tell him—what?—that Johnny and I were friends and therefore I couldn't see him anymore even if he moved to New York? That made no sense.

Okay, I'd go out with Vinnie T that night as planned, play it by ear, and hope Johnny didn't find out because he'd be certain to read something into it. I returned Vinnie T's call and told him sure, we were on, and that I looked forward to seeing him again.

My stomach growled. I'd been too worked up to eat breakfast. I went next door to Pete's Café to stoke up. "Got any of that cream of carrot soup?"

He did, so I stayed and ate. Pete joined me at the table. "You were amazing at our meeting," he said.

"I don't know what got into me."

"Whatever it was, I'm glad it did. Some of our members were headed down a damned scary path. You stopped them cold. Nobody else had the guts. I'm proud of you."

"Julia found out about it and came by Midnight Millinery," I told him. "She thanked me for my support and gave me a cheesy foam rubber Statue of Liberty hat."

Pete chuckled. "Looks like you've got a new friend."

Elliot walked out from the back of the restaurant. "Toilet's fixed."

"You're a miracle worker, Elliot." Pete gave him a twenty-dollar bill. "Want to stay and have some lunch with us?"

"I'll have to take a rain check on that. I've got to see Anna. The bakery's got a window stuck open and it looks like rain." He smiled and slipped out the door.

"Good to have him back," said Pete.

"What's the story with Elliot anyway?" I asked.

"Like everybody else in this city, he's fighting for a little bit of space and looking for another job."

"What kind of work?"

"I thought you knew. Elliot was the building super over at the Hudson Shadow. When the board fired him, he lost not only his job but his home too. That's why he's on the street."

"Why'd they fire him?"

"I don't know."

I was stunned. Yet another person with a motive to kill Royce Montmyer. I didn't think Elliot had done it, but I sure wanted to know the circumstances of his firing, how the board had handled it, and what Royce Montmyer's role had been. Maybe Elliot had known too much about the illicit activities in the garage. As soon as he got back from fixing Anna's window I'd ask him.

I'd just got back to Midnight Millinery when a fancy shiny metallic green car pulled up in front. Dweena, in a dazzling red jumpsuit and strawberry blond banana curl wig, hopped out of the driver's-side door, rounded the car, opened the shotgun door, and yanked Kathilynda, then Nado out of the car. She ushered the squabbling duo into Midnight Millinery.

Nado? Kathilynda? Dweena? What the hell. This was better than I'd hoped for.

"Indeed," explained Dweena. "I followed Kathilynda to the United Nations, lurked on the fringes of her tour, which she left early to avoid the long lines in the gift shop. That's where she ran into Nado. They started screaming at each other. I offered them a ride, in fact I insisted, which reminds me, I really should get this fine specimen of a vehicle to a less conspicuous location. I'll be right back."

For the second time in as many days Midnight Millinery became a battle scene. I couldn't tell what Kathilynda and Nado were fighting about—something about Greece perhaps, which made no sense, although it tied in to the UN. I assumed that like most fighting couples whatever they were fighting about had absolutely nothing to do with what they were mad about.

Kathilynda stopped to catch her breath. Nado did the same. I seized the opportunity to ask, "Nado, where the hell have you been?" He told me, as amazing as it seems, he'd been to all the places Kathilynda had looked, in the same order, including, today, the United Nations. She'd been on the French language tour; he'd been on the American. "It was like we'd never parted," said Nado.

"Yeah," sneered Kathilynda. "We picked up our fight right where we left off."

I didn't care about their fight. "Where did you stay at night?"

"Oh that," said Nado. "After I ditched that cop car, I ran into the first place I found open that early, an all-night organic restaurant run by a pack of vampires. Well, they're not really vampires, at least I don't think so, the sun doesn't seem to bother them, but they sure as hell look the part. It's like a theme restaurant. They showed me how to make organic borscht. I showed them a thing or two about hot dogs. In gratitude they let me stay in their storage room."

More vampires? Perhaps later I could digest that information. At the moment, all I could say was, "You shouldn't have run." Nado started to speak. I held up my hands to stop him. "I know, I know, Turner and McKinley, the detectives who were taking you in, weren't terribly clear. I've talked to them. They never thought you murdered Royce Montmyer."

Nado looked at me and scratched his head. "Murder? Did somebody get murdered?"

This was too much. I collapsed onto my vanity stool; Jackhammer jumped up on my lap. I scratched his head and stared into space. Kathilynda took over and told Nado about the murder. She got enough of the story right that I didn't have to intervene.

Nado said he hadn't seen a thing, that he'd been drunk-as-a-skunk passed out, then Kathilynda started shouting again saying he drank too much, and he said you'd drink too much too if you had to crash in that noisy garage, and you wouldn't believe some of the stuff that happened there, which didn't surprise me at all. I asked him to elaborate, but he was too busy fighting with Kathilynda. The subject turned to Greece again. I was trying my damnedest to figure that out when Dweena came back with a bottle of champagne. "A celebration. Nado is found."

"Great," I said.

She popped the cork like a pro. Bubbles spilled down the side of the bottle. She and I celebrated while Nado and Kathilynda battled.

29

Kathilynda and Nado made up. I'm not sure how it happened. Dweena and I had moved out of range of the fight. I was telling her about Taffy, the location scout and the hooker I'd met, when all of a sudden we noticed the silence. Nado and Kathilynda had stopped yelling and were clinched in a teary hug.

"Cute," said Dweena.

I lifted my champagne glass. I'd soon have my apartment back.

Turner and McKinley would be thrilled when I brought them my fugitive ex-husband. Possibly even more thrilled than if I promised them an invitation to the wedding Johnny wasn't having. Possibly thrilled enough to give me the skinny on the 911 tapes.

First I had to convince Nado to go.

"Are you out of your mind, or do you think I'm out of mine?" He crossed his arms and gave me a look of defiance.

"It's the New York City water supply," said Kathilynda. "I'm convinced they put something weird in it. Makes New Yorkers nuttier than a bakery full of fruitcakes. Brenda Sue's a sad example of what can happen."

The three of us were back at my apartment. Nado, after

remarking on the weird furniture that hadn't been here when he last saw the place, plopped down on the banana couch. Kathilynda dragged out all her shopping bags and showed Nado all the junk she'd bought.

"You *have* to go," I said in a vain attempt to get his attention.

She trotted out the turquoise teddy.

He stroked the soft fabric and looked at his wife. "Nice."

"Hundred percent silk," she said. "Fifty percent off. Bloomingdale's."

It was no use. I went into the kitchen to make a cup of coffee. While I waited for the water to boil, I pondered what to do. I could always call Turner and McKinley and tell them I had their man. However, they'd be easier on Nado and more obliging to me if he turned himself in.

I poured the water into the filter and watched it swirl around the coffee grounds. I came up with a way—not very nice, but worth a try. "Oh Nado, would you please come out here a minute?"

In all the excitement I hadn't had much of a chance to look at him. Now the first thing I noticed was his dopey accidentally avant hair style. It still looked like a flattop gone to seed, only the top was taller and the sides had grown prickly. As soon as he cleared the doorjamb, I reached around him, slammed the door shut, grabbed on to his shoulders, and backed him up against the refrigerator. There was very little room to maneuver with both of us in the tiny kitchen. "If you don't go to the precinct," I whispered, "I'll tell Kathilynda."

He looked puzzled. "Tell her what?"

"Oh, I don't know," I said, musing. "Maybe I'll tell her what *really* happened the night of Johnny's party, how you and I—"

"But nothing happened."

I smiled. "Hey, it's your word against mine. She already thought the worst once."

"You'd lie to Kathilynda about something like that?"

"If I were you I wouldn't put it to the test."

I kicked the door open and let him squeeze by. "Thanks, Nado. It's good we had this little talk."

He went back into the room. "Honey," he said to Kathilynda. "I think Brenda Sue's right. I have to face the music and turn myself in to the police."

As Nado and I walked down Hudson Street toward the precinct, I said, "Turner and McKinley will no doubt try to scare the living daylights out of you, but they won't bust you for stealing their car."

"I bet they're plenty pissed."

"That's an understatement. They'd love to toss you in the slammer and throw away the keys, but to do so would call attention to what you did, which would once again remind their peers what they did, which was to lose their vehicle, which made them the butt of every joke. If I were you I'd be real nice to the detectives."

Nado stopped in front of the White Horse Tavern. "I remember this place. It's right over here that . . . Hey, where's the hole?"

The hole in the street, the hole Turner and McKinley ran their car into, the hole that gave Nado his opportunity and henceforth caused no end of problems for me and Lance and even Kathilynda, had been filled up again.

"Gone," I said, "but don't worry. It'll be back someday."

"What is all the digging for?" asked Nado.

"Nobody knows anymore. It's simply a fact of life on Hudson Street. The ever-present background against which all else unfolds."

"It wouldn't happen in Belup's Creek."

"Face it, Nado, nothing happens back in Belup's Creek."

＊　　　＊　　　＊

I stopped in front of the precinct and gave Nado a last-minute pep talk. "Remember, the policeman is your friend."

"I don't know about this, Brenda Sue."

"Come on," I said. "It'll be fun. Something you can tell your grandkids."

"Grandkids? Kathilynda's not—"

I pushed him through the door. Inside I nodded to a couple of uniform cops I knew and then headed straight up the narrow staircase. No one stopped us or asked where we were going. Nado seemed impressed that I knew my way around.

To keep the element of surprise, I hadn't phoned ahead. I figured the detectives would be in, what with the low crime rate and all. I peeked into their cubicle. Turner had his expensively shod feet up on his desk. I didn't see McKinley.

I poked my head in. "Afternoon," I said.

Turner looked up, started to smile, but cut it short when he saw Nado. "I'll be goddamned," he said. He swung his feet to the floor and glared at Nado.

Nado swallowed hard and kept his mouth shut.

McKinley strode in, smiled at me, did a double-take when he saw Nado. "Son of a bitch," he said. He too glared at Nado.

I felt sorry for Nado. The fourteen freckles on his nose stood out in high contrast against his noticeably paler skin. He looked from Turner to McKinley. "I can explain," he said. Then he got a surprised look on his face, like he couldn't believe he'd said that. The next time he opened his mouth, nothing came out.

I took over. "It was all a misunderstanding," I said. "Nado thought you were running him in on vagrancy charges because he was living in his van."

"Vagrancy?" said McKinley. "We don't do that. We're detectives, for chrissakes."

"You know that, and I know that, but Nado didn't know

that. He's not from these parts. It was his first time in New York.''

Turner slammed his fist on his desk. "I suppose where Nado comes from it's okay to take an official police vehicle for a joyride and dump it within spitting distance of another precinct?''

"Where Nado's from, the cops are known to be rather brutal. Head hitters. Gut slammers. They don't care if they leave bruises. And so, unattuned to the more benevolent nature of big-city detective professionals such as yourselves, poor Nado was scared out of his wits."

"We only wanted a statement," said Turner.

"Did you happen to mention that to Nado?"

Turner and McKinley both looked at each other and shrugged.

"See what I mean?" I said. "Anyway, that's all water under the bridge, right?"

"Pretty damned murky water," said Turner.

McKinley made a face. "Shaky damned bridge."

The detectives got over it. They were far too interested in what Nado had seen the night of the murder to dwell on the messy details of their own humiliation.

Nado, who seemed so sincere he was tough to doubt, stuck to his story that he'd been in a drunken stupor. "Three sheets to the wind. I didn't know anybody got murdered until Brenda Sue told me."

They went over the same questions again and again. "Did you see anything? Hear anything? Feel anything? Smell anything?"

"No, no, no, and no."

"Shit," said Turner. "You really don't know anything, do you?"

Nado shook his head.

"Rough case, huh?" I said.

"As if you don't know," said Turner.

"It's a tough one, all right," said McKinley. "Killer may

as well have been from Mars. There's a hundred people with thousands of motives, and not one of them checks out.''

"Maybe I can be of some help," I said.

"Here we go again," said Turner, lifting his eyes toward the heavens.

Ignoring that, I plunged ahead. "A lot of illegal stuff went down in that garage."

"Went down? My goodness, Ms. Midnight, aren't we hip to police lingo," said Turner. "I suppose Mr. Verlane has kept you on top of things. We know about the criminal activity that *went down* in the garage."

"Did you know that Royce Montmyer was having an affair with a married woman?" I hated to steer the conversation so dangerously close to Lance.

"Yes, Ms. Midnight," said McKinley.

"It's the first place we looked," said Turner. "Both wronged spouses have ironclad alibis."

"Both?"

That meant they didn't suspect Lance.

Over the last few days tiny thoughts had flickered across my consciousness, thoughts that Lance was the killer and had hired me to find out who knew what so he could keep one step ahead. What an incredible relief. I felt a thousand pounds lighter. I couldn't suppress a smile.

"I see you like that Ms. Midnight," said Turner. "Of course we know that Mr. Chapoppel asked you to look into the matter and despite our warnings you've been hanging around the Hudson Shadow."

"No way," I said. Then I saw the expression on Turner's face. "How did you know?"

"Same way we knew that Mr. Chapoppel didn't do it. Your friend Lance Chapoppel was under surveillance at the time of the murder. He is not, and has never been, a suspect in the murder of Royce Montmyer."

"Surveillance? What for?" I remembered Lance had said he was being watched. At the time I chalked it up to paranoia brought on from too many late nights designing noodles.

"Someone, we believe his estranged wife, anonymously reported that Mr. Chapoppel was building sophisticated bombs in his apartment. We investigated, the Feds investigated. Nobody found nothing but a bunch of noodles. We kept him under surveillance to be sure."

Nado must have felt the conversation had moved safely away from him. "Why would an estranged wife want to do that?"

I leveled my gaze at him. "To make trouble for an ex, or in this case a soon-to-be ex. Tempting, no?"

Nado looked down at the floor. "Oh."

"Actually it's pretty funny," I said. "Susan wanted to make trouble for Lance, but in doing so she assured he was in the clear for the murder of her lover."

"Not only that," said McKinley. "She also provided an alibi for Mrs. Montmyer, who was our other most likely suspect."

"The hooker raid?" I said.

"Not bad, Ms. Midnight," said Turner. "You do get around. You must know that someone reported one of the hookers had a bomb."

I nodded. "It had to be Maris Montmyer. She hired a hit man and needed an alibi for herself. If you listen to the nine-one-one tapes—"

Turner shook his head. "Close but no cigar. We noticed a familiar MO."

"Modus operandi," said McKinley for Nado's benefit.

Turner went on. "We listened to those tapes. They confirmed our hunch that Susan Chapoppel, not Maris Montmyer, called in the meat market bomb scare. Apparently Mrs. Chapoppel likes to report bombs. She solves a number of problems that way. She used a false report to cause trouble for her almost ex-husband and used a false report to cause trouble for her lover's wife."

"Susan saw Maris in the meat market that night."

"That's what we figure," said Turner. "Susan Chapoppel was having dinner in one of those new restaurants, she saw Maris Montmyer walk by, hatched the plan, made the call from her cellular phone, and watched the whole bust from her window seat."

"So it really wasn't Maris Montmyer who called it in."

"Afraid not, Ms. Midnight, but you get an A for effort. Not bad for a milliner."

"How about this?" I said. "Maybe Susan Chapoppel had a fight with Montmyer or was having second thoughts or something and she wanted to get rid of him. She could have hired a hit man to blow him away and gone to the restaurant to give herself an alibi." I didn't believe that myself, but McKinley's reaction made me mad.

He snickered. "Once again, Ms. Midnight, you've been watching too much TV. You've got hit men on the brain. That might happen on *Tod Trueman*, but never in real life."

"Speaking of Tod," said Turner, "we hear Johnny Verlane is back in town. Did he get that movie deal?"

"He turned down an offer."

"Johnny said no to Hollywood?"

"He did, and rightfully so. The honchos wanted to move Tod Trueman to Iowa, make him a sheriff, give him a wife, and kids, and a pig farm."

"Get out of here," said McKinley.

"It's true," I said. "Lemmy wanted Johnny to jump at the chance, but Johnny stuck to his guns. They had a big fight."

"Johnny oughta dump that chromedome buffoon agent of his," said Turner.

Nado piped up with, "Lemmy Crenshaw is a cool guy. When I met him at Johnny Verlane's party—"

"*You,*" roared Turner. "*You* were at Johnny's party?"

"Sure," said Nado.

It seemed like a really good time to leave.

*   *   *

On the walk back up Hudson Street, Nado was greatly re-lieved. He bopped along, swinging his arms, like he didn't have a care in the world.

I felt good too. Things were winding down quite nicely. Johnny was here, Nado and Kathilynda would soon be there, Lance was in the clear, Royce Montmyer's murder was back in the hands of the police where it belonged, and my summer line was strong. There remained one dark cloud on the horizon—my date with Vinnie T. I had to tell him we had no future.

30

Nado and I bumped into Julia as she wheeled her casket through the lobby of my building. It was the first time I'd seen it. Julia had on another bright baggy muumuu. She flashed an equally bright sunny smile, and boomed, ''Hiya neighbor.''

I mumbled something appropriate and tried to brush past her to get on the elevator.

''Hey, what's your hurry? Aren't you going to introduce me to your friend?''

I straddled the elevator door. It banged against me, then bounced open and banged against me again. ''Nado Sharpe, Julia Pond.''

''Pleased to meet you, Nado.'' She pumped his hand enthusiastically.

''Groovy haircut,'' said the casket in a raspy pre-recorded voice.

On the way up in the elevator Nado said, ''Whoever said New Yorkers aren't friendly?''

Nado bragged to Kathilynda about his adventures at the precinct and told her the casket had complimented his hair. Kathilynda said he'd damned well better get a haircut before they got back to Belup's Creek.

I dragged the phone into the kitchen and called Lance Chapoppel. I was prepared to leave a message, but the live version of Lance picked up. I got right to the point. "Great news. You're in the clear. You're not a suspect. You never were a suspect. Not only that, but Kathilynda found Nado. He'll tell your co-op board you knew nothing about him living in your parking space."

Lance asked a whole bunch of questions. I answered and filled in the details.

"I told you someone was watching me. Susan is beyond belief. This will help me out when we negotiate the divorce settlement. How could I ever have married such a woman?"

"I'm afraid that question will go forever unanswered."

"Who do the cops think murdered Royce Montmyer?"

"Not you, not Nado, not Maris, not Susan, so who the hell cares which broker, buyer, seller, drug dealer, car thief, or prostitute did the deed?"

"You're right, it doesn't matter."

"Where've you been anyway? I was worried."

"Yeah, I know. Sorry about that. I had to get away for a while. My life's completely screwed up. My wife left me, my noodles look like your last year's hats. The noodle thing sent me off the deep end. However, I consulted with my lawyer and he came up with a solution. Brenda, how would you like to have a noodle named after you? The Brenda goes great with pesto. You'll go down in culinary history."

"I'm flattered. I don't know what to say."

"Then it's done. And dig this. A cereal company has shown interest in a sugar-coated version."

I carried the phone back into the room in time to hear Nado and Kathilynda talk about getting the van tuned up so they could hit the road to home. Music to my ears.

"Do you know of a good auto mechanic?"

"No, but I'm sure Dweena does. Give her a call. She's in my book. Meanwhile I've got to get out of here."

I got the brown sheath and a pair of patent leather heels out of my closet and slipped into the bathroom to get dressed. When I came out, Nado said, "Looking good, Brenda Sue. Got a hot date?"

"I'll bet she's seeing Vinnie T," said Kathilynda.

"Vinnie T?" said Nado. "What's he doing in New York?"

"Business," said Kathilynda. "Belup Development is either buying or getting bought by some big New York company. Vinnie is doing the deal. He took Brenda and me out to this really fancy restaurant."

"Vinnie T is a creep," said Nado.

"You're just jealous," said Kathilynda.

"I am not. Why is Brenda going out with him? I thought she and Johnny Verlane . . ."

I made an effort to tune them out, but it was hard. They started screaming about Greece again, then Vinnie T, and something about Belup's Creek. When they got around to me and Johnny for the second time, I took that as my cue to exit. "I'll be back later tonight to get Jackhammer."

I went over to Midnight Millinery to get the black straw hat. I put it on and was adjusting the tilt when the phone rang. It was a fax from Margo with a note: "Here's an early look at the layout! I think it looks great!!" I watched over the machine as four more pages ground out in slow motion, to reveal, inch by inch, the magazine layout. The machine beeped that it was finished. I tore off the paper, crammed it into my purse, and left.

Off in the distance, somewhere over New Jersey, I saw dark angry storm clouds churning toward New York. I almost went back to get an umbrella, but the bus came right away. I figured it'd get me to Vinnie's hotel before the storm hit.

I settled into a seat and took out the fax, glad to have something to look at on the ride uptown. The photos had been cropped to show a lot of each hat and mere hints of dresses, a common practice. Naturally, I was elated. I wondered how the soon-to-be-famous dress designer felt about it. According to the article that zigzagged around the photos, he was a man who "knows his target market and has aimed his line accordingly." Buzzwords.

The article went on to describe how the designer had started out in a one-room East Village tenement making dresses for downtown friends, then friends of friends, and then friends of friends of friends, and then finally, boom. He was the next big thing. Would I ever be the next big thing? Probably not. I never thought in terms of my target market, and . . .

Wait a minute. Target market?

I put the fax away. I thought about target markets, markets, and targets, but mostly about targets. What if Royce Montmyer's killer hadn't hit his target? What if Royce Montmyer was not the target?

It made perfect sense. Even Turner and McKinley had said there were lots of people and lots of motives but none of them checked out. Royce Montmyer had been in the wrong place at the wrong time. He'd been killed in a shootout between rival drug dealers, or hookers, or car thieves, or brokers, buyers, and sellers, or some permutation thereof.

I found it oddly comforting that the murder of Royce Montmyer was a real crime gone bad, hardened criminals who'd screwed up, bullets gone haywire, instead of a cozy little murder among acquaintances over real estate or romance or the stuff acquaintances kill each other over.

Turner and McKinley would be thrilled; no matter what Lemmy Crenshaw thought, there was still crime in New York, enough to keep a couple of detectives gainfully employed.

Before I knew it the bus deposited me in midtown and roared off. I got lucky; it hadn't started to rain.

During the block-long walk to Vinnie's hotel I tried to refocus. I couldn't let my momentous realization about the murder of Royce Montmyer distract me from my purpose. Vinnie had done a lot of hinting about him and me. If he was serious I had to put a stop to that kind of thinking.

I got to the hotel a few minutes early, so I sat in the grandly decorated lobby behind a potted palm and watched people parade by. I pretended it was cocktail hour in the sophisticated art deco 1930s, an exciting time to be in New York. The Empire State Building and Chrysler Building were brand-new, and all the women wore really cool hats.

When it was almost time to go I flipped open my compact, checked my hat and lipstick. In the mirror I saw a familiar figure getting off the elevator across the room. It was Richard, the guy Vinnie was working with. When I turned to look, he waved and came over.

"Another stunning hat," he said. "I've got to get my girlfriend down to the Village to see your little shop."

"I'll make sure she finds something she likes," I said. "Is Vinnie up in his room?"

"He most certainly is. He's getting all spiffied up for your date. If you asked me, I'd say the guy kinda likes you."

Vinnie had a reservation in a restaurant on the top floor of the hotel. Kathilynda would have been disappointed; it didn't spin around. However, it had a great view. We were seated in a quiet corner. We watched the day darken prematurely as the storm clouds surrounded us. Dramatically romantic.

"Kathilynda found Nado," I said. "She ran into him at the United Nations."

"Really? That's great news."

"You can say that again. They kissed and made up and now it's like they're on their second honeymoon."

"How much longer will they be in New York?"

"Not long, I hope."

"Yeah, I bet you're tired of sleeping at your shop."

Kathilynda strikes again. Damn her anyway.

"Kathilynda wasn't supposed to tell you that," I said.

"You're supposed to think I have a penthouse with gobs of guest bedrooms."

"Hey, I may be from Belup's Creek, but I do understand the reality of New York real estate. It's a good thing I do, because this deal seems to be happening."

A waiter splashed ice-cold water in our goblets. Another brought a basket of fresh-baked, still-steaming breads. Menus were dropped off, specials recited. We ordered. Vinnie chose a high-priced California red wine. "We have a lot to celebrate."

I couldn't let this go on any longer. I couldn't bring myself to say anything either. This was a very tough situation. I'd never been good at this boy-girl kind of stuff. I lingered over the rolls in the basket, finally chose one, and buttered it very slowly. "Uh, Vinnie, there's something I have—"

"Brenda, I am so sorry, but you'll have to excuse me. I just remembered something I forgot to tell Richard. I really should call him. I'll only be a second. Don't go away."

I could not believe it. Business. Men. Businessmen. Yuck. It reminded me how lucky I was to have Midnight Millinery. I didn't make deals for a living, I made hats. It was very concrete.

Vinnie was gone much longer than a second, long enough for the wine to come. I went ahead and had some without him. It was okay, though I'd have preferred French.

Vinnie came back the same time our food arrived.

"Bad news," he said. "I'm afraid I'm going to have to hurry through dinner. Richard . . . well, what can I say? It's business. You know how it is."

Vinnie bolted from his food. I picked at mine; I'd rather not eat at all than eat fast. Under normal circumstances I'd have been angry. But these were not normal circumstances. Actually, this had worked out quite nicely. The whole purpose of my seeing Vinnie was to let him down easy. I no longer felt any obligation to do so. Not for old times' sake, not for anything.

During our very brief dinner, it started to rain. A huge clap of thunder sounded and a bolt of lightning lit up the sky, the buildings.

"Now, that's a sight," said Vinnie.

We finished eating. The storm pounded the city. Then, just as quickly as it began, it was over. So was dinner.

We got up from the table. Vinnie wiped his mouth and pecked me on the cheek. "I'll make it up to you. I promise."

I pecked him back. "It's all right. Really."

Together we got the elevator. "Go out with me tomorrow night?" said Vinnie. "Please. I'll come down to the Village."

To make things easy I said, "Okay." I'd call him tomorrow to break the date.

Vinnie got off on his floor; I continued down to the lobby.

A string of cabs lined up in the drive in front of Vinnie's hotel. I got in the first one, told the driver where I was going, leaned back, and relaxed. As far as I was concerned, Vinnie was history. With that out of the way, I was free to think about Royce Montmyer, and the fact that he hadn't been the target. I'd think it through tonight, then tell Turner and McKinley tomorrow. They'd better not laugh at me this time.

The cab pulled away from the hotel and stopped at a red light. As we waited, I felt the tiniest twinge of regret and turned back to take a look at the grand hotel. There was Richard, headed toward the door, on his way to see Vinnie, I supposed, to discuss whatever it was they hadn't discussed before. He moved fast. Just like a businessman. An airport van pulled alongside, momentarily blocking my view of him. As it passed by, it blew out a lot of exhaust, worse even than Nado's van. It left Richard coughing.

Good, I thought, and immediately felt guilty. Richard hadn't done anything to me. For that matter, neither had

Vinnie. It's just that his rushing off had been so insulting, it caused me to lose sight of the fact it had worked out for the best.

The closer I got to the Village, the better I felt. Everything really was back to normal. It wouldn't be long before I was back in my apartment and I wouldn't have to think of Nado or Kathilynda for a long time. I already wasn't thinking about Vinnie or Richard. Well, that wasn't exactly true. Thinking I wasn't thinking about something was pretty much the same as thinking about it. All of a sudden what I was thinking wasn't very pleasant. I was thinking how when I first saw Richard I thought I'd seen him somewhere before. I thought he might be from Belup's Creek. Now I remembered where I'd seen him before and it sure wasn't Belup's Creek.

31

I had the cab drop me off on West Fourth Street in front of Midnight Millinery. I watched as it sloshed away on the glistening wet cobblestones.

I didn't see Elliot around. He was probably still wherever he'd gone to get out of the rain. Too bad. It would have been nice to ask him a couple of questions, but I figured I could do without.

I looked into the window at Pete's. The café was busy and Pete looked harried. On a quieter night, I might have bothered him, asked if he remembered any specifics.

I'd been right about one thing all along: The man who paid Elliot to get lost wasn't a bum. Homeless men don't hand out hundred-dollar bills. About everything else, I'd been dead wrong. The man was no writer. He wasn't doing an article on the homeless for *New York* magazine.

I slipped into Midnight Millinery. I kept the lights off so no late-night customers would disturb me and sat down at my worktable to think everything through. I didn't much like my conclusion. Too bad it wasn't more like a bad hat. I couldn't change the trim, or tilt the situation, or turn it around backward, or give the brim a new twist.

Lemmy was right; sometimes reality sucked.

I couldn't alter reality; however, I was pretty sure I could catch a killer. First, I had to get Nado and Kathilynda out of my apartment.

The night had turned beautiful in the wake of the storm. The entire populace of the West Village had taken to the streets, to breathe in the clear night air. Any other night I would have grabbed Jackhammer and joined the throngs, but this wasn't any other night.

A sliver of light came out from under Julia Pond's door. I hoped that meant she was home and still awake. I rang her bell. When she answered, I quickly stepped inside her apartment. "I need your help."

I hadn't been in Julia's apartment since Randolph, the classic rotten-to-the-core neighbor, had been in residence with his exercise bike and two tons of arrogance. Julia was hardly the exercise bike type. Yet her apartment surprised me. I expected it to look like one of her muumuus. Except for the talking casket in the foyer, the decor was remarkably tasteful. Clean simple lines, fresh colors. Ikea Moderne.

Julia bustled around. She gathered up several catalogues from the couch and shooed Irving away. "Sit here," she directed. "Would you like a refreshment?"

"No thanks." I imagined joke ice cubes with flies embedded. It was nice of her to ask, though.

I told her what I wanted her to do. I didn't go into lengthy explanations, but told her only what she needed to know. "The situation is urgent."

She listened to my plea, asked a few questions. When I was done she squinted her eyes, frowned, slowly shook her head, and seemed about to say no. Then she surprised me. "What the hell? I'll do it. I've got to take the casket out anyway. Besides, it sounds like fun."

Everybody has their own idea of fun.

I let myself into the apartment. It was dark. Jackhammer charged into the foyer and jumped up into my arms. "Hey, big guy."

I went into the room and flipped on the overhead light.

Kathilynda sat up, groggy, and rubbed her eyes. "Back so early?" she asked. She had on a white I LOVE NEW YORK T-shirt with a big red heart instead of the word love. Nado had on a black version of the same shirt. Like her, he sat up, rubbed his eyes. "What time is it?"

"Ten-thirty," I said.

"We didn't expect you until *much* later," said Kathilynda.

"If at all," added Nado with a leer.

Kathilynda hit him with a pillow—my pillow. "I can't wait to hear all about you and Vinnie T. Is he gonna move to New York?"

"We had dinner," I said.

"And then . . ."

"That's all. He was in a hurry."

"Well," said Kathilynda, "I guess sometimes the sparks just don't fly, though you'd think after all this time—I mean, like high school, for chrissakes—something would have happened."

There was no time for banter. "What did you two fight about right before Nado left?"

"None of your business," said Kathilynda.

"Talk to me about grease." When I overheard their kiss-and-make-up argument, I kept hearing that word. Since they'd just been at the UN I thought they were talking about Greece, which made no sense. Grease, now, that made sense.

"What about it?" said Nado.

"That's what you two were fighting about, right?"

"Yeah, so what?"

"I need details," I said.

Kathilynda shot a vicious look at Nado. "Nado doesn't care about the environment. I caught him dumping the grease from our hot dog grill into Belup's Creek, not just once, but a lot of times. It was his brilliant way to cut costs.

I tried to make him see the big picture. That's what the fight was about."

"As usual," said Nado, "Kathilynda is making a mountain out of a molehill. Instead of paying a rip-off artist to haul the grease away I disposed of it myself. It's no big deal. Everybody does it."

"Like who?" said Kathilynda.

"The fried chicken place does it. Talk about grease. Jeeze. The burger joint. Also, your friend Vinnie T. I don't hear you complaining about him. I guess his shit doesn't stink. He was there late that night with some of those guys from Belup Development. They dumped stuff in the creek too. Hey, if one of the biggest firms in town can get away with it, why not me?"

"Why would Vinnie T dump grease into Belup's Creek?"

"I didn't say it was grease. I don't know what it was, maybe some kind of building material."

"Did he see you?"

"Oh, you better believe I made damn sure of that. I flipped him the bird. I never did like that guy."

"You're jealous 'cause he was cooler than you in high school," said Kathilynda.

"He's not cooler now," I said.

I told them what was up and what they had to do. They protested. I told them it was no joke. Then I took them next door to Julia's.

Things, and I'm talking things in the large sense, have a way of turning out real weird. Kathilynda and I had a lot of history together. Nado and I, even more. We'd been married. Snippets of ancient memories surfaced into my consciousness—bits of conversations, the clang of a high school locker slamming shut, the buttery smell of popcorn at the drive-in.

I transported myself back to Belup's Creek. Back then, and from that perspective, I examined what I was about to do. No way. Never in a billion years, not in my wildest imaginings would I have dreamed up the current scenario. Despite the severity of the situation, I cracked up. I laughed until tears ran down my face. I simply could not help myself.

Julia opened the lid on her talking casket. It made the appropriate spooky creaking sound, which made me laugh even harder.

"You don't have to laugh," said Kathilynda.

"Yes, Kathilynda, I do. Now get into the casket."

With a shudder she backed in. "I hate you, Brenda Sue."

"You do not," said Nado. "Brenda Sue's looking out for us."

Kathilynda grabbed Nado's arm and pulled him inside.

"That's right," I said. "Now squish together real close. That's good. With that, I shut the door on the talking casket.

I turned to Julia and said, "Take 'em away."

"I musta been nuts to agree to this," said Julia. She rolled the talking casket and its live human cargo around the corner to the elevator.

"Have a nice trip."

I would have loved to accompany Julia and her talking casket on their nightly promotional walk through the Village, but it wouldn't have been prudent. If someone was watching it would have been too obvious. Was somebody watching? Maybe. Maybe not. Better safe than sorry. Besides, how many times in a lifetime would I get the opportunity to pack my first ex-husband and his second wife into a promotional talking casket?

I'd have loved to gloat longer, but I had too much to do.

I called Chuck. "Breakfast. Seven o'clock tomorrow morning. My apartment."

"What's going on?"

"Can't explain now."

"You cooking?"

"No. Pick up some doughnuts on your way."

I called Johnny and had pretty much the same conversation except I told him to pick up the coffee. "Be sure to get lots of extra sugar for Chuck."

"Glad to see you," said Elizabeth. She wiped her hands on paint-spattered jeans. "The Dude and I needed a break anyway."

I breathed deep. "I love the smell of paint."

"Yeah, me too. I miss it."

The three of us sat on the floor and stoked up on coffee and pineapple ginger cookies, surrounded by half-built built-ins. I told them what the deal was.

"I'm so sorry," said Elizabeth. "You must feel terrible."

"Actually I feel pretty lucky. And I did get to put Nado and Kathilynda in a talking casket. That's got to count for something."

"What are you going to do, tell Turner and McKinley?"

"No. I have a better way. I'm going to show them. You know how they are. Actions speak louder than words. The thing is, I need your help."

"Count me in," said Elizabeth.

Dude Bob frowned. "What exactly do you want us to do?"

Elizabeth gave him a dirty look.

"It's all right," I said. "He's right to ask. The object is to keep innocent bystanders, both pedestrians and vehicles, away from the Hudson Shadow garage tomorrow evening for a half hour or so. I figure the best way to do it, without attracting undue attention, is to stage a film shoot. You two will be the advance crew. You'll carry clipboards and walkie-talkies. If anybody approaches, turn them away."

"Brilliant," said Elizabeth.

Dude Bob looked skeptical.

"Really," said Elizabeth. "That kind of stuff happens all the time around here. No one will question a thing."

"Okay," said the Dude. "I'll do it."
"You'll need to coordinate with Chuck."
"Fine."

Jackhammer and I stayed in the apartment that night. He conked out immediately. I thought and rethought and worked out most of the kinks in my plan. Toward dawn I got a little sleep.

32

I woke up to the sound of Jackhammer's toenails clicking on the floor. He circled the mattress a couple of times, then plowed into the back of my knees. I opened my eyes and found myself surrounded by Elizabeth's furniture, which was now mine. It was definitely not the day to decide whether the banana couch should face the window. I looked at the clock. Good. I still had plenty of time to take Jackhammer for a walk before meeting with Chuck and Johnny.

Jackhammer headed straight for a pile of garbage bags in front of the Italian restaurant, the same restaurant I would have taken Vinnie to if things had turned out differently. I pulled Jackhammer away. "Garbage'll give you a belly-ache."

Chuck showed up right on time. "Hey, Brenda. You look awful, like you haven't slept in a week."

"Thanks."

He set four cardboard boxes on the coffee table. "Chuck Riley doesn't bring just any doughnut. Sensing a special occasion, I went up to Twenty-third Street and got us four dozen original glaze Krispy Kremes."

Moments later Johnny arrived with the coffee.

I talked. Chuck and Johnny inhaled Krispy Kremes. The doughnuts were done long before I was.

I didn't know how best to tell the story. After a couple of false starts, I ended up beginning with the end. "Vinnie T did it. Or rather, he hired Richard to do it."

"Who's Vinnie T?" asked Johnny.

"Who's Richard?" asked Chuck.

To Johnny I said, "Vinnie T is an old acquaintance."

Chuck smirked. "He's the guy who Kathilynda says Brenda's had a crush on since high school."

"Is that who you've been seeing?" asked Johnny. "That's just great. I go away and you date a murderer."

"I haven't been *seeing* anyone. Vinnie T and I went to dinner. I thought for old times' sake. He apparently had something else in mind."

"I'll bet," said Johnny.

"As to your question, Chuck, Richard is a hit man."

"Why would Vinnie T want to kill Royce Montmyer?"

"He didn't. He wanted to kill Nado."

"I think you better back up," said Chuck.

I took his advice. "Okay, from the beginning. Vinnie T and Nado never liked each other."

"Because of you?" asked Johnny.

"No. Not because of me. Just because. Now, fast forward to more current time. Nado dumps grease in Belup's Creek, he sees Vinnie T also dumping and gives him the finger."

"Very mature," said Chuck. "What did Vinnie T dump?"

"I don't know. Whatever it was, he sure didn't want Nado to know."

"Johnny nodded gravely. "Probably a DB."

"A what?"

"Dead body," said Johnny.

Chuck frowned. "Why didn't Vinnie ice Nado on the spot?"

"There could have been witnesses," I said, "or maybe

Vinnie T had to check with his boss first, or maybe he didn't have the means to do it. As far as I know he doesn't carry a gun. Anyway, Nado returns from his mission at the creek. Kathilynda's mad that he dumped grease, they have a huge fight, he takes off in his van and tells her he's on his way to New York to see me. Thanks to Kathilynda, Vinnie finds out where Nado is headed. You with me this far?''

"I think so," said Chuck.

"Yeah," said Johnny. "You have stupendous taste in men."

I continued. "From here on I'm only guessing. I think Vinnie hired Richard to kill Nado. I don't know if Richard is a real hit man or somebody Vinnie had worked with on the business deal. Given the way he bungled the job, I'd say he's an accountant who happens to own a gun. Richard needed to keep an eye on Midnight Millinery so when Nado showed up he could kill him. Richard had a problem. How can he stake out the place without attracting attention to himself? Solution: He pretended to be a bum. Who is more invisible than a bum? He wanted the street to himself, so he paid Elliot to get lost for a while. The first thought that crossed my mind when I saw Vinnie with Richard was that he was someone I'd known a long time ago in Belup's Creek. You know, vaguely familiar. When I realized where I'd seen him before, everything fell into place."

Johnny shook his head. "I should never have left town."

"Anyway, Richard waited on West Fourth Street. When Nado showed up, Richard followed him until he was ready to do the deed, then he shot him. Except he missed and plugged Royce Montmyer instead. Richard freaked out and split. Turner and McKinley nabbed Nado. Nado freaked out and split."

"Why didn't Richard pop Nado when Nado first showed up at Midnight Millinery?" asked Chuck.

Johnny explained. "In the movies, hit men, or accountants-turned-hit-men, often stalk their victims. It makes for more suspense.''

"I've got it," said Chuck. "Maybe he was waiting for Vinnie's check to clear."

I went on. "So Vinnie T came to New York to make sure the job got done right. Meanwhile Nado disappeared. Everybody's looking for Nado. I told Vinnie T that Kathi-lynda found Nado, before I realized he wanted him dead. I had to hide Nado and Kathilynda." I told them about the talking casket.

"Sorry I missed that," said Chuck.

"What now?" asked Johnny.

"I have a plan to trap Vinnie and Richard."

"I have a better plan," said Johnny. "Chuck and I will march you straight down to the precinct and you will spill the beans to Turner and McKinley. That's the safe, rational, foolproof plan."

I shook my head. "Say I do that. Say, given my track record or the fact I recently got Nado to turn himself in, the detectives actually pay attention to me. Say they even believe me. What can they do? Question Richard? What if meanwhile Vinnie T hightails it back to Belup's Creek? My plan is good. It'll work. At least listen. That won't hurt."

Chuck and Johnny grumbled. I plunged ahead and out-lined the plan. I didn't stop for questions. "So Richard and Vinnie T will be trapped in the garage. One of them will be armed, probably with the gun that killed Royce Mont-myer. Turner and McKinley will be on the scene to make the arrests. It's simple. It's elegant. What can go wrong?"

Chuck rolled his eyes. "Plenty."

He had a long list.

Johnny's list was even longer.

I answered most of the questions to their satisfaction.

"I don't know, Brenda," said Chuck. "I still say there are too many variables."

"Look, if Vinnie doesn't take the bait, I promise I'll go to Turner and McKinley. I have to do something soon. I can't leave Nado and Kathilynda in the back room of Julia's Trick Shoppe forever. Last night was already one night too many.''

"Bet they're pissed," said Chuck.

"I imagine they are."

"I can't believe you really sent them through the Village in a talking casket," said Johnny. "To tell you the truth, I find the whole talking casket concept a bit much to believe."

"It really exists, and I really sent them away in it, and it really couldn't happen to a more deserving couple."

"Remind me not to get on your bad side," said Chuck.

"Does that mean you'll do it? You'll help?"

"Yeah, I guess."

"How about you, Johnny? Are you in?"

"I don't know. My part's a lot more difficult than Chuck's."

"What do you mean by that?" said Chuck.

"Well, it is," said Johnny. "Just for starters, before we even get to the garage, I've got to convince Turner and McKinley, who are mad at me, to give me yet another driving lesson."

"Invite them to your wedding," I suggested. "Tell them to mark the day in their calendars."

"What wedding? I told you that was a publicity stunt."

"Turner and McKinley don't know that."

"You're asking me to lie."

"I only mention it as a last resort. It'll get you back on their good side."

"Until I don't get married. What then?"

"Hey, stuff happens. People break up. Plans change. So, mention your wedding, then tell them you need more lessons in how to drive like a cop for your movie deal."

"Another lie. I don't have a movie deal."

"Make something up, but not the Iowa sheriff. I already told them you turned that down."

"There's no other way?"

"Right offhand, I'd say no. Come on, Johnny. Tod Trueman would be up to the challenge."

Johnny looked as if he were in pain, as if I had literally twisted his arm.

"If things work out," I said, "Turner and McKinley will be very happy. They'll have you to thank for getting them involved."

"And if things screw up, they'll have me to thank for getting them involved."

"Nothing's gonna get screwed up."

I hadn't expected it would be so tough to convince Chuck and Johnny to go along with my plan. Chuck especially. He usually loved stuff like this. The entire incident with Elizabeth and Dude Bob had put him out of sorts. Chuck's feelings for Elizabeth were no secret. I remember one time Lemmy had teased him about it. "Chuckeroo," he'd said, "Elizabeth is old enough to be your mother, or even your mother's older sister."

"Yes," Chuck had said, "but the important thing is, she's not."

After Chuck and Johnny left, I gave Dweena a quick call and told her what I needed. "No problem," she said.

We made arrangements to meet at the Hudson Shadow.

Johnny thought his part was hard. I had to call Vinnie T and dangle the bait to get the ball rolling. It was a good thing I'd agreed to see him again.

This was one hell of a way to get closure.

The hotel operator put my call through to Vinnie's room. It rang three times before he picked up—enough time for me to go through several stages of panic. This had to work.

Deep breath. I tried to sound perky. "Good news. Kathilynda and Nado are headed back to Belup's Creek much sooner than I thought. My apartment is almost mine again."

"Fantastic," said Vinnie. His voice held steady. I'd have loved to have seen his face.

"The bad news is they're leaving tonight. I have to see them off, for old times' sake. I guess that pretty much messes up our date."

"It doesn't have to," said Vinnie. "What time are they leaving?"

"Around nine. I'm supposed to meet them in the Hudson Shadow parking garage. Believe it or not, after all this, Nado's van is still parked in my friend's space."

"Why don't we plan our evening around the Sharpes? I could meet you at your shop, say nine-thirty, ten."

"You sure you don't mind?"

"Not at all. What are the Sharpes doing today?"

"Running around like a couple of maniacs, cramming in as much as possible. Kathilynda says, 'So many souvenirs, so little time.' "

Vinnie laughed. "Until tonight, then. I'm looking forward to seeing you, Brenda."

"Thanks, Vinnie, for understanding. I'd have hated to miss Nado and Kathilynda."

"I can dig it," said Vinnie.

33

Chuck walked briskly beside me. "Nice night for a hanging," he muttered.

I too got caught up in the mood. "Yeah, right."

Actually it was a nice night. Too bad I was too tense to appreciate it. Too bad I was walking with Chuck to the showdown at the Hudson Shadow parking garage. Too bad about a lot of things.

"I assume Johnny successfully bamboozled Turner and McKinley into giving him another driving lesson?" said Chuck.

"Yes," I said. "He called me this afternoon. The wedding invitation worked like a charm. He told them—"

"Please, Brenda, if you don't mind, I don't want to hear about weddings right now, not fake weddings or real weddings or any kind of goddamned weddings in between."

"Sorry." He had it much worse than I thought. "Do you want to talk about it?"

"No."

I glanced over at Chuck. He looked straight ahead, refused to make eye contact. I knew it was the wrong time to bring up Dude Bob, but I had no choice.

"You and Dude Bob will need to coordinate to make sure—"

Chuck cut me off. "I know what I have to do."

239

Neither of us said any more until we got to the Hudson Shadow.

"Quick checklist," I said. "You've got the controller, walkie-talkies, and cellular?"

"Yep."

"I have the signs you made up for the corridor. Dude Bob and Elizabeth will be here soon. I see that Dweena's already here. I guess that's it."

"I guess it is."

"Good luck."

"Yeah."

Chuck veered off and walked around to the side of the building. I met Dweena at the lobby entrance.

"What's with him?" asked Dweena.

"He's upset about Dude Bob and Elizabeth."

Dweena caught me eyeing her microskirt.

"I know," she said, "chartreuse is over. I think I'll dye it navy blue."

"It's not that," I said, "but do me a favor and stick to the periphery of the lobby."

"I know the drill," she said. "Shiny floor, right?"

"Right."

"So what do you think about navy for fall?"

"If I were you, I'd go straight to black. It's much more powerful."

The revolving door placed us right in front of the doorman's station. Dweena quickly moved to the side. I smiled at the doorman, nodded my head toward Dweena. "She's with me. We're both working on that project with Mr. Chapoppel."

In more ways than one, we skirted the edge of the lobby to the elevator.

Dweena and I were alone in the basement, a fact which I took as a good omen. The most complicated part of my plan concerned keeping innocent bystanders out of the garage. Chuck had printed up signs for me to hang throughout the corridor that led to the inner door of the garage: CLOSED FOR NECESSARY EMERGENCY REPAIR. PLEASE USE OUTSIDE GARAGE DOOR. SORRY FOR THE INCONVENIENCE. THE MANAGEMENT. I taped them up.

"What happens when people go around to the other door?" asked Dweena.

"I hope no one will want to get into the garage in the short time we need it. If they do, I've got Elizabeth and Dude Bob pretending to be setting up for a film shoot. They'll stop everybody except Richard and Vinnie T. Then they'll let Turner and McKinley roar into the garage. As a further safety measure, Chuck rigged up the garage door controller so that it will override any other signals. Nobody can get in unless Chuck opens the door. After everybody's in, he'll shut it tight as a clam until I call his cellular."

"You're getting very good at this."

"Thanks. I'd rather be making hats."

I hung the last of the signs on the inner garage door itself. Dweena and I went into the garage and I made sure the door locked behind me. Then we scoped out the place, looking for a good car to hide in.

"Oh my. I cannot believe our luck," said Dweena.

"What is it?"

"This vehicle I stand before. Notice the license plate."

I should have known. "Diplomat."

"This is a very special diplomat, a very paranoid diplomat. We've got ourselves a bulletproof automobile complete with tinted windows."

Dweena got a small tool out of her faux leopardskin clutch bag. In the blink of a false eyelash we were on the inside looking out. Waiting. I checked my watch twice.

I figured Vinnie T and Richard would be on foot. That way it would be much easier for them to slip unnoticed into the garage in the wake of someone else going in or out. Of course, they would have no idea that Chuck would open the door specially for them.

I held my breath when the garage door creaked opened. As I expected, they were on foot. What I didn't expect was the gut-wrenching awful feeling I got when I saw Vinnie T. I had very much wanted to be wrong about him. But I was right. The plan was moving along. The door closed.

Vinnie T and Richard split up and cased the joint. They met up again near Nado's van and stepped into the shadows. It was almost like they weren't there.

The garage door mechanism started up again. The door lifted and two cars quickly rolled down the incline. Two cars? What had Chuck done? The cars pulled up next to each other and popped their respective trunk lids. Two men exited, one from each car. Both walked around to the rear of the cars. One wore a black suit; the other, navy blue.

Not those goddamned drug dealers again. As Lemmy Crenshaw would say, craparama.

"Which part of the plan are they?" asked Dweena.

"This is the part where everything gets all screwed up."

"Oh."

Moments later the squad car raced into the garage, siren blaring, with Johnny behind the wheel. Johnny, Turner, and McKinley were here to save the day. Now things started to go right, except they were already wrong, so what was right wasn't really right anymore.

I'd repressed the reason why Johnny needed frequent driving lessons. It wasn't only that he couldn't drive like a cop. The fact is, Johnny couldn't drive. Period. He couldn't drive like a cop, or even like a stoned-out half-crazed cab driver.

In all the excitement, at high speed, he overshot the sharp turn coming into the garage. He managed to make it inside, but just barely. He skidded and smashed the squad car into a three-foot concrete-block guide wall.

My heart stopped. I'd killed Johnny and Turner and McKinley.

The siren continued to wail.

The alleged drug dealers stared at the squad car.

I didn't see Vinnie T or Richard anywhere.

It seemed as if hours went by before I detected activity in the squad car. I heard the familiar voices of Turner and McKinley, cursing a blue streak. Then, according to plan, the driver's-side door opened and out came Johnny. He appeared undamaged.

I hadn't killed anyone yet.

According to plan, I opened the door of the diplomat car and screamed, "Watch out. They're armed."

In the original plan, my statement was meant to refer to the gun either Vinnie T or Richard would have, which would surely turn out to be the murder weapon. The statement was intended to spur Turner and McKinley into action. Since things were all screwed up, when I said, "They're armed," I didn't mean Vinnie T and Richard. The arms I referenced were the guns in the hands of the alleged drug dealers. Those guns were now pointed at Johnny.

Johnny ducked down behind the door of the squad car, as he'd done many times on the *Tod Trueman* set, only this time the cameras weren't rolling.

Everyone froze in their respective positions.

I'd liked to have seen an EEG of the collective brain activity as all the players tried to figure out exactly what the hell was going on.

The drug dealers figured it out first, although they got it wrong. They each understandably concluded that the other was in cahoots with the authorities. The guy in the black suit slowly brought his gun around and pointed it at the guy in the navy suit. Then the guy in the navy suit pointed his gun at the guy in the black suit.

Dweena whispered. "You're right about navy. The black is so much more commanding."

I looked over at Dweena and saw that, like me, she was terrified.

Turner and McKinley are big-city detectives. They are trained to figure out what happened after the fact. I have my own opinion as to their level of expertise, but right then my opinion was quite beside the point. What mattered right then was that they got enough figured out to get Johnny back into the car, where it was safer, especially for an actor who was pointing his finger at two very pissed off and confused armed drug dealers.

As for Vinnie T and his colleague Richard, I don't know what they knew or when they knew it. I doubt they figured out that the whole setup was a trap to catch them. I doubt they guessed my role. Again, that's beside the point. What mattered was that they'd be quick to perceive the need to scram.

That much I was able to figure out.

I scanned the garage, looking for any movement. I spotted Vinnie T and Richard creeping toward the inner door that led into the basement. No problem. I knew it was locked. I'd locked it myself.

Then I watched in horror as Vinnie T turned the knob with ease and pushed the locked door open. He and Richard barreled through.

Goddamn it anyway. Somebody must have unlocked the door from the other side. Over Dweena's protests I got out of the bulletproof diplomat car and ran after Vinnie T and Richard. I yelled, "Turner. McKinley. Stop them." I was operating in complete no-plan mode. I was determined to stop them. I'd gone to far too much trouble to let them get away.

I darted through the door behind Vinnie T and Richard. Just in time I slammed on my brakes. In front of me was a pile of fallen humanity. In addition to Vinnie T and Richard, there was Rita the woman from the laundry room, and a ladder, all tangled up together.

And a gun skittering across the corridor.

I pounced on the thing. Then very gingerly picked it up.

"Shit," said Rita. She picked herself up and patted her body to check for damage.

Vinnie T and Richard got back on their feet and tore off down the corridor toward the elevator.

I pointed the gun at them. "Stop, or I'll shoot."

They stopped, turned around. "It doesn't have to be like this, Brenda," said Vinnie. He took three steps forward.

I shook the gun. "I mean it," I said. "I know how to use this thing."

He took two steps back.

While the drug dealers kept each other at bay and Johnny radioed for help, Turner and McKinley snapped into action and came running to me. They had no way of knowing the extent of Vinnie T's and Richard's crimes, but they knew something was surely up and didn't want anybody to leave the scene. There'd be plenty of time later to sort out who was guilty of what.

I handed the gun to McKinley.

34

What had gone wrong? Why did Chuck let the drug dealers in? If it hadn't been for Rita, tyrant of the Hudson Shadow laundry room, Vinnie T and Richard would have escaped.

Rita, it seems, had been totally undeterred by Chuck's laser-printed emergency repair signs. She saw the closed corridor as a once-in-a-lifetime opportunity to steal cable television services. She was teetering on a ladder, busy splicing a cable line, while on the other side of the door just inside the garage the shit was hitting the fan.

When Vinnie T and Richard barreled through the door, they rammed into the ladder, which sent it, Rita, and Rita's wire cutters, crimpers, and alligator clips all crashing down to the ground.

Back inside, the garage was one big muddle. I didn't know what Johnny had told the dispatcher when he radioed for help, but it sure did the trick. Two dozen cop cars poured in through the open garage door one right after the other. Who let them in? Had Chuck left the garage door open? Or had he opened it when he saw them coming? I'd been way too busy chasing after Vinnie T and Richard to call him.

I went back to the diplomat car. "What's happening?" asked Dweena.

I shrugged. "I don't know." I took the cell phone out of my purse and called Chuck's cell phone.

No answer.

Meanwhile the flood of police cars had jammed into a gridlock. Sirens wailed. Horns honked. Cops cursed.

Turner and McKinley had their hands full dealing with two sets of alleged bad guys and Rita.

Johnny rose to the occasion. He mounted the car that belonged to the black-suited drug dealer and directed traffic with a suave Tod Trueman–like flare. He flung his arms this way and that in a beautifully choreographed sequence, and told the cops where to go. He stopped once to brush his thick dark hair away from his smoky gray eyes, which, now that I could compare eyeball to eyeball, absolutely did not resemble Vinnie T's.

Vinnie T, handcuffed and unhappy, talked to Turner. His eyes frequently rolled toward Richard. And Richard? He too was handcuffed and unhappy. He talked to McKinley. His eyes frequently rolled toward Vinnie T.

The drug dealers, also handcuffed, clammed up. Neither was saying nothin' without his freakin' lawyer.

Rita cursed the cable company, Vinnie T and Richard, Turner and McKinley, the drug dealers, Johnny, me, Dweena, and the Hudson Shadow. She threatened to sue us all.

Johnny, Dweena, and I got to ride to the precinct in an unmarked car driven by the ponytailed undercover detective I'd seen snickering outside Turner and McKinley's cubicle after Nado absconded with their vehicle. He had on a Day-Glo tie-dyed T-shirt.

We were the first to pull out of the parking garage. I looked anxiously up and down the street. No sign of Chuck. No sign of Dude Bob or Elizabeth.

"Excuse me," I said to the cop. "Did you happen to see a film crew out here when you came in?"

"Looked more like a brawl to me. Two citizens duked it out."

We pulled up to a stoplight. The cop whirled his head around, flashed a huge smile at Johnny. "Love your show, man, especially how you always get the girl at the end."

The precinct was deserted. Most of the cops were still at the garage. The ponytailed cop quickly ushered us into a cramped office. It was even grimmer than Turner and McKinley's tiny cubicle and smelled like cigarette butts, although I didn't see any around.

Another detective sauntered in. This one had a shaved head, tight jeans, wraparound mirrored sunglasses, a sleeveless mesh muscle T-shirt, and a well-tended three-day stubble. When he saw Johnny he said, "Are you really him?"

"He is indeed," said the ponytailed cop.

Against a backdrop of a blown-up map of the precinct they staged a good cop/bad cop routine, asked a bunch of stupid, irrelevant questions, then switched roles and asked pretty much the same questions. When Ponytail played good cop, his voice sounded smooth, like a voice-over from a greeting card commercial. When he played bad cop, his voice boomed and shook the room. Each time the guy with the shaved head asked a question, he turned his head in profile, first one way, then the other.

This was all for Johnny's benefit. According to Johnny, just about everybody wants to be an actor. And they all think actors get jobs for other actors. If that were true, there'd be no agents. Lemmy Crenshaw would either be mopping floors or practicing law.

When they were done with the impromptu audition, they both handed Johnny a business card. On the back each scribbled his home telephone number. "In case you think of anything else."

Throughout the interrogation they pretty much ignored Dweena and me, which was good because I didn't want to talk about it. Unfortunately, before we were let go, Turner and McKinley got back and sought me out. They wanted to talk about it. With me. Alone.

"Dweena and I'll wait for you," said Johnny.

"Thanks."

Turner and McKinley took me back to their cubicle, shut the door. "All right, Ms. Midnight, would you mind telling us what the hell was going on in that parking garage? Don't say you just happened to be sitting in a bulletproof diplomat car, minding your own business, discussing fashion with your friend."

"It's a little complicated," I said.

"Take as much time as you need," said McKinley.

So I told them everything I could without implicating Chuck or Dude Bob or Elizabeth. "Rita was a lucky accident." I tried out a smile. It got me nowhere.

The detectives scowled at me.

"Check out that gun. I'm positive it's the same gun that killed Royce Montmyer."

"We're positive too," said Turner.

"Did you beat a confession out of Vinnie T and Richard?"

McKinley brought his face in front of mine. "That's not funny, Ms. Midnight."

"But, as it turns out," said Turner, "not too wrong. The confession part, that happened. Not your friend Vincent Torrence, but the other guy, Richard. The guy's an accountant, for chrissakes. Sang like a bird."

"Which illustrates," said McKinley, "what happens when nonprofessionals stick their noses where they don't belong."

Dweena, Johnny, and I started out the front door of the precinct. "Whoa," said Dweena. "Check this out."

The media had arrived in full force. West Tenth Street was clogged with news vans. Reporters with expensive haircuts and designer suits jockeyed for position. It seemed a bit much for the situation.

Johnny sensed the question before either Dweena or I asked it. "Oh that," he said, with a dismissive wave of his hand. "When I called it in, I told 'em Tod Trueman, Urban Detective, was pitched in a life-or-death gun battle with the forces of evil."

We quickly retreated. To avoid the assembled reporters we slipped through the side exit and cut through the driveway to Charles Street, a practice the cops usually frown on.

Dweena, Johnny, and I headed straight for Angie's to rendezvous with Chuck, Elizabeth, and Dude Bob. As usual, the bar was packed, but I finally spotted Chuck's carrot-colored mop of fuzz. He was facedown on the bar. No sign of Elizabeth or Dude Bob. "Over there," I said, and pointed.

Dweena, Johnny, and I pushed our way through the crowd.

"Chuck?"

He lifted his head. His face was a mess. A black eye had started to form. "Guess I screwed up pretty bad." He clutched his middle, moaned, and dropped his head back on the bar.

Tommy brought over a red wine for me, dark beer for Johnny, seltzer with a lime twist for Dweena, and a paper cup full of ice and a towel for Chuck. "I tried to get him to go to St. Vincent's," he said.

"Did Chuck tell you what happened?" I asked.

"Only that I should see the other guy," said Tommy.

"Dude Bob?" I asked.

Chuck lifted his head, smiled a lopsided smile, and collapsed again.

Dweena wrapped the ice in the towel and held it up to Chuck's face. "I've seen worse," she said. "He'll be just fine."

"Here comes Elizabeth," said Johnny. He held his arm over his head and waved. "We're over here."

Elizabeth hurried over. "Is Chuck okay?"

"Yeah," said Dweena. She took the ice pack away so Elizabeth could see the damage.

Chuck moaned, "Dude Bob's worse than me?"

Elizabeth said, "You better believe it. Two shiners and a fat lip."

Tommy brought Elizabeth an anisette. Then he, Elizabeth, Dweena, Johnny, and I all blurted out at the same time, "What the hell happened?"

"You first," I said to Elizabeth.

"Everything was going smoothly according to your plan. Chuck manned the door, Dude Bob and I diverted pedestrians and cars. Then Chuck and the Dude got into an altercation. I believe it was over who was supposed to tell whom what to do. It escalated. The result, as you no doubt already know, is that neither did what they were supposed to do when they were supposed to do it. Who were those guys who got into the garage anyway?"

"Drug dealers," I said.

"Where's Dude Bob?" asked Dweena.

"He's at my apartment," said Elizabeth. "Sleeping. I'm afraid when he recovers I'm going to send him back to Montana. I need my space."

Chuck lifted his head. His lopsided smile was positively beatific. "I'll help you finish the built-ins." He lay his head back down on the bar.

Johnny walked me home. "Don't look so glum, Brenda. It's not like your plan didn't work."

"It's exactly like my plan didn't work. Simply put, my plan didn't work. I failed to account for human foibles."

"Everybody does that. I wouldn't worry about it if I were you. Bottom line is that the bad guys got caught, with a couple of drug dealers and Rita thrown in for good measure, although they'll surely let her go."

"It was stupid and dangerous. It was a bad plan."

I felt lousy because my bad plan messed up, and even

lousier that it had taken me so long to figure out that Vinnie T was a creep.

Jackhammer bounded into the foyer. I'd been gone long enough to merit an extra-special greeting. He didn't care if my plan worked.

I called Lance Chapoppel.

"You wouldn't believe all the commotion over here," he said. "I could see it all from my window. First somebody was setting up a film shoot, then a fistfight broke out between two guys. One of them kind of looked a little like Chuck, though I don't suppose it was. Then at least two dozen cop cars roared up. I don't know what the hell's going on."

"They caught Royce Montmyer's killer in the basement of your building."

"How do you know?

"I was there. The cops got the killer and the gun and a confession."

"It's really over?"

"Do you hear that sound? The fat lady is belting it out."

It may have been over for Lance, but I had a couple of loose ends to tie up, namely Kathilynda and Nado. I couldn't leave them in the back room of Julia's Trick Shoppe forever. Could I? I have to admit, I was tempted.

Considering the fact I had to awaken her, Julia was cheerful. She whistled a happy tune all the way to her store. She didn't even grumble when Jackhammer stopped to lift his leg every twenty feet or so along the way.

She unlocked the two padlocks, rolled up the gate, and unlocked the door to the store. Together we rousted Kathilynda and Nado from the back room.

"It's about time," said Kathilynda.

"What happened?" said Nado.

"You're safe. Vinnie and Richard are in the lockup."

We all walked back together. I let Nado and Kathilynda

into my apartment and lingered in the hallway to talk to Julia.

"I don't know how to thank you," I said.

"Don't bother," she said. "We're even."

"You mean we can go back to being enemies again?"

She smiled, stepped into her apartment, and slammed the door.

I brought Kathilynda and Nado up to date.

Nado shook his head. "I always knew that Vinnie T was no damned good."

Kathilynda said, "I still say he looks like Johnny Verlane. A little."

35

I was draping a swath of taxicab-yellow diaphanous silk over a tiny pillbox form—a procedure that's much trickier than it sounds— when the bells on the door jangled. I didn't have to look up to know it was Turner and McKinley. I'd gotten off far too easily last night. I heard the sound of their expensive leather shoes on the wood floor. They stood over me, their bodies blocking the sunlight.

Jackhammer took one look at the two of them and slunk into the storage closet. Lucky dog.

I sighed, fastened a swirl of silk with a pin, and looked up at the two detectives. "I had a feeling you'd be coming around sooner or later." Of course I'd hoped for later.

Gray and black stubble poked out on Turner's face. McKinley's eyes were red. They'd been up all night. They did not smile or bother with a good morning.

For a change, McKinley sat at the vanity and let Turner pace the floor. A couple back and forths and Turner stopped in front of me. "Ms. Midnight, Detective McKinley and I have had time to discuss the events of last night. I find it necessary to repeat. Your scheme was stupid and dangerous."

"Dumb, dumb, dumb," said McKinley. He sounded like a bass line in the background.

I had nothing to say in my defense. I happened to agree

254

with their assessment. I looked down and ran my finger along the wood grain of my worktable. I thought of the tree it had been sliced from, the lush forest where the tree had once lived and stretched toward the sun. Birds had tweeted in its branches.

"However," continued Turner, "your stupid plan worked."

Surely, I'd not heard right.

McKinley stopped his dumb, dumb, dumb refrain. "What my partner is trying to say, is thank you."

I had to hear it again. "What?"

"Thank you," said Turner.

I cupped my hand to my ear and cocked my head.

"Thank you," said McKinley.

That was enough.

After that, we all relaxed. Jackhammer dragged a crescent-shaped scrap of felt out of the storage closet. He added it to his pile of fabric and sat on top of it.

"Do you really come from Pork Belly?" asked Turner.

"Belup's Creek," I said.

"Whatever. I just got off the phone with the authorities there. Your Vincent Torrence had big plans. Your car-thieving ex-husband, while illegally dumping grease, witnessed Mr. Torrence supervising the placement of concrete blocks in Belch Creek."

"Belup's," I corrected. "That's pretty much what Nado thought. Vinnie T dumped building materials."

"No, Ms. Midnight. You did not listen carefully. I did not say Mr. Torrence had dumped anything. The placement of blocks was a precision operation. Mr. Torrence attempted to alter the flow pattern of the creek in such a way as to flood the property of a rival developer."

"So it wasn't a DB."

"What the hell's a DB, Ms. Midnight?" roared McKinley.

"Dead body."

Both Turner and McKinley rolled their eyes.

Turner continued. "When your ex flipped the almighty bird, Mr. Torrence greatly overestimated his cognitive ability, reported to his boss that Nado was on to them. Boss ordered Torrence to make sure Nado didn't blab. He hired Richard, who blew the job, so Torrence came to New York to make sure the job got done right."

Pretty much what I thought. "What will happen to Vinnie?"

"It's kinda tricky since he wasn't the actual shooter, but whatever was gonna happen legal-wise suddenly got a lot worse. Last night that creek . . ."

"Belup's Creek."

"Damn thing flooded, spilled over its banks. Only it didn't flood the rival developer's land like it was supposed to. Mr. Torrence was in New York when the last concrete blocks were dumped into the creek. Whomever he left in charge screwed it up big-time. The flood sent Mr. Torrence's boss's own personal house ass-over-end. Boss is real pissed."

"This isn't the kind of boss you want to piss off," added McKinley, "if you get my drift."

I got it.

At last, Kathilynda and Nado were headed back to Belup's Creek. This time, I met them in the parking garage for real.

Kathilynda stood outside the van surrounded by dozens of shopping bags. "Oh, it's you. Hi, Brenda Sue."

Nado crouched down in the back of the van. He poked his head out and said. "This must be déjà vu for you."

I peeked inside the van. Every cubic inch was stuffed with shopping bags.

"We put your dresser over there," said Kathilynda. She pointed to a dark corner of the garage.

"Okay," I mumbled. Later I'd worry about the dresser, but right then I had something else on my mind. I had to do the last thing in the world I ever thought I'd do, and I didn't know how to do it. For inspiration, I thought of

Turner and McKinley. They'd done the unthinkable and survived. "Uh, Kathilynda . . ."

"Yeah?" She handed Nado a bag.

"Thank you." I spit it out, all at once, machine-gun fast.

"What the hell for?" She handed Nado another bag.

"That thing with Vinnie T in high school—you called . . . disguised your voice. If you hadn't . . . well, maybe . . . what I'm trying to say is that since he turned out to be a creep, it was a good thing I never got to go out with him back then, when I was much more impressionable."

Kathilynda heaved a bag into the van, took a deep breath, and let me have it loud and clear. "Look, Brenda Sue, I'm goddamned sick and tired of your crap. This is the last time I'm gonna say it. I did not call you and pretend to be Vinnie T. I did not talk through a hair dryer tube. I did not disguise my voice in any manner at any time. I did not break your goddamned date with Vinnie T."

I waited for the shock waves of her voice to dissipate. "Somebody did."

"Not me."

"Well then who?"

Kathilynda handed another bag to Nado, only Nado had disappeared into the recesses of the van. "Nado, where the hell are you?"

Suddenly Kathilynda and I looked at each other. We realized the same thing at the same time. "Nado," she said.

I nodded. Nado.

We climbed into the van. Nado was keeping very busy rearranging a pile of shopping bags. He whistled to himself like he hadn't a care in the world.

"You!" Kathilynda and I lunged for Nado's skinny neck.

Somewhere, hovering about in all of this, was a lesson. I'd spent years not liking Kathilynda for something she hadn't done, when there were so many other perfectly good reasons not to like her.

Nado confessed. "Only I didn't use a hair dryer tube;

that was a handkerchief stretched over the phone."

"Why, Nado?"

"I had a crush on you. I always knew Vinnie T was no damned good."

Kathilynda gave him the evil eye.

He put his arm around Kathilynda. "I had a crush on you too," he said. "I would have done the same for you if Vinnie'd asked you out. After all, I did marry both of you."

"What about those calls about where you were?" I asked. "Did you make those too?"

"Nope," said Nado. "Those must have been legit responses to that poster you put up. Awful picture, by the way. I look like some kind of dweeb."

By the time they were actually leaving, as Nado gunned the motor trying to get the van started, tears welled up in my eyes. I found strange words coming out of my mouth. "We'll have to get together like this more often." A big mistake, I realized, and qualified, "Well, maybe not exactly like this, but . . ."

The engine turned over.

Kathilynda waved good-bye.

"It's been real," said Nado.

And they were gone.

Once the Sharpes hit the road, things swiftly got back to normal.

I reclaimed my apartment and moved Elizabeth's banana couch over by the window. Jackhammer pigged out on green beans and threw up on the couch.

I gave my old dresser, the one I'd stored in Nado's van, to Rita. The cable company chose not to press charges against her. Instead, they gave her a brand-new TV, a cable setup, and free lifetime service, in exchange for the rights to use her story as an example of what happens when you try to steal cable service. She put her new TV atop my old dresser and tried to figure out how to get the premium channels.

Dweena repositioned the bulletproof diplomat car on a
daily basis. Finally the diplomat gave up, sold the car to
some drug dealers, and bought a bicycle.

The neighborhood business association dissolved. Pete
was philosophical. He said everything has its time. Julia's
Trick Shoppe stayed and thrived and sponsored a women's
basketball team.

Maris Montmyer's check for the mourning veil and hat
bounced.

Like I said, back to normal.

One afternoon the landlord's limo pulled up. He waddled
into the shop with yet another "niece" wiggling behind his
cloud of foul cigar smoke. This niece didn't resemble the
other niece, and neither niece resembled the landlord or his
wife, or probably anyone remotely related to the landlord.
This time, with this niece, I was ready. I made no threats,
but I *did* inquire as to his wife's health.

He took the cigar out of his mouth, gave me a dirty look,
and said, "Fine."

"That's nice," I said.

While the niece tried on hats and pouted in the mirror, I
had a friendly little chat with the landlord. "You know,"
I said, "it's funny how things turn out sometimes. See, I've
got this friend Elliot, he's an experienced building super,
and he needs a job. I notice you've got several buildings
around here in need of a qualified super."

The landlord frowned a deep face-furrowing frown,
shook his head. Before he said no, I held up my hand to
silence him. "Oh my. Your *niece* looks lovely in that hat,
don't you think?"

The landlord was a quick study. "Have your friend get
in touch."

*   *   *

Johnny had a party to celebrate the fact that he'd officially turned down that movie deal that would have turned Tod Trueman into an Iowa sheriff. As a by-product of that decision, he'd fired Lemmy. Then he rehired him. Even so, Turner and McKinley were invited. They told me they were glad Johnny had broken off his engagement because it meant more parties and more guest starlets.

I didn't bring a date to this party. Not even an ex-husband. I'd spent a lot of time pondering the past, and the present as a product of the past, and the future as a product of the past and the present. So, this time when Johnny walked me home from his party and we were standing in front of my building and he said it was time to talk about this just friends crap, I was ready. I knew what I wanted. This time, Lemmy did not come screeching around the corner in a cab to spoil the moment.

DEN OF ANTIQUITY MYSTERIES

by
TAMAR MYERS

LARCENY AND OLD LACE
78239-1/$5.99 US/$7.99 Can

As owner of the Den of Antiquity, Abigail Timberlake
is accustomed to navigating the cutthroat world of rival
dealers at flea markets and auctions. But she never thought
she'd be putting her expertise in mayhem and detection to
other use—until her aunt was found murdered . . .

GILT BY ASSOCIATION
78237-5/$5.99 US/$7.99 Can

A superb gilt-edged, 18th-century French armoire Abigail
purchased for a song at estate auction has just arrived
along with something she didn't pay for: a dead body.

THE MING AND I
79255-9/$5.50 US/$7.50 Can

Digging up old family dirt can uncover long buried
secrets . . . and a new reason for murder.

SO FAUX, SO GOOD
79254-0/$5.99 US/$7.99 Can